"India? Are you all right?"

She couldn't tell Jack what was on her mind, so she bit back her questions about her daughter's first days with him and Mary and changed the subject. "I love to look at photos, but I always want to know the stories behind them."

"Colleen is like that, too. Unfortunately, we couldn't tell her much. Mother Angelica only told us Colleen had a normal delivery. You don't seem surprised to hear she's adopted. Has she already told you?"

India nodded in time to the beat of her own heart. Jack's question tempted her again to enter a dreamworld, where Colleen would get used to the idea of her true identity, and Jack would forgive her for her lies.

"J-Jack," she stuttered, "Colleen's birth mother could tell you all about her birth. Have you never wondered about her?"

His vehemence gave aw~~~ ~~~~~~~ ~~~~~ling about the "birth m~~~~" ~~~~~ ~~~~~~ mother. That's all I ~~~~~~~~ ~~~~~~~~~ the idea of some wom~~~ ~~~~~~~~~~ ~~~~rom us. I still think al~~~ ~~~~~~~~~~~ ~~~ose stories on the news...."

His voice trailed off, and India tried to hide her utter dismay. Averting her face, she scrambled for composure. He'd given her a swift, detailed answer. If she tried to tell him the truth, he'd think she'd come to steal his child.

ABOUT THE AUTHOR

Anna Adams grew up battling for position with four brothers and five male cousins. Her grandma, concerned when Anna built a tree house that resembled a condo for a family of four, gave her the gift of a Harlequin romance novel and told her that young women (Anna was twelve and—*please*—no longer a "girl") could combine other, even more exciting adventures with their architectural accomplishments.

With wholehearted joy, Anna plunged into a world of strong women and loving men who knit their lives together no matter what obstacles stood between them. Now Anna can't believe she's lucky enough to add her stories to the ones that came before her. She hopes to bring the same delight she's known to other readers. She just wishes she could share that cool reading spot, too.

Anna lives in Georgia with her jazz guitarist son, Colin, her swims-like-a-fish daughter, Sarah, and her hero of twenty-one years, Steve.

HER DAUGHTER'S FATHER
Anna Adams

HARLEQUIN®

TORONTO • NEW YORK • LONDON
AMSTERDAM • PARIS • SYDNEY • HAMBURG
STOCKHOLM • ATHENS • TOKYO • MILAN • MADRID
PRAGUE • WARSAW • BUDAPEST • AUCKLAND

ISBN 0-373-70896-3

HER DAUGHTER'S FATHER

Visit us at www.romance.net

Printed in U.S.A.

To Mamie—who gave me that first book.

To Colin and Sarah—may life bring you the love
you've given me.

And to Steve—I still listen for your voice on the phone,
your key in the door. You love like a hero.

PROLOGUE

ON NEW YEAR'S EVE, in the basement of St. Genevieve's Home for Unwed Mothers, India Stuart gripped a small flashlight between her teeth and bent over a locked filing cabinet. Seconds ticked like frantic heartbeats in her head.

She'd learned how to pick locks from a book, but her hands hadn't trembled this way when she'd practiced at home. Like the attorneys she'd consulted and Mother Angelica, who'd run the home since before India had come here to give birth, the lock remained firm.

She didn't take burglary lightly. Fifteen years ago, she'd stepped outside the rules and made one mistake that had taught her never to rebel again. She glanced at the window she'd climbed through. Headlights on a waiting car flashed twice.

Her father, encouraging her. He was only trying to help, not alert the local police. "Dad!" She redoubled her efforts. A bead of sweat trickled down her nose. Had he flashed the lights before? Even at a time like this, she and he did not know how to communicate.

She tightened her moist fingers on the tools. Any minute Mother Angelica might materialize to engulf her in voluminous black robes. No, at night, Mother Angelica only ventured from her room to investigate the sound of a gallon of ice cream bouncing across the kitchen tiles. India still remembered.

Inhaling a shaky breath, she started over. Use a gentle touch. Persuade the lock. Don't force it.

With a metallic thunk, it finally gave and sprang outward. Astounded, she stared at the cabinet. A moment of truth. Fifteen years of hopes and dreams and regrets, all concentrated in one shattering second.

She yanked the handle on the *S* drawer.

Smith, Smith, Smith—how many frightened young women had borrowed that name? Finally, a Smythe and two Snyders. She ran her fingertips over the folder tabs. Sprayberry, Spritzer? At last, a Stewart, and another, and then—Stuart, India. Even in the dim light her folder looked old.

Fifteen years.

She tugged at the file. Wedged between the others, it stuck. She tugged harder, but left it halfway in, so she wouldn't have to figure out where it belonged when she finished with it.

Prying the folder open enough to see the writing on the pages inside, India shone her small flashlight on Mother Angelica's spidery scrawl. She searched for the name she'd tried to imagine for too many years, the name of the child she'd given up for adoption.

Colleen Stephens.

India squeezed her eyes shut, holding in terrified joy. This moment was worth any danger. She shook herself, remembering her father outside. Getting him arrested wouldn't improve their strained relationship.

She dug a small notebook out of her pocket. Her knees wobbled as she wrote down her daughter's address. Arran Island, Maryland. So close. She'd always been so close. India stared at Colleen's adopted parents' names. Jack and Mary Stephens. She hoped they loved Colleen the way she'd wanted to. She vowed not to hurt them as she jotted down their names and then threaded the file back into its slot.

She shut the drawer and pushed the lock back into place.

Quickly she turned off the flashlight and stowed it in her pocket. Across the room, her father's wrench, upright and gleaming in the moonlight, still braced the window open.

She clambered to the window ledge and eased the wrench out. Then, she forced a space large enough to wriggle through and tumbled out onto the grass. As she leaned back to tug the window down, her father gently revved his car's engine.

She scrambled up the slight rise and pushed through shrubbery that grabbed at her clothes and skin. Gravel scrunched under her heels as she skidded to the front passenger door and yanked it open. Breathing hard, she slid into the seat. The man behind the steering wheel, all in black, his hair a shock of steel, tilted his head in a silent question.

"Colleen Stephens. Arran Island, Maryland." India choked on the words, amazed she had gone to such lengths, but unbelievably glad.

For a moment, Mick Stuart's eyes reflected her happiness. He sobered abruptly. "So you found out her name. Let it go now. Get back on a plane for Seattle and take that job. Hire someone to find out if she's all right."

The last plane she'd boarded for Seattle had broken crosswise on the runway, burst into flames and changed her life forever. Dragging herself through smoke so thick she almost had to chew it, she'd seen her bland life for the safe picture of responsibility she'd created. She'd thrown away her parents' love and hidden her own for them so deep she didn't know how to find it anymore. Since Colleen's birth, she'd kept herself from loving anyone.

As she'd struggled into clean air, she'd known—to go forward, she had to confront her past. Later, flat on her back with a broken leg, she'd had plenty of time to face the truth. Giving up her child had been the wrong decision for her to make. She couldn't change the choice she'd made, but she needed to know Colleen hadn't suffered because of her.

Now, adrenaline pushed her to snap a sharp reply to her father's suggestion she put her daughter behind her. She swallowed old resentments. "I was looking to run away once and for all when I considered that Seattle job. I'm tired of running. For the same reasons I want to mend my fences with you and Mom, I have to know Coll—she's safe."

Grunting, he eased the car into gear and drove toward the wrought iron gate. "I know the accident changed things for you, but India, you're looking back with hindsight. You have a master's degree in library science. You have security I couldn't provide for you when you got pregnant. You must know we were right. What would you have made of your life if you'd had to care for a child?"

"Dad, my heart still hurts for her. When I woke up in that hospital bed, I knew I had to make my peace—and not just with you and Mom."

India turned her face to the window. Neither of her parents knew the guilt and shame that had haunted her as she'd carved out her competent life. She'd taken her degrees and then taken jobs in small towns and big cities close to a "home" that no longer felt like hers. Doing unacknowledged penance, she'd lived near her parents and hidden her true feelings—an easy feat, because she couldn't bear to see them often enough to let them have a good look at her.

"I won't meet her or talk to her. I don't want to hurt her family, but I have to see she's happy and safe."

"You were sixteen years old. Forgive yourself. Forgive your mother and me. You need a family of your own. You need to let someone love you."

"I can't *let* anyone love me until I know she's safe. I've believed I abandoned her. I just need to see she's safe."

For the first time, he backed down. "It's my fault. If my business hadn't failed… " Trailing off, he maneuvered the car into the street and anonymity.

"No, Dad." India stared at his face, rugged and lined from the years he'd spent painting other people's houses in Virginia sun and weather. "I made the final choice. It was easy to blame you and Mom, but everything changed when that plane skidded down the runway. I took the easy way out—with my baby and with you."

"You've worked hard for everything you have."

"I've worked at not getting hurt, at not letting anyone love me, including you and Mom." India eyed the thick, wavy strands of his hair. "You didn't have to come tonight."

"I couldn't let you come alone. I owe you this, and tomorrow, I'll arrange for an ad in the Arran Island paper. Someone will need a housepainter." Reaching across the gearshift, he patted her knee. "And his able apprentice. Your mother is going to manage the business while I help you—as long as I remember how to run the equipment after all this time in the front office."

India splayed her fingers over the ache in her chest. To find her own way, she had to see she'd done right by the child she'd never even held. She'd looked back for too long. From today, she looked forward. No fear, no guilt.

Mick slowed the car for a traffic light. "If we can just get one house, we may find out everything we need to know."

India's smile took all her acting ability. She talked brave, but she felt wary. The huge chance she was taking could break her family apart all over again.

"What's the matter?" Her father's gaze searched hers in the dim light.

Twisting in the seat, she pressed the back of her head

against the cool window. "I just made you an accessory to breaking and entering."

Mick curved his mouth. "You got my wrench back, right?"

CHAPTER ONE

"HAYDEN, I DON'T NEED YOU and Nettie to help me raise my own daughter." Jack Stephens pushed away from the worn kitchen table and his half-eaten lunch. His former father-in-law scraped back his chair, too.

"We know you're a good father to Colleen, but she's grown even more rebellious since we were here at Christmas. While you're busy with the boat, let us help you."

Intense March sunshine flooding through the window hurt Jack's eyes. The boat. Two months ago, a storm like the hand of God had pushed his boat ashore. Since then, he'd worked on a friend's boat during the day and made repairs on his own in the evenings. Maybe Colleen had acted up more since then, but his busy schedule hadn't started her one-girl rebellion.

No, she'd changed when Mary died. Nearly three years ago. He shied from the uncomfortable truth. Colleen had stopped talking to him after her mother died.

Jack shoved his plate onto the counter. "You've worked up to this all morning, haven't you? No wonder Nettie wanted a girl's day out." Hayden Mason's diminutive wife had insisted she and Colleen needed new clothes for the spring festival tonight. "Did Colleen ask you to talk to me?"

"Of course not," Hayden said, picking up his own plate. "Unless you approve, we won't even tell her we want to stay."

Like a living, breathing entity, Jack's small kitchen seemed to squeeze him. "What if I don't approve?"

Hayden narrowed his gray eyes, Mary's eyes, but Jack wouldn't let memories of Mary soften his impatience with her managing parents. His parents, too, after all these years.

"I don't want you to stay. You and Nettie come between Colleen and me. When you're here, she turns to you first, and I can't reach her."

"Maybe she needs us." Hayden took Jack's shoulder. "I don't want to hurt you, but you two can't talk to each other anymore. You don't understand each other."

"She doesn't have to understand me. She has to do what I tell her to do and be where I tell her to be. She forgets she's fifteen, and I'm her parent." Jack broke off. Tough talk, tougher than he meant, but his anxiety for Colleen made him feel weak, out of control. "How could you and Nettie do a better job? You pave her way with gifts. Look at that leather jacket Nettie bought her last weekend."

Hayden sighed reflectively, as if the black and silver-buckled, biker-gang special clanged in his memory, too. "Now, Nettie made a mistake there. She swears Colleen showed her a different jacket. One with a velvet collar." Hayden shook his head. "But Colleen also told her how much she misses Mary. Has she told you?"

"What kind of man do you think I've become?" Taking Hayden's plate, Jack avoided his eyes. "I know how much Colleen misses her mother."

"But has she told you? Has she cried in *your* handkerchief?"

At the sink, Jack stared out the window at the green-blue bay. Colleen hadn't shed one teardrop in almost three years, not when the police called to say Mary's car had gone off the road, not when he'd come home from Mary's hospital bedside two weeks later to tell Colleen her mother was gone.

Colleen seemed to want him to believe she regarded her mother's death with the same stone-cold apathy she extended toward every word he spoke, from "I love you" to "Call me *before* you stop at your friend's house."

"We'll work out our problems." He tried to sound sure. Colleen was his little girl. Why didn't he know how to reach her? "Maybe you and Nettie should stop running interference for her."

"You need time to get your boat back in the water. Colleen needs attention. We can give both of you exactly what you need. Let us stay, just until you finish repairing the boat and get your business back on track."

Pressure beat behind his eyes as Jack stared at the older man. Maybe Hayden was right. If Colleen had talked to Nettie about Mary, maybe she'd find a way to talk about the other things she couldn't tell him. "What about your house in Baltimore?"

"Nettie's cousin in D.C. will check on it. Besides, we're not so far away that we can't go home if we need to."

Even as Jack opened his mouth to give in, the front door slammed open. Colleen's usual entrance. Leaving Hayden behind, he hurried through the kitchen archway. In the dim light, he saw what Colleen had done to herself while in her grandmother's care.

Her hair, much darker than the honey-blond it had been that morning, stood on end. Exaggerated paleness painted on her cheeks and eyelids stopped Jack cold. She smiled through black lips. Behind her, Nettie hovered, cautious as Colleen ought to be.

"What have you done?" Jack clutched at his slipping temper. Who knew parenting could scare the hell out of a grown man? His daughter needed him, but he couldn't figure out what she needed. "Colleen, what have you done to yourself?"

Adolescence hadn't robbed her of all her good sense. A hint of anxiety finally entered her eyes. "I had a makeover."

"A makeover?" She looked like one of the living dead. Jack eased in a deep breath. Their arguments followed the same pattern. Step one—he lost his mind. Step two—she clammed up. Step three—silence deepened the gap between them. "Go upstairs and clean your face. We'll talk about this in a few minutes."

"I paid for the makeup, Dad." Squaring her shoulders, Colleen lifted a Macy's shopping bag. "I plan to use it."

Jack stared at his daughter, pointedly ignoring Nettie and Hayden, who were blind to the fact they didn't help Colleen when they financed her mistakes. "How did you pay?"

She hesitated, reluctant to involve Nettie, keeper of the moneybags. She bit her lip and shifted her shopping to her other hand. "Grandma gave me the money."

Nettie scooted around her. "Now, Jack, honey, I know this looks bad." She was as reluctant as Colleen to come clean. "I didn't know—I thought, what's the harm in a little makeup? I—"

"But where were you when she did this?" As he switched on the hall light to see his daughter's hair, Jack's fuse burned a little shorter. He turned Colleen's head so that the spiky ends glinted. "Purple?" Appalled, he let her go.

"No. Burgundy." Colleen tapped her palm gently over the points.

Her hair looked like an eggplant sunburst.

In one more rescue attempt, Nettie nudged Colleen farther behind her and lifted one hand to her own shoulder. Clenching her face in an exaggerated grimace, she rubbed her shoulder, as if her muscles ached horribly. With a side-ways glance, she made sure she'd lured Jack's attention away from Colleen. "I indulged in a short massage." She tilted her head toward her granddaughter. "I've been under a little stress, you know."

Hayden showed up at Jack's side. "Nettie." His voice dripped disappointment.

"I know. I know." Her show of guilt made Jack want to laugh and shout at the same time. Nettie dropped her head. "I don't know how I—"

"Dad, this isn't Grandma's fault." Colleen stepped in front of Nettie. "I tricked her."

"I'm the adult, Colleen." Nettie muscled back in front of her granddaughter, forcing Jack to retreat a step or two. She patted her own perfect silver coiffure with delicate weariness. "I should have paid closer attention."

Their protective dance softened Jack's heart. Leaning against the wall, he pressed his palms to the cool plaster. Since Mary's death, Colleen had held her emotions tight. The joy he'd loved in her seemed muted, and she showed him only frustration. He'd tried to give her privacy, because he understood her need. Later he realized she'd stopped telling him her troubles. Only when she'd begun to act out anger she refused to discuss had he realized he should have pried.

He couldn't punish Colleen for withdrawing when he'd let her go to give her time. She missed Mary, but she refused to talk to him about her grief. He'd thought he understood because his own pain and sorrow had felt so private.

Maybe if he let Nettie stay, Colleen would find a way to talk to her.

Jack swallowed a huge lump in his throat. *Why can't she talk to me?* But before she went and did something to herself he couldn't undo, she had to talk to someone. And Nettie made her care more than anyone else could.

All three of them waited for what he'd do next. "Go wash your face, Colleen," he said again. "I don't want you to wear that stuff to the festival tonight."

A slight, relieved smile curved her mouth, but she held it back. "I'll do something about my hair, too."

Reluctant to look too closely at the damage, Jack allowed himself a brief nod. "Your grandpa and grandma are going to stay awhile, until I finish the boat."

Colleen hesitated, looking from Nettie to Hayden. "Great. Two more keepers."

Jack pushed away from the wall. "Cut it out."

She headed for the stairs, the heels of her ankle boots tapping on the pine floor's wide planks. She whirled, planting her hands on the balustrade to look down with pink cheeks and stormy eyes.

"Don't be mad at Grandma, Dad. I've tricked you before, too."

He didn't trust himself to speak until Colleen slammed her door, and its echo let the air out of him. He turned and took Nettie's hand. "I'm sorry it's not a more exclusive club." He glanced from her to Hayden. "Are you sure you still want to stay?"

"YOU LOOK FINE, INDIA. Stop worrying, and try to have a good time. Tonight's your chance to meet people who might tell you something about her." Her father lowered his voice on the pronoun.

India smoothed the hem of her new plaid skirt over her thighs and felt conspicuous. "She might be out there." India nodded at the festival crowd that snaked around the cavernous high school gym. "I feel like a kid, myself, in this. Maybe I'll call Mom tonight and ask her to send some of my things."

Mick handed her a plastic cup of pink stuff. "Try this. A little girl wearing that same skirt poured it for me. I've never seen hair her color—purple, I swear. I'm not sure I could mix paint to match."

Smiling despite choking tension, India held the glass at her lips. "Thanks, Dad. I feel better now."

Mick ran his hand over her gauzy sleeve. "Your eyes look like big blue marbles. Relax."

India shifted away. After all these years, she hardly knew how to accept her father's comfort. She twisted the blond strands of her ponytail. She'd tried so hard to protect her parents, she'd forgotten how to go to them when she was afraid.

And she was scared stiff. What would she say if she met Colleen? Nothing. She couldn't intrude in Colleen's life. She had to run away as she had so long ago.

She'd kept running until those few terrifying moments on a burning plane had taught her what was important. Family. Living down the past before it ate up the future. She'd been all appearance before, but now she wanted to feel the emotions she'd hidden from, as long as she did nothing to hurt Colleen. "What if she's here? What if I meet her accidentally?"

Mick sipped his own drink, somehow understanding her mid-thought conversation. "She might also be at home, tucked up in her own bed. She might be out of town. Don't get your hopes up."

India rubbed her index finger through the condensation on her plastic glass. "I'm not secretly hoping to run into her."

Hurt bruised her father's gaze. "I'm not saying you'd try to see her, but you're *my* daughter, and I don't want you hurt."

India took a deep breath and plunged into the heart of the matters between them. "I know what you've done for me.'' After he'd dragged his business back from the edge of bankruptcy, he'd put away his brushes to manage his company from a desk in a comfortable office. Until now. ''I know you only came back into the field to give me an excuse to come here, but we could be lucky. Maybe we'll meet someone tonight who'll tell us Colleen lives in a fairy tale, and we can finish painting Mr. Tanner's house and go home.''

''You could walk right into her, and she wouldn't know you.'' Mick turned, almost blocking out the mob behind him. ''We can leave now if you want, if you have second thoughts.''

''No.'' A woman in a bright red dress floated on a clear path for Mick. Their landlady at Seasider Inn looked different tonight, without her square white pinafore and her cat's-eye, tortoiseshell glasses. India shoved her cup into her father's hand. ''Here comes Viveca Henderson. I need some air.''

Warily Mick turned. ''Yeah, she likes me too much. I think I'd better mention your mother to her again. Where are you going?''

''Outside, to the high school's dunking booth.'' Reluctant or not, she'd come here to find out about Colleen's life. ''The sooner I find someone who'll gossip about her, the better.''

Bright lights illuminated the parking lot. India passed an apple-bobbing barrel and a kissing booth, manned by girls in cheerleader uniforms. Could one of them be Colleen?

In the booth's shadows, India glimpsed a young girl in the same skirt she'd bought. India smoothed her hem again. In this light, she couldn't tell if the girl's short cap of hair was purple. Suddenly the girl tried to pull away from the boy at her side, but he held on. Leaning down, he spoke close to her ear, and she slid her arm around his waist.

Hesitating, India studied the crowd around the girl and boy. No one else seemed to see trouble. When the boy turned the girl toward the parking lot, she went willingly.

The cool breeze brushed a paper hamburger wrapper past India's ankle. What would Colleen be like? Would she have a boyfriend who looked too old for her? Would she seem even younger than the girl with the purple hair?

Rubbing her goose-bumped arms, India watched the people enjoying themselves too much to notice the weather or the children. She wished she'd brought her jacket along. Even if it hadn't matched her froufrou lacy blouse and plaid skirt.

She'd vowed not to meddle in Colleen's life, and keeping vows was her strength. Yet deep inside, she had to admit she'd thought she might see Colleen here tonight. She couldn't help wanting to look ''cool.'' After she'd sorted through her serviceable though faded jeans, the painting overalls her father had provided, or the one good dress she'd packed for just in case, she'd trekked to the nearest mall on the mainland.

Ridiculous.

What would Colleen Stephens care about a stranger's wardrobe?

A sudden, urgent cry stopped India beside a large wooden planter. She stared back into the crowd, waiting for another cry, but she heard nothing. Just children's voices and party sounds.

She scanned the little ones weaving in and out of the festival booths. All happy, many laughing. But that one voice, for a moment, higher than the rest—India pushed nervous fingertips through her hair. While the frightened cry still echoed in her head, she turned toward the parking lot's edge.

With so many cars here, every house in town must be empty. She craned her neck, searching for—what? Almost before she realized she was hearing it again, the thin, high voice arched over the fun once more.

India made a beeline for the sound. In the weaker light beyond the open lot, cars stood in rows. Three rows back, the tall, gangly boy from beside the kissing booth tried to tug the purple-haired girl into a cherry-red sports car while two more girls dragged at her other arm. They all struggled in silence now.

Suddenly the two other girls broke away and ran toward the festival crowds. India had eyes only for the girl who still clung with both hands to the roof of the boy's car.

"Get in," he shouted. "Get in or you'll never see me again."

Intimately familiar words, in a different context, in a more dangerous situation than when her long-ago boyfriend had threatened her with them, deepened India's instinctive rage.

"I won't go with you when you're like this." The girl tried to arch away from him, but he only pushed harder.

Her friends ran up to India. Their great relief hurt her. They were just little girls, caught in a bad game of grownup.

One intercepted her. "He's been drinking. Our friend— Please help us."

India broke into a run. "Go get more help."

"Okay."

With heightened senses, she heard their footsteps fade behind her. In the false light, the paint on the boy's car looked warm and wet. As she rounded the hood, India slapped her palm on the metal. She would have jumped on it to make him turn away from the girl. He whirled, fists clenched.

"Hey! That's my car." Slurring the words, he flailed his arms, to reach for India.

But she bowed her body out of his reach and stationed herself between him and the girl, who stood now, stunned and still.

"Do you think you're a big man, because you can bully a girl like this?" India sized him up at about seventeen. At least six inches taller than she, and forty pounds heavier, he was mad and drunk enough to be plenty mean. She didn't dare break her gaze from his to check on the girl.

Completely unintimidated, he marched toward India, his fists again at his sides. "Who are you?"

"The woman you'll have to go through to get to her." She braced her hands on her hips and hoped the girl stayed behind her. Bouncing on the balls of her feet, India waited for him to strike—and for instincts that had dragged her this far to tell her what to do next.

The boy stopped. "You don't know her. You don't belong here. Who are you?"

"We've covered that. Where are your parents? Do they know about you?"

"Know what about me?" He stumbled forward. "You hit my car."

Backing into the girl, India eased her away from the car. She risked a quick glance inside. No keys on the seat. She couldn't see the ignition.

"Go home." India pretended she wasn't afraid. "Before this girl's friends bring the police back. And next time, pick on someone your own size."

"I'll—" Before he could say what he planned to do, a man appeared out of darkness.

"Keep your filthy hands off my daughter." He hauled the boy around to face him. With his fists full of the kid's collar, the man studied the girl behind India. "Colleen, are you hurt?"

India stiffened. Her heart lodged in the back of her throat. *Go now. Run, before she sees you.*

Somehow, she couldn't move.

"Colleen!"

"I'm fine, Dad." The girl edged around India, her voice a young echo of India's mother's. Rachel sang like an angel. She sang lullabies her grandchild would never hear. And this child spoke with Rachel's voice.

India wobbled. Plaid skirt and purple hair brushed into a thick cap. The girl who'd served Mick the glass of pink punch.

More than one Colleen might live on Arran Island.

India stared at the man. Strong and inflexible as granite, from wide, high cheekbones to the dent in his chin, his face softened as he searched his daughter for injury.

"Are you sure you're not hurt?" Her father, he had the right to stay and make sure. He would take her home and comfort her—and hopefully talk to her about boys who drank too much and threatened young girls.

Before Colleen could answer, her friends slipped through the cars to surround her with tears and relief. She collapsed into their arms, instead of in her father's.

Why? Teenaged angst? Or something deeper, some problem that might motivate a young woman to look up to a boy like Colleen's bad choice.

India lifted her hand to the girl with the fuzzy purple hair. More than one Colleen might live on Arran Island, but she doubted it. She took one step backward and then two more. Before anyone noticed her again, she faded into the darkness.

CHAPTER TWO

INDIA GLANCED FROM the adjoining door to her father's room, to the old beige phone on the bureau. For the first time in years, she craved the comfort of her mother's serenity. She dialed.

Her mother picked up on the first ring. India broke into her hello. "I saw her, Mom, but she's in trouble."

"I should have come with you, too." Through the telephone lines, Rachel Stuart's voice sounded tinny and far away and too much like Colleen's.

"She has purple hair, and a boy tried to drag her into his car. I think he's her boyfriend. If I hadn't stopped him, he would have hurt her."

"Her boyfriend?" Rachel squeaked.

"What kind of parents let their daughter date a boy like that? She's not old enough to date. Even I know she's not old enough. Maybe I know better than anyone."

Rachel's response came more slowly. "Daughters sometimes do things their parents don't know about."

India tightened her hand on the phone. "How am I supposed to answer that? I don't want to hurt you, but I have to hope Jack and Mary Stephens are more suspicious than you and Dad."

"So do I, but don't leap to conclusions. Wait awhile."

Impatient with the same Zen-like acceptance Rachel had shown her in similar straits, India lashed out. "I don't plan to use this as an excuse to announce I'm her mother, but

I hope her real parents won't give her the freedom to hang herself.''

Rachel's silence lengthened. Finally she took a tolerant breath that sounded nearer than her voice. ''Maybe she made one innocent mistake tonight. Honey, don't push me away again. I'm glad you called me first and that you want to talk to me, but I'm not sure how to help you. I don't want to suggest anything that will make you turn away from me, but I really don't believe you can judge Colleen's family situation by one incident. Stay there. Keep your eyes open.''

India shook her head, alone again with decisions about the child she'd given up already. She shuddered. Talk about repeating history. When she'd known she was pregnant, she'd turned first to her mother. And Rachel's answer? *Give the child to someone who can make her a good life.*

''I'm sure you're right, Mom.'' Old habits died hard. She couldn't help saying what her mother wanted to hear. ''I'll get Dad. He'll want to say good-night to you.''

WHITE PAINT PERMEATED the fine black bristles of the brush India dragged carefully over the window ledge. *What am I going to do?*

Dip the brush in the paint-spattered can.

I promised not to involve myself in her life.

Wipe the bristles against the can's lip.

But he could have hurt her—and her father knew him. Her father wasn't surprised to find them together. India turned her face away from paint fumes that rose with the brush, but she had to look back to paint the trim her father had primed.

''Time for lunch, honey.''

She jumped at Mick's hesitant voice from below her.

Was she so transparent he felt he had to be gentle with her? "You can take off the kid gloves, Dad. I'm all right."

"I guess, but let me be perfectly honest. Your mother's worried about you, and I'm not supposed to trust your usual 'I'm all right' response." He climbed her ladder's lower rungs, forcing her to hold on or topple off. "You've lived close by, and you always showed up on the required occasions, but you were always all right. You didn't want college tuition. You never asked me to help you with stuff a dad's supposed to do, get your keys out when you locked them in the car, paint your apartment. I guess time between you and me stopped when you were sixteen. I'm not always sure what to say to you or how to put it, but I'd like you to try to trust me."

India shook her bangs out of her eyes and offered a contrite smile that felt strained. "I didn't abandon you and Mom. I let you help me make a bad decision, and even though it was completely my decision, I haven't felt comfortable with you since."

Mick took the brush from her. "Blame us for it. Be as angry as you can, but stop hiding from me. I came here to help you. When will you forgive me enough to think of me as your father again?"

"I'm guilty, not angry. I've even *wanted* to blame you and Mom, but I know better."

"Excuse me, Miss—Mrs.—Ms.—ma'am."

Startled by the gravelly, unsure voice, India leaned around her father. The ladder swayed, but the tall man below steadied it as if she and Mick weighed nothing. Instinctively, her heart ricocheting in her chest, India grabbed her father's wrist. "Dad."

"I'm Jack Stephens." The man, his blacker-than-black hair in silky curls that stroked his up-tilted head, eyed them with embarrassment. "I couldn't hear you until I got close enough to realize I was interrupting."

India gripped the aluminum ladder's cool edge. What had she said? What could he have heard? Nothing that would expose her connection to Colleen, but plenty she and her father should have discussed years ago in private.

"No." Mick curved his hand around India's. "We're on our way down. I came up to remind my daughter the Fish Shop stops serving lunch in twenty minutes." With a quick pat, he released her hand and started down. "I'm Mick Stuart, and this is my daughter, India."

Skipping the last several rungs, Mick dropped to the ground. Taking his cue, India tried to remain calm. *Act normal.* She clung to the sides of the ladder, but at the last minute, she couldn't risk touching Jack Stephens. Even brushing against him would feel like involving herself with Colleen. She skipped the same rungs her father had, to leap away from Jack.

Confusion lined Jack's broad forehead. She searched his face, high cheekbones, dark chocolate eyes that returned her intense interest. Jack smiled. He looked far younger than the forty-two she knew him to be.

His smile called up every defense she'd ever constructed. This man was her child's father. Colleen's father, as India could never be her mother.

"Hello, Mr. Stephens." India stepped to Mick's side. "My father handles the business. Dad, I'll go on to the Fish Shop and order for you, okay?"

"No, wait." Jack reached for her arm, but she pulled away. As his fingers drifted through air, he looked slightly embarrassed. "I came to see you. I believe we met at the festival."

India swept her ponytail over her shoulder. Nervously she inspected the pale yellow strands splayed across her palm. "No, I think I'd remember."

"You helped my daughter. I'd like to thank you."

For fifteen years, she'd handled every situation life

tossed her way, including a plane crash and a heart that stayed empty no matter how hard she tried to fill it. She might not have made the right choices, but she'd chosen. She flipped her ponytail back and took control. "How did you find me, Mr. Stephens?"

"Jack. My name is Jack." He shrugged his broad shoulders. "This is a small island. I just asked if anyone had seen you, and a friend told me Tanner'd hired you and your father to paint his house."

India couldn't hold back an admiring smile. He'd worked her own plan against her. "You didn't have to come. I'm sure anyone would have helped your daughter. She didn't want to go with that boy anyway."

In obvious relief, he braced his hands on his hips. "I can't tell you how happy I am to hear that, but I can say how grateful I am for what you did. Colleen's friends said Chris almost dragged her into his car."

So Chris was his name. India tried to look through Jack's handsome self-consciousness to the man beneath. Shouldn't he know what kind of boy this Chris was? His grip on the kid's neck implied he'd understood.

"Fortunately, she held on until I got there." India wiped her hand on her shirt and held it out to him. "Thanks for stopping by. I was glad to help."

Sliding one foot forward on the grass, Jack took her hand. India released her fingers from his, uncomfortable with a sudden warmth that sizzled up her arm. She noted the dusty jeans that clung to his muscled thighs, the faded Georgetown sweatshirt that stretched across his chest beneath a dark blue field jacket. How did a fisherman get so dusty?

The same pale dust flecked her father's clothes, but he'd spent the day stripping old paint off Mr. Tanner's trim. Had Jack lost his fishing business since he'd adopted Colleen?

Could this situation disintegrate any faster? Maybe she was jumping to conclusions. She needed time to think. At any moment, Jack might see something of Colleen in her. She couldn't let him have even the smallest suspicion. She had to escape his observant gaze.

"I'm starving, Dad. Mind if we go now?"

Mick's weathered skin flushed with embarrassment at her brisk tone. India squeezed his arm, amazed he didn't see her point.

He hung back. "We shouldn't leave our equipment out, India."

She turned him toward Mr. Tanner's crushed-shell driveway. "It'll be fine. Come *on*."

"I'll walk with you." Jack's deep voice stayed at her side as he lengthened his stride to keep up. India looked anywhere but at him.

At the top of the driveway, she slid into the passenger seat of her father's panel truck. Mick took his time coming around the hood, talking to Jack Stephens in quiet words she couldn't decipher. Tapping her feet on the floor, she was breathless when her father finally lifted a farewell hand to Jack and opened the door.

"Nice to meet you," Mick called.

Jack nodded. His questioning gaze made him look vulnerable, despite his height and work-hardened body. Wind lifted his silky jet curls again. India shifted in the truck seat. What color would Colleen's hair be under all that purple?

WAITING FOR COLLEEN outside the Arran Island House of Beauty, Jack tipped his soda can up. The cool drink tasted good on such an unnaturally warm spring day. As he dragged the back of his hand over his mouth, he eyed the woman balancing her groceries, her keys and the bulky

D.C. newspaper while she pushed through the grocery's front door.

In baggy overalls and a dark blue shirt, with the sleeves rolled up her slender arms, she looked more child than woman. Her long corn-silk ponytail didn't help.

If not for her, Chris Briggs might have hauled Colleen into his car. He might have killed them both, driving under the influence. With a shudder, Jack took another swig of soda that bit at the back of his throat.

His father-in-law came out of the market carrying his own copy of the newspaper. Hayden nodded toward India Stuart as he passed behind the commercial van emblazoned with the words, Stuart Painting. He spoke to her, but she shook her head. With a friendly shrug, he crossed the street in four strides and stepped onto the curb beside Jack. "She's the one?"

Jack nodded. "She'd rather spill everything in those two bags than ask for help."

Hayden grinned. "I offered. Did you?"

"No." Jack smiled, unsure of his response to India. "I figured I'd irritated her enough when I thanked her this morning."

Hayden thwacked the paper against his thigh. "She's cute, though."

"Cute?"

"Go over there and help her, son."

Jack opened his own truck's door. "I have enough woman trouble, and I thought you stayed on to help me."

Hayden cocked an eyebrow at the apparent non sequitur.

Jack looked at Hayden with affection. "Your advice just keeps getting worse."

Watching India Stuart, Hayden came around the truck and took the other seat. "Yeah, I guess. Maybe she's too young for you."

Shouldn't the guy feel some sort of loyalty toward

Mary? Jack danced uncomfortably around thoughts of her, himself.

He'd tried. He'd tried as hard as he could with Mary, accepting her accusations when she'd told him he'd driven her to do what she'd done to their marriage. He'd wanted a child as badly as she had. But as he peered through the House of Beauty's plate glass window, trying to identify which shadow belonged to his daughter, Jack wished he'd never found out the truth about Mary's affair. Wished he'd never known she'd settled for him only to keep the child they couldn't make together.

"There she goes."

Jack thought Hayden meant Colleen, but when she didn't stroll through the beauty salon's doors, he turned to the other side of the street in time to watch India's van rumble dustily away. Jack curled his fingers around the steering wheel.

"When I thanked her, she acted almost angry. She couldn't wait to get rid of me."

Hayden offered a sage nod. "People don't like to get involved. Maybe she's just a nice woman who helped Colleen because she couldn't pass a child in need, but she doesn't want to be thanked. Wouldn't you have helped a child in Colleen's position?"

Being in the right place at the right time didn't explain the ice in India Stuart's dark blue eyes. "I think there's more. She had to force herself to look at me." He pushed her from his mind. "Colleen is my first concern. I'll talk to Chris as soon as he crawls out from under his rock again."

"Didn't you speak to his mother?"

"I tried to talk to Leslie, but she isn't the same since Tom left them. The whole time we talked she nursed her youngest, and her twin boys climbed all over us. I think Chris requires more energy than she can give him. I suggested he should help more, and she told me he puts all his time and money into that fancy car of his.''

Hayden bounced his fist against the knee of his trousers. ''You'll find him. Hey, if he won't listen to you, maybe you can set that Stuart woman on him again. From what I hear, she held her own.''

''I can't afford to see the humor.'' Jack broke off, pleasantly surprised as Colleen pushed carefully through the shop door.

A breeze lifted her honey-blond hair into her eyes. Impatiently she brushed it away with a furtive glance, as if she didn't want anyone to see her without her purple rebellion.

Jack's relief evaporated. ''I don't think she gets it yet, either. Maybe I should have her thank India Stuart in person, too. It's only polite, and admitting her mistake to a stranger might make her see how big it was.''

AFTER THEY PUT AWAY THEIR equipment the next day, India and her father headed to the town square for an open-air market Mrs. Henderson had told them about. The local library sponsored a booth that sold used books. India stopped there first.

''You're new in town,'' the woman behind the wooden counter said. ''I'm Nell Fisher.''

India held out her hand. ''India Stuart. Mrs. Henderson told my father and me the market opens here every week.''

''Yes.'' The other woman waved a work-gloved hand at the people who strolled up and down the neat rows. Now that the weather had gone back to chilly normal, everyone wore coats that flapped around them and rubbed the wooden stalls. ''We probably have something you'd like. I recommend Clem Tyler's hydroponic tomatoes, and Reverend Goodling's wife tats beautiful lace collars and cuffs, if you're in the market.'' An excellent saleswoman, she pointed over her shoulder, at a rocky lean-to with its back to her stall. "And, of course, the requisite tie-dyed-anything-you-ever-wanted-to-wear booth."

India laughed. "Do you always participate?"

Mrs. Fisher nodded. "When I can get away. I don't have an assistant just now, so I have to close up while I'm here, but I hope to turn a couple of the youngsters into patrons, while their parents shop for better prices than we can get in the stores out here. You'll notice we don't have room for a mall, and we pay the price for our isolation."

India picked up a dog-eared copy of *Peter Pan*. "Do you read to the children?"

"If I gather a large enough crowd. You seem pretty interested."

India hesitated. Gossip ran both ways. Would a house-painting librarian make Colleen's neighbors suspicious? But no, she and her father had agreed on what she should say, to cover her failings as a painter. She was helping him out, the best he could afford. "I usually work as a librarian. I'm on sabbatical, and my father needed a hand."

"Really?" Interest lit Mrs. Fisher's eyes. "And how long do you plan to stay on the island?"

"Depends." India's breath grew short. "We don't know how much business we'll find for my father."

"Maybe you'd like to help me out if you have some free time in the evenings. We have a volunteer program." Mrs. Fisher lifted a stack of books onto the counter. "I just don't have a volunteer to man it at the moment."

"Volunteer?"

"Yes. Unless you're too tired in the evenings?"

"No." Drawn to the work she loved best, India leaped at the chance for more contact with the people who lived in this community with Colleen. "I'd love to help. My father might be able to spare me for a couple of hours some days, too."

"Good. Drop by the library tomorrow—" Mrs. Fisher broke off as a gleaming car braked at the curb next to the stall.

Hard to miss that car, or the girl who climbed out to stand, impossibly tall, unexpectedly uncertain. She'd washed that purple right out of her hair. With the palest brown cap of silky strands hugging her chin, she looked exactly like pictures of India's mother at fifteen.

India gripped the pole supporting the library booth. She should run for all their lives. This slender child, teetering on the razor blade of adolescence was definitely the daughter she'd given up.

Warmth, as big and bright as the sun, and twice as powerful, exploded in India's chest. She wrapped her arms around herself as if she could contain the astounding happiness that burst and blossomed to life inside her. She felt the same compulsion she'd had the day Colleen was born, to count all her fingers and toes, to make sure she was all right. And just as she hadn't then, she couldn't now. India moved her head from side to side. How could this happen?

"Hi." The girl twined her fingers in front of her. "My name is Colleen Stephens."

India managed a stunned nod. "I figured." She cleared roughness from her throat. Her heart pounded a drum solo. "I met your father."

"He told me." With an apparent eye for reinforcements, Colleen looked back at the car.

Her reminder of the boy who waited behind the steering wheel dragged India back to reality in a heartbeat. "You came with him?" she asked before she knew she was going to.

Colleen blushed. "Chris isn't always like he was that night at the festival." She swallowed hard and stared at Mrs. Fisher until the older woman moved to the back of her booth. Colleen thrust out her hand, offering to shake. "I just wanted to thank you."

India spiked a swift glance over Colleen's shoulder. Did Jack know she was out with Chris? She took her daughter's hand. It felt small and warm and totally vulnerable.

Her heart contracted. Chris could hurt this child so easily, and she didn't even recognize the danger. Protective instincts rose in India, as strong as if she'd raised Colleen from day one. Instincts she had to check.

"Colleen!" A tall white-haired man's sharp voice made the girl jump.

"Grandpa," she said, turning around.

"I take it you're with him?" The man tilted a contemptuous chin at Chris, and India swallowed a cheer.

"You're embarrassing me." Colleen looked stealthy. "He's not a bad guy."

Her grandpa shared India's doubts, but he broadcast them, not caring Colleen had left the car door open. "Has that boy had anything to drink today?"

"No." A quick blush reddened her skin. "We had a Coke after school. He's not like that."

"All the same, I'll take you home." The man looked at India. "You must be Miss Stuart."

"My grandfather, Hayden Mason." Colleen rammed her hands into her pockets. "I'm not coming home with you, Grandpa. I'm old enough to take a ride from a friend without you calling the angst police."

"I have no idea who the angst police might be, young woman, but I'm taking you home. Say goodbye to Miss Stuart."

"India."

He looked startled, and India realized he welcomed her contribution to the conversation no more than his granddaughter's. "India, then. Colleen, I'm busy this afternoon. Come now."

Colleen twisted her mouth in a frown India recognized. It usually came just before her mother put her foot down so hard the house rumbled. But Colleen gathered her wits with a wary look at Mrs. Fisher. "Goodbye, Chris," she called, a hint of panic edging her voice.

Without another word, he yanked her door shut and squealed away on smoking tires. India planted her feet firmly on the ground, instead of comforting Colleen, who broke her heart with a forlorn expression.

Colleen followed her stern grandparent as he turned, but she looked back at India. Defiance and a puzzled awareness struggled in her eyes. India dragged herself to her full height. If she couldn't stay out of Colleen's life without looking like a cyclone victim, she needed to leave. Colleen offered a halfhearted smile and lifted one hand that quickly flopped back to her side as her grandfather reached for her other sleeve.

India waved back, but Colleen looked away so fast, India wasn't even sure she saw. Realizing her daughter had truly come and gone, India shivered, finally feeling the cold air that snaked into her heavy sweater. She stopped waving and wrapped her arms around her waist.

"Great. I've turned into Granny Clampett."

Mrs. Fisher leaned across the booth's counter. "I didn't know anyone your age ever saw that program."

"JUST TALK TO HIM, DAD," Colleen whispered through the small opening in her doorway. "I'll never be able to show my face in front of my friends."

"What friends? Even you said Mrs. Fisher and India Stuart were the only ones close enough to hear.

"And Chris."

"Chris is out-of-bounds to you. He's too old, and he tried to hurt you."

"No one understands him except me."

"I understand him, and that's why I've told you to stay away. I need to be able to trust you, Colleen."

"Trust me? If you did, you wouldn't set Grandpa on me. Did you have him follow me after school?"

Jack almost laughed, but her frustration made him empathetic. Mary had told him how strict Hayden could be. "No, but he can't walk away when he sees you doing something dangerous."

"I don't want him here if he's going to embarrass me like that. He was worse than you."

Jack really had to hold back a grin. Maybe he owed Hayden some gratitude. "I'll talk to him, but try to see this afternoon from his point of view."

"No, thank you." She shut her door with a firm click.

Jack turned, wanting to whistle. She hadn't thrown herself back into Chris's car, and she'd come to him for help. Parenthood looked a little brighter tonight. He'd better find Hayden and explain the art of making good ideas seem as if they'd come from Colleen first.

He ran down the stairs, two at a time. Hayden looked up from his paper in the living room.

"We need to talk." Jack sprawled on the sofa. "You made me look good to her."

INDIA FIDDLED WITH THE SWITCH on the paint sprayer she was trying to clean. "Dad, I can't make this thing work."

"Let me see it."

But as she turned to him, paint and cloudy water spewed from the nozzle, covering Mick in a smelly cloud. He stopped, a frame from an old cartoon. She couldn't help laughing as he pulled off his glasses and stared at her, his eyes circled perfectly in white.

"Spray painting the boss?" he teased in a tone that promised retribution.

As he grabbed for the nozzle and she fell, a truck pulled

up at the edge of Mr. Tanner's driveway. Somehow, India knew who'd be driving.

"Jack."

He leaned out his window, worry creasing his forehead. "I'm sorry to bother you again. Have you seen Colleen?"

India clambered to her feet. Mick stood swiftly beside her. "What's wrong?" she demanded.

"We haven't seen her." Mick glanced down the road. "Shouldn't she be in school?"

"She should be." Jack shielded his eyes, more from their gazes than from the sun. He seemed intent on the sails just visible over deep trees at the end of the road. "Sometimes she goes to the marina. I thought she might have passed by here."

Chris and his shiny car tumbled in India's mind. "No." She wished him on his way so she could look for Colleen without his knowing. Mick's elbow in her ribs startled her.

"Tell him." Mick nodded toward Jack, his ghostly face not funny anymore.

"Tell me?"

India stared at her father. "Tell him?"

"About yesterday."

"I know what you want me to tell him, but Dad—"

"Tell me what?"

India grimaced. "I'm sorry. I'm being thoughtless, or maybe we're both butting in." She glanced her father's way. "You probably already know, but I ran into Colleen yesterday. She wanted to apologize. And Chris was with her."

"Hayden told me. You haven't seen her today?"

"No."

With a thank-you wave he hit the gas and headed toward the marina. India stared after the dusty cloud that rose behind him. "I'm supposed to stay out of her life, Dad. Remember?"

"At the cost of her safety? What if her grandfather hadn't told Jack?"

"I feel like a tattletale. I wish I could go look for her, too." But she'd given up that right fifteen years ago. India reached for the sprayer they'd left on the ground. "How serious do you suppose this is?"

Her father answered with silence. For several seconds, he only stared at her, his thoughts and his gaze uneasy. "It was serious with you."

"I don't know what to do. What if I'm as big a threat to her as Chris? What if she finds out about me, and they didn't even tell her she was adopted?" She glanced at the road again, clear now of Jack's dust. "Where is her mother anyway?"

"Maybe she works out of town."

"I pictured a close-knit, Beaver Cleaver family." Jack's hurt had deepened her concern for him, as well as for Colleen. It confused her. Worse, it seemed to create a bond between them. She still felt the emotional brush of his telling gaze, swiftly averted to hide his thoughts.

"India, be careful with that. You could cut yourself—"

Too late. She let the sprayer tumble to the ground and covered the gash on her palm with her other hand. She eyed her father, thoughts of Jack and Colleen weighting the air between them. "None of this was supposed to happen."

CHAPTER THREE

NARROWING HER EYES against the glare of the sun off polished chrome handles, India pushed through the drugstore doors and angled away from the soda fountain to the stocked shelves. She'd left her father cleaning the Tanners' yard. He'd offered to drive her, but she'd taken the long way, hoping for a glimpse of Colleen.

India turned down the aisle of first-aid products. She'd never considered what she might do if the baby she'd handed over to Mother Angelica had grown into a fifteen-year-old in trouble. Though he obviously loved her, Jack couldn't manage to keep Colleen from making one bad decision after another.

Were Colleen's actions merely those of an average girl of fifteen?

India stopped in front of the bandages. Frustration made her shift on restless feet.

She picked up a tin of Band-Aids. Dinosaurs. Not one serious-looking box in the row. Teletubbies, dolls with big hair, birds with big hair, even soldier gargoyles hulking across adhesive battlefields, but not one plain Band-Aid. And no answers to her questions, either.

"Grandma, what about this one? Golden Auburn? How could Dad object to Golden Auburn?

India dropped the tin. As it rattled across the floor, she ducked after it. Colleen's voice. She knew it with a mixture of delight and apprehension that clenched her stomach muscles. But "Grandma"? Colleen was playing hooky with her grandmother?

"Are you kidding? Your dad would throw Grandpa and me into the street." The light voice paused. "Frankly, I couldn't blame him. Absolutely no more hair color for you, Colleen."

"Auburn, Grandma. A-U-B-U-R-N. Not burgundy this time."

India rose slowly as Colleen inexorably turned her head.

"Trouble," the older woman said, not noticing her granddaughter's wandering attention. "T-R-O-U-B-L-E. Can you spell disaster? Put the dye back, and let's go home."

Recognition faded slowly to ambivalence in Colleen's gaze. India nodded, relieved she wasn't with Chris. Colleen lifted her chin in unwilling acknowledgment.

"I saw your father." India spoke before she had time to think twice about whether she should. "He's looking for you."

At least four inches shorter than the girl by her side, Colleen's grandmother also turned. A faint tint of lavender in her silvery hair hinted at Colleen's love of color. She grabbed her granddaughter's shoulder. "Oh, dear. I forgot the note. Did you speak to your teacher before you left? Did you ask for your assignment for tomorrow?"

Colleen grimaced. "I didn't go to last period. My other teacher, Mrs. Denton, held us late. They never call parents, Grandma. I figured you'd give me a note tomorrow morning, and I'd straighten it out."

The older woman hunched her tiny shoulders. "You might as well buy the dye. I'm swimming in soup now." But as Colleen grabbed a box off the shelf, her grandma snatched it away. "Don't you know a joke when you hear it? Let's pay for the rest of this and—" She broke off as the miniature ship's bell above the drugstore door clanged. "Uh-oh."

By the time India turned, Jack had already seen Colleen. His relief, potent as India's, seemed to confuse his daughter. India felt like a tennis spectator.

"Dad?" Colleen took the hair color from her grandmother and shoved it back onto the shelf. "I had a dentist's appointment."

Jack's smile took India's breath away. He looked so young, his wide mouth masculine and yet terribly tender.

"I forgot," he said. "Your assistant principal called to say you'd missed your last period class. Thanks for taking her, Nettie."

"I forgot the note. I'm sorry, Jack."

He shook his head, a man who'd fought free of danger. "No problem."

India sucked in a deep breath that somehow made Jack see her. For the slightest moment, they shared silent, heartfelt relief. Comforted and afraid all at the same time, India tried to withdraw. She had to get out of here before he began to wonder why Colleen mattered so much to her.

"Nettie, did Colleen introduce you to India?"

"Not yet, Dad." Colleen's exasperation sounded blessedly adolescent.

Jack seemed to agree. His grin widened. He walked toward India, only to narrow his gaze as he stared at her hand, still wrapped in the clean white cloth her father had produced from the depths of his truck. Her heart beat a strangely disturbing rhythm at his concern. She made an instinctive move for the door, but Jack blocked her way.

"Are you all right?" Spoken so close, the words skittered over her skin. Before she could answer, he wrapped his large hand around her forearm. Even through her dismay, she enjoyed the heat of his skin, the weight of his large, capable fingers.

No. This, most of all, wasn't supposed to happen. She tried to pull away. "I'm fine."

"Jack," a bluff voice said, "good to see you out of the boatyard." A burly man came out of the office behind the counter. He spelled S-A-F-E-T-Y to India.

"I just need these Band-Aids." She brandished the dinosaur tin like a trophy.

The man looked at her, startled. "Yes, you do. Your hand is bleeding."

Colleen and Nettie hurried around the shelves at the other end of the aisle. India ping-ponged back to Jack. "It's already stopped. I only cut it."

She wrenched away from his dark gaze, rationalizing her strange response to him. He knew things about Colleen that were forever lost to her. Little things, like her favorite ice cream. Big things, like the whys and wherefores of her belligerence toward him.

She tugged out of his grasp, but her arm felt cool where he'd touched her. Cupping her injured hand between her waist and the Band-Aids, she hurried to the counter. "How much are these?" She risked a last glance at Colleen, who stared back with curiosity.

Despite all her best intentions, India's mouth curved. Gladness overwhelmed her as she memorized the girl's sharp chin and soft cheeks, the graceful sweep of her poor distressed hair. Colleen smiled back, a real smile this time.

India's insides crumpled.

Her daughter. The tiny infant she'd loved and longed for and entrusted to Mother Angelica. No longer a mystery, but flesh-and-blood real, and for once in a safe place. Colleen looked like a miracle.

"Wait, that cut's dirty." Impossibly oblivious to the longing India wore like a coat, Jack Stephens strode to her side. "Do you need stitches?"

She shook her head and dodged his reaching hand. "No."

Nettie leaned in and gently plucked the edges of the cloth away. "It doesn't look good, young lady."

Jack covered the cut again and eased his shoulder in front of the older woman. "Careful, Nettie. You know how bleeding makes you queasy." To India, he was all business again. "The clinic's close. I'll drive you."

Though tempted, India came to her senses. She'd do a lot to snatch a few more minutes with Colleen, but in the end, it was too risky.

"I don't need to go." She dug change out of her pocket and waited for the man behind the counter to ring up her purchase. "I have to get back to Mr. Tanner's house and help my dad."

Jack explained to Nettie. "India and her father are painting the house."

"Are you?" Nettie's polite, old-fashioned manners deepened the burden of India's lie.

"We're almost finished, actually," India blurted, unnerved enough to say the first thing she thought. "I guess we'll head back to Virginia soon."

"You want a bag for this?" The man behind the counter pushed the tin toward her.

"No, thanks." She opened the lid and took out a large Band-Aid she managed to open with one hand and a little leverage from the other.

"Here, let me help you." Jack took the Band-Aid from her and put it on the counter. "What do you have to clean her cut with, Al?"

The man passed Jack a small, square package that contained a medicated wipe. India pulled it from Jack's fingers.

"I'll do it." She swabbed her cut, wincing as the treated wipe stung. Before she could reach for the Band-Aid again,

Jack picked it up and peeled off its backing. His bemused smile set off loud alarms that clamored up and down her body. He'd *never* understand why she was so reluctant to accept his aid. Not if she could help it.

He smoothed the bandage over her palm with exquisite gentleness and a wry look at the dinosaur springing across the colorful background. "Nice ornithomimus. How do you suppose they print the whole name on there?" His roughened, calloused fingers irritated her skin with pleasure and scattered her wits.

She pulled away. "Small dinosaur. Big Band-Aid." This man was not just her daughter's father. He was married to her daughter's mother. She scooped up her tin. "Thank you again."

So willing to lend aid to a stranger, Jack disconcerted her. She tugged at the strap of her overalls. Had she and her father stepped into another world when they'd crossed the long, low bridge to Arran Island? Or did people just naturally help each other in a small community? She flexed her sore hand.

"Can you drive?" Jack asked.

"I drove here." She peered around him, though he seemed to take up half the room. "Goodbye, Colleen." She had to mean it. She fought a lump in her throat. "Nice to meet you, Nettie." Was Nettie Jack's mother, or Mary's? She'd never even know.

"WHERE'S INDIA FROM?" Nettie asked.

Colleen slid across the truck's seat and bumped the rearview mirror out of place with her forehead.

"Are you okay?" Jack patted her head and readjusted the mirror. "I don't know where she lives, Nettie. Maybe Virginia, since she said they were heading back there. I guess she and her father go where they find work. Al told me he remembers an ad they placed in the paper a month or so ago.''

"Oh no. Their business must be off.'' Softhearted to a fault, Nettie leaned around Colleen. "And the only work they found here was the Tanners?''

Jack nodded, his attention split uncomfortably between Nettie and India's image in his mind, her feminine, soft body lost in her overalls. Water blisters on her palms puzzled him. "I assume so.''

"Then you'll have to find them something else,'' Nettie said.

He almost hit the brakes. "You mean find another job for them?'' His daughter's amused expression caught his eye. "How am I supposed to find another house for them to paint?''

"You know everyone on this island. Whose house needs paint?''

Jack cast a glance at the bay on his side of the truck. Fishing didn't provide the living it had for his father and his friends' fathers. "Who can afford new paint?''

Nettie settled back in her seat. "Just go through each of your friends, Jack. You'll come up with someone. A young girl like that, giving up her life to work for her father. Where is her mother anyway?''

"Maybe she likes to paint,'' Colleen suggested.

"Do you like to work with your father?'' Nettie made it sound like duty on a garbage scow.

Tense, Jack waited for Colleen's response. She took her time.

"Well, no, not really.'' She caught hold of his wrist, but quickly released it. Fifteen-year-olds must never show affection. "You don't treat me like one of your employees, Dad. You always have to instruct me, like I'm a kid.''

Her explanation hurt his feelings as much as her first answer. "You've never worked the nets for me, Colleen.

You've only sanded paint since we've had the boat out of the water. Did you know how to sand before I showed you?''

A mocking laugh gusted out of her mouth. "How hard is sanding? I can figure out how to push a piece of sand-paper back and forth.''

Jack tightened his hands on the wheel. "Let's let this go for now. I've enjoyed the past hour with you, and I'd like to stretch it as far as we can.''

To his astonishment, Colleen laughed. A sweet, rich peal of laughter he'd known all her life. He grinned. Somewhere inside her lingered his little girl, the child who'd once firmly believed he knew all the answers.

"You know, Dad, Marcy's mother has been after Mr. Shipp to paint their house.''

"Marcy?'' Jack knew the girl. "How's her eyebrow ring working out?''

"We're talking about her house. Honest, the paint looks as bad as Mrs. Shipp says. Maybe we should stop by there.''

Her sincerity reeled him in. Jack nudged her shoulder, teasing. "All right, but I have to know one thing, and tell me the truth.'' She looked so worried, he almost laughed. "Did Marcy pierce her own eyebrow?''

"Dad!'' She shoved back, which apparently didn't count as affection.

"All right, but your eyebrows are off-limits. Agreed?''

A FEW DAYS LATER, Colleen couldn't remember the laugh-ter she'd shared with her father. With one swift glance at him sanding the bow of the *Sweet Mary,* she dropped over the boatyard fence. Chris waited, engine running, behind a stand of trees that hid his car from her father. Boiling with resentment, Colleen slid into the passenger seat.

"What did he say to you?" Chris didn't even wait for her to speak before he turned into the street.

Colleen twisted on the vinyl. "Everything. He just kept on. He said if they had nothing to teach me I'd be bored, but making straight A's. Then he started on how I wouldn't be able to get into a good college."

Chris snorted. "How can he expect you to know what you want to do for the rest of your life? I'm eighteen, and I don't know."

Colleen held a careful silence. Her father wouldn't be surprised to hear that. "He said I let you change me, that I've been different since you came along—like I needed you to tell me school is a waste of time."

"Since I came along?" Chris's derisive laugh raised prickles of discomfort along Colleen's spine. He leaned over for a swift, hard kiss. "I don't see a thing wrong with your attitude. Maybe I should talk to your dad, myself."

"He's not kidding, Chris. He really doesn't like you."

"Do I care?" Chris nosed the car to the curb. "He doesn't have to like me as long as you do."

Pretending to check the buckle on her boot, Colleen shifted away from Chris's hand. Lately, when he touched her, he made sure she knew what he wanted and how hard he'd try to take it.

She edged another thin slice of space between them. "You could try more with Dad. My grandparents agree with him, and they all try to keep me from seeing you."

Chris slammed his fist on the gearshift. "I'm tired of Jack Stephens. Who does he think he is? I heard the bank came sniffing around to see how much work he's done on the repairs. He's a deadbeat, Colleen."

She might be mad at her dad, but Chris's opinion made her madder at him. She shrank against the car door. "Don't talk about him that way."

Chris burned her with angry eyes. "I'll bet you don't tell him to shut up when he talks about how bad I am."

"I didn't say shut up." She wrapped her palm around the door handle. "He *is* my father."

Chris snatched a handful of her sweatshirt. "Maybe it's time you picked one of us. Look at the way I treat you. Are you loyal to me or to a guy who acts like you're a baby?"

Unwilling to admit Chris frightened her, even when he forced her to recognize her fear, Colleen tightened her hand on the door. "You want me to choose between you and my dad?"

"Yeah, between me and some guy who'll be lucky to keep one of those old broken-down nets on his boat. He thinks he's such a man."

Colleen opened the door with a slow screech of metal against metal. "I called you because I needed to talk to you. You say you care about me."

Chris softened his grip on her shirt, trying to turn his palm against her breast. "I say I love you."

She shoved him away. "I've asked you not to do that."

His pupils glittered. "Maybe you are a baby after all." His voice hissed like a snake.

Truly afraid now, she slid backward out of the car. He laughed when she landed on the pavement on her bottom.

"Maybe I am a baby, but I'll walk from here." She scrambled to her feet, hauling her short skirt down. "Okay?"

"No, it's not okay. Don't act like this. You always try to ignore me when you're mad. We're just arguing."

"I wanted to talk."

"You *want* me to guess what you want. I know what I need."

As if that settled everything, he pulled the door shut and drove off. Colleen stared after him, her legs shaking. He drank more than she ever let on, because he hated living in this small town where everyone knew his life inside and out. But Colleen didn't think he'd had anything today.

He'd left her in the middle of the street, said terrible things about her father. And he'd tried to grope her again. Could her dad be right about Chris?

What had he meant by that crack about making him guess what she wanted? She'd told him, in every way she knew, not to touch her like that. And how was she supposed to tell anyone what she wanted if no one ever listened to her, anyway?

She turned toward the marina, more alone than ever. If only her mother hadn't died. Colleen swallowed hard. Even after three years, she missed her mom, but she couldn't talk to her dad about that, either. No matter how much she wanted him out of her business, she hated the look of pain that still came into his eyes when he didn't think she noticed.

And Grandma. *Poor Grandma needs someone to look after her more than I do.* If only her mom...

At the top of the hill, Colleen paused. She'd meant to ask Chris to take her to the marina. Looking out at the water, at the sailboats bobbing all around her, she felt clearer, calmer. But today she missed her mother, and her mother had never liked the bay.

She'd resented the water like another woman who stole Colleen's father away, and sometimes even Colleen had wondered why he'd worked such long hours. She scuffed her feet in the gravel at the edge of the road.

Her dad and mom had loved each other, but they'd had problems, like every other married couple she'd ever heard of. Her dad's grief had been real after her mom died. Why did everyone believe she couldn't see what went on around her?

Colleen hesitated on the road. She couldn't go home.

Grandma badgered almost as much as her father about grades. Maybe she'd go to the library. She'd entered her favorite picture of her mom in their exhibition of island families. They hadn't sent it back yet, so maybe they'd used it. Her father certainly hadn't missed it from the piano.

Too busy looking for signs she'd spent ten seconds alone with Chris, he couldn't seem to see their problems went deeper than her choice of a boyfriend. Chris was right about one thing. He already saw her as a woman. She mattered to him, but her father still believed she was a baby. Because of his attitude, even strangers like India Stuart treated her like an infant.

India Stuart. A perfect match for Dad. A worrier who had no problem ''helping'' even though it meant butting into someone else's life. Colleen scuffed her feet deliberately along the rough pavement. She tried to forget how scared she'd been of Chris. He'd been completely sober the day he'd driven her to thank India for her help, and he'd given her a lift even though he'd believed India ought to apologize to him for hitting his car. Nothing wrong with that.

NELL FISHER ROSE WITH INDIA and offered her hand across the desk. ''I'm so glad you came in. I can't convince my regular patrons they have time to read to the toddlers or shelve books, or even read back titles for me while I do inventory.''

India lifted her shoulders, uncomfortable with omissions in the picture she'd drawn for Nell. But she might learn more about Colleen here, and then she could go home as she'd told Nettie she was going to. ''I'm glad you can use me.'' They turned together to the door of Nell's small office. ''I'll see you on Saturday morning at nine for the toddler's story time?''

Already distracted by the unusual number of people crowding into the main room to see the historical society's display of island family photos, Nell nodded. As she drifted away, India searched for Viveca Henderson.

Her landlady had invited her to see this exhibition. India had jumped, just at the off chance of seeing a photo of Colleen as a small girl, as an infant if Viveca could recognize her. But did she need any more regret? Because surely she would grieve even more if she stumbled on a record of Colleen's life.

India found Viveca at the exact spot where she'd left her, a perfect vantage point. Viveca leaned into India's shoulder and nodded at the young girl with honey hair who was disappearing around the first panel of photographs.

"That Stephens girl. Her father ought to worry more about her than about his boat." Her voice rang tartly. "Are you ready, dear? How nice of you to help Nell out." She held her vintage fifties skirt away from the crowd. "You know, I always liked Colleen until she started going around with that Chris Briggs."

India no longer wanted to hear island gossip about Colleen. In fact, she bit gently at the inner skin of her cheeks to swallow a defensive response.

The first lady of the Seasider went on. "She's making decisions she'll regret one day."

India curled her nails into her palms. The woman could be too right. *Am I not living proof?* Though she'd hoped for just this kind of opportunity, she couldn't take it now. Instead, she wished she'd stayed home, where she'd never have known the townspeople had already begun to judge Colleen.

Small towns. They provided loving arms or bitter verdicts. No in-between in a small town.

Hoping to change the subject, India pointed at the first

line of pictures, of women in crisp white shirtwaists and full skirts and men proudly flanking their fishing boats.

"Do any of these families still live here?"

Mrs. Henderson obliged. India cruised along at her side, only half taking in Captain Torquay and the shark he'd netted one day with his shrimp, or the Honorable Honoria Madison, the mayor's wife who'd run away with a traveling milliner.

"No, Viveca, you're wrong about Honoria. She was my great-great-great-aunt, and I happen to know...." A woman India didn't know spoke up.

India ducked out of the conversation, impatient to see the later photos, the ones from the past fifteen years. She strolled through the panels, drinking in the good library air, flavored with old and new books and casually stored newspapers. She missed this world.

She turned a corner and saw Colleen. A study in concentration, the girl might have been completely alone. She saw nothing, appeared to hear nothing except memories suggested by the photo that held her attention.

Her look of utter loneliness drew India on reluctant feet. She'd been right to stop Chris from taking Colleen with him that night, but she was completely wrong to speak to her now, to intrude on the privacy her daughter had drawn around herself. Colleen could never be her child. And she couldn't let herself forget that.

But Colleen didn't notice her. Over the girl's shoulder, India stared at the picture in its simple silver frame. A beautiful woman laughed with love at Jack as he curved his arm around her and smiled into the camera. Something about his smile... The vulnerable curve of his mouth sparked an uncomfortable pang in India's heart, but the woman's blissful face intrigued. Her blond hair, as pale as sea foam after a storm, clung to the woven shoulder of Jack's sweater. Her eyes overflowed happiness.

Mary Stephens, at last. Ashamed of her involuntary envy, India pressed her hands to her belly. "Is she your mother, Colleen?"

As if India at her side didn't surprise her, Colleen stretched her hand to the finely carved frame. Her eyes glowed, brilliant yet subdued, like light seeping past the door of a closed room. She rubbed one fingertip around the woman's face.

"That's Mom. She died three years ago."

CHAPTER FOUR

DEEP SADNESS HELD INDIA silent in the face of Colleen's lingering grief for her mother. Colleen kept her eyes trained on the photo.

"They adopted me when I was only a few hours old. Mom always said adopted children were luckiest, because their parents chose them. I felt pretty lucky until she died."

Aching for her, India lifted her hand to touch the girl's arm, but she kept her comfort to herself as Colleen turned with an accusation in her eyes.

"Why does everyone in this town take Dad's side about Chris when no one knows him the way I do?"

"I can't speak for everyone else."

"Why do you, then? What do you think you know about Chris that I don't?"

Nothing here had turned out as India had expected. Her daughter no longer had a mother. *And I can't step in.* She couldn't tell the truth, and she definitely didn't want to lie. Not now, when she needed to most.

"When I was your age, I made a mistake." Putting her hand on her throat, India felt for the lump that made talking difficult. "I don't know how to tell you this. I've never talked to anyone about that time. I hurt myself and my parents—I hurt too many people. Maybe, when I saw you with Chris, I thought of that. Maybe I just don't want you to be hurt, and I don't know Chris except for what I saw of him that night at the festival."

"What makes you think your past has anything to do with me?"

Reaching behind herself, India gripped the lip of a bookshelf. She'd already confessed too much. "Colleen, I know—I *know* you think nothing bad will happen to you. You can tell right from wrong. You can't imagine why you'd make a foolish decision."

Her wide eyes slightly softening her air of haughtiness, Colleen stepped back. "Yeah? So?"

"I don't want any girl your age to go through what I did."

"No one in this town believes I'm capable of thinking for myself."

"Maybe you should think about your grandparents and your father. Think of the place you live and how these people look at you."

Colleen raked her fingers through her hair, a gesture so familiar to India it brought instant tears to her eyes. Colleen might have been India's mother in youthful form. India bit the inside of her cheek again. No crying, no whining. *I can take this. She's the important one.*

Colleen only shook her head in disgust. "I know how they talk. To them, I'm a child. You're a complete stranger, and even you gossip about me." *Stranger* came out of her mouth like an epithet.

"Colleen!"

India's tears vanished at the harsh rasp of Jack's voice. She turned. Tall and male, he vibrated with the wrath of an angry parent.

"Apologize." Silk in his voice chased apprehensive shivers down India's back.

"Dad, I—"

He stopped her with a fed-up look. She tilted her chin.

"I'm sorry, Miss Stuart." Without warning, she relaxed, the stiffness falling out of her body as she tried to claim all of India's attention. "Sometimes I let my temper go, but I understand what you tried to tell me."

Touched beyond bearing, India turned to Jack. "She had a right to be upset."

"I know you left the boatyard with Chris." Jack closed in on his daughter. "That's what this is about, isn't it? You have to get me back because you're too young to date an eighteen-year-old boy?"

Colleen's pink blush spread. She grabbed the loose cloth of his sleeve, evidently surprising them both. "I wouldn't do that to you, Dad. I don't like sitting in that boat shop, and the dust hurts my head. I just wanted to see—" She broke off and pulled her hand away, trying to retire back into her adolescent shell. Her eyes drifted over Jack's shoulder to the photo of him with Mary.

As he followed her gaze, his face tightened with pain, but only long enough for him to catch himself. "Let's go, Colleen."

"Dad, I'm sorry."

In the grip of need she didn't understand or trust, India curled her fingers over the hard, strained muscles in his forearm. Why were they so reluctant to talk about Mary Stephens? What had happened to make them so protective of each other? She had no right, but she wanted to make it better. "Maybe you should—"

He stepped away from her, in a hands-off gesture she couldn't ignore. In a moment of startling clarity, India realized her concern for Jack stood apart from her burgeoning, maternal anxieties for Colleen.

India backed into one of the panels. Mercifully, Colleen and Jack were too fixed on each other to notice.

His hands shook on Colleen's sleeves as he turned her toward the door. Rooted to the floor, India ached to do something. Clearly Colleen regretted letting Jack find out she'd needed to see her mother's picture.

India tossed her ponytail over her shoulder. Had he considered renewing the paint on *his* house? A watery smile curved her mouth, but Jack's shadowed eyes cut to her heart again.

"I wish I'd learned to swim better," she said as she watched them leave. "I'm in way over my head here."

"India?" Viveca Henderson's voice preceded her hand on India's shoulder. "To whom are you speaking? Are you aware you're quite alone?"

As INDIA SLIPPED INSIDE her hotel room, Mick came through the adjoining door, holding a towel to his chin as if he'd just finished a shave. His smile made her feel normal again.

"We've had company," he said.

"Who now?"

"I left his name—" Mick crossed back into his own room, and India followed in his footsteps. He bumped into her as he turned with a business card he took off the desk. "What's wrong with you?" he asked.

"We have to get out of town."

"You sound like a Clint Eastwood movie."

India snatched his towel away. "Mary Stephens died three years ago. Colleen can't talk to Jack, and Jack's heart is broken."

Mick stepped back. "You expected a fairy tale?"

Though they'd disagreed so often for so many years, Mick's pragmatic acceptance of Colleen's family comforted India. She might be overreacting if he didn't panic with her. "I like happily-ever-after, Dad."

"So you want to run away before you see if she gets one?"

"Run away? I've tossed myself nearly into the middle of their problems. I have to get out before I confess who I am."

Mick shook his head. "You won't. You know you can't."

"I'm dying to." India slumped on his neatly made, rust-colored hotel comforter. In the silence, water dripped from a faucet. The heater struggled to live but gave in with a gurgle. India lifted her head. "Thank you for coming with me. I'm so grateful I can be honest with you."

"See? I don't know how many times I've told you to come to me when you have a problem. Tell me about Jack's heart."

She froze. "I usually don't come to you because you hear and see too well."

"We painters." He waved an admonishing finger at her. "People talk to us. You might think bartenders hear it all, but give a man a paint can, and he looks like he's waiting to solve all your problems. Remember Tom Sawyer."

"He worked his way out of painting."

Mick gave a move-it-along motion with his right index finger. "Jack's heart?"

"Colleen came to the library to look at her mother's picture, but Jack was in the picture, too." Searching for the meaning underneath, India frowned. "Maybe she wanted to see her parents together again? Anyway, I don't think she told him she was coming to the library. I think they'd had some sort of argument, and she'd pulled a disappearing act."

"Familiar story."

"You mean for her? No, you mean me, but I only disappeared when you couldn't help me anymore."

"Your mother and I are your family, just like Jack is Colleen's. We were supposed to help, especially when you needed us most. Look at Colleen. She's the same age you were when you got pregnant. Now, make me believe she could provide for a child of her own."

India refused to contemplate his homespun truth, but

neither could she take the absolution he offered. "When Jack showed up, he asked her where she'd been. Instead of answering, she just looked at the picture, and he looked, too. I've never seen anything like the pain in his eyes, but he covered it up so fast I almost thought I'd imagined it." She rubbed her chest. "No, I didn't imagine it."

"You like Jack." Mick leaned against the desk.

"I'm confused about Jack, because he's Colleen's father."

"He's a good father, but why won't she talk to him?"

"Exactly." India slapped her hands against her thighs. "And that's the one question I cannot ask them."

"I think you might hang yourself on several questions." Mick straightened and held out the business card. "Like I said, we have a new client."

India tilted the card toward the weak gold and green lamp. "Leon Shipp. Power Trucks for Power Men?"

"He wants us to paint his house. We could stay another week or so." Mick nodded at the card. "If you think we should."

"No, I don't." She blushed. "But I volunteered to help with toddler story time at the library, so we have to stay until Saturday."

Mick laughed. "Run to the familiar? I'll call this Leon and tell him to expect us tomorrow morning. Okay?"

India tilted her head sharply to one side. "I'm afraid."

As if she were his little girl again—and she'd been a daddy's girl once—Mick sank onto the edge of the bed beside her and tucked her cheek against his rough shirt. "I know you won't hurt anyone—well, except yourself, and I'm here this time to help you if you make that mistake again. I don't want you to spend fifteen more years wondering what might have been."

"She's your granddaughter, too. And she's Mom all over again."

His chin moved up and down against her forehead. "Mmm-hmm."

Miserably she clutched his sleeve. "I wish I could give you back everything I took from you."

"Shh. You refused to take anything from us, India."

"I love you, Dad."

As she absorbed her father's silence, she realized how long it'd been since she'd last said those words.

Mick cleared his throat. "I'd paint Leon Shipp's house and his entire fleet of bumper cars to hear you say that again."

India smiled. "Power trucks, Dad."

"Whatever. Try not to ruin the moment, honey."

AT THE TOP OF THE HOTEL'S rickety wooden steps, Jack hesitated. By the time he reached India's door, his courage damn near deserted him. Whatever she'd said to Colleen at the library had made his daughter more receptive to him. On the way home, he'd kept silent, afraid anything he said to Colleen might only push her further away. But the moment he parked the truck, she'd announced she wouldn't see Chris anymore unless they met within a group of her friends.

Which ought to cut down nicely on their time together. And Jack didn't intend to look that gift horse in the mouth.

Still puzzled over India's unexpected powers of persuasion, Jack stared at her sea-salted, pale gray door. He rubbed his palms against his jeans. Sweaty as a teenage boy's, they bumped over the denim. If he didn't knock now, he never would. He owed India an apology for the brusque way he'd treated her at the library, especially since she'd managed to help his daughter.

He'd shut down the moment he realized Colleen had come to see her mother's picture. Memories of Mary sprang a truckload of feelings on him, just when he felt least prepared to deal with the past. Hayden had snapped that photo of them together the day they'd heard Colleen was coming.

Jack hated that picture. He wondered that no one else had ever seen the truth in his eyes. That morning, Mary had told him Mother Angelica had called. At the same time, she'd confessed she'd made love with another man. She'd said she couldn't go on with their marriage without coming clean. The man had been one of the island's summer people, and Jack hadn't let her say his name.

"I just wanted to remember what love felt like without a purpose."

Mary's words still tore him apart with a deeper emotion than he'd ever felt for her again. Both desperate to have a child, they'd tried every crazy procreation theory anyone suggested. In some horrible, too-sane recess of his mind, he'd understood what she'd meant about needing a different kind of love.

In the same breath as her confession, she'd asked him to stay with her and adopt the infant girl Mother Angelica had offered them. How many times over how many years had he wished she'd kept her secret?

Able to feel such strange compassion for Mary, he'd believed he would be able to forget her betrayal. He never had. He'd loved her still, but he'd never loved her in the same way. He'd hidden from the truth behind work and behind his and Mary's mutual joy in Colleen. She'd used him to keep the baby who'd, in a way, cost them their marriage. He'd accepted the compromise.

Why now, outside India Stuart's room, had he lost his long-standing ability to shield himself from those memories? Impatient, he stepped forward and pounded on the door.

Startled at the shotlike echoes in the otherwise silent street, he peered at the windows around him. His resolute knock had sounded more like police on a raid. Just the kind of commotion to raise a dozen or more Arran Islanders.

Nobody answered the door. He knocked again, more gently, just in case India had ducked behind her bed at his first demand to be let in. Still no answer. He turned toward the stairs, feeling foolish. All that idiotic soul-searching, just so he could apologize to an empty room.

Glancing down the street to the bay, he saw India before he'd gone down one stair. In silky blue shorts and a white oversize tank top, she ran through the waning sunshine like a grasshopper, all arms and legs that flailed in way too many different directions.

He laughed to himself. "Exercise is exercise. I thought she'd be more graceful."

Her clumsy stride didn't detract from the taut line of her thighs or the sweet curve of her upper arms. Jack tightened his hand on the stair rail. *Oh, my God—I just ogled her.* Again he surveyed the surrounding windows. Thankfully, not a single curtain twitched. And India came toward him.

"Jack?" she panted as she crested the hill.

A stride like that ought to leave her out of breath. "India," he returned, descending the steps two at a time. Movement made him feel less asinine, less as if she'd caught him loitering outside her door. Since she had.

"What's up?" Her deep blue gaze narrowed. "Is Colleen all right?"

Well, at least she didn't assume he'd come on his own behalf. "She's fine, better even. I don't know what you said to her, but you must have gotten through."

India's guilty start piqued his interest. "What do you mean?" she asked in an innocent tone he didn't trust.

"She promised not to see Chris alone again."

"You mean like on a date?"

He nodded. "Finally, one for our side." *Stop stalling. Say what you came to.* "I'm sorry I was rude earlier."

India backed up as if she'd stepped on a cat. "Not at all." Color flooded her cheeks. Her gaze ducked his. "You were busy with your daughter."

"What *did* you say to her?"

"I just—" She swallowed. The muscles in her throat tightened above the nest of her sharp collarbones.

"You just what?" Heeding a sudden need to know the texture of her skin, he trailed his finger through the beads of moisture that hugged her rounded shoulder. Unexpected desire raced in his blood. His mouth watered to taste her taut skin just beneath her jaw, where her pulse fluttered even faster now than when she'd stopped running.

Did his nearness affect her, too?

India looked down at his finger against her skin. Jack jerked his hand away and tried to remember what she'd last said. "You just what?"

She tilted her head, her defiant expression astonishingly like Colleen's. "I admitted I'd used some bad judgment when I was her age that hurt my family." The words spilled from her, as if they weighed too much to carry inside.

Jack frowned. Surprised. He didn't want to know after all. "I appreciate your help, and I don't know how to say this without sounding harsh, but I'm not sure she needs to hear about anyone else's bad decisions." He stopped, realizing he'd insulted her, though she remained stoic. "I mean—judgment."

"She wanted to know why no one trusts Chris."

"Why won't she talk to me?" He shut his mouth, reluctant to follow in his daughter's footsteps and pull India any deeper into their lives.

"I know I meddled, but the mistakes she can make are

even more dangerous than the ones I made at her age. I should have thought harder before I spoke to her.''

Jack hesitated. ''I'm grateful for her change of mind about Chris, but I don't know if she should be talking to you about family matters.''

How could Colleen share her confidences with a stranger? Even a stranger who ran like a tipsy centipede and, in moments like rare treasures, smiled as if she knew how to make the most out of joy. Colleen should talk to him.

Now India's smile turned brittle. ''I'm sorry if I over-stepped.''

''No, I can't imagine you did.'' She'd disappeared that night at the festival. She'd all but refused his gratitude for helping Colleen. ''I'm being rude again, but Colleen confuses me. I always thought her diaper days would be the hardest. You can't go to the bathroom without making sure someone keeps an eye on an infant, but now she's a teen-ager, I suddenly realize how much more she needs guidance.''

''Even if she refuses to believe she does?'' India finished for him.

Maybe she had known how to talk to Colleen without saying more than she should. What mistakes had India Stuart made? What had she done that made her so anxious to help his daughter?

He lifted his chin. ''You must know fifteen-year-olds. Nieces? Nephews?''

''No, I'm an only child.'' Color stained her cheeks again, beautiful pale pink that deepened the blue in her eyes. ''I've just worked with children.''

Intrigued, Jack settled one foot on the stair behind him. ''You volunteer?''

India wrapped her arms across her rib cage. Her fingers looked too slender, splayed over her shirt. Her gaze became shuttered with reluctance. "I work at the library at home. I'm helping my father this spring. If you'll excuse me, Mr. Stuart, I'm still sweaty, and the weather's changing again."

A librarian? She'd waited all this time to mention it? Why? "What did I say that turned me into Mr. Stuart? I was Jack when you ran up."

India scooted past him, her back to the opposite rail. She must have run along the bay, but the salt on her skin was perfume. Drying, it left interesting, powdery patterns. Would her fragile wrist taste different than the full, earthy curve of her mouth?

She braced one hand on her hip and the other against the wooden building, as if she heard his thoughts. Restraint tightened her tone. "You asked me not to pry. Maybe you shouldn't, either?"

He hesitated. One step closer, and he'd ask her questions a single man asked a single woman. Like why she was so afraid of the awareness that ran like a current between them.

But he wasn't just any single man. As he searched the shadows on India's face, he remembered he was a fisherman who worked on another man's boat so he could pay to repair his own trawler. His daughter barely spoke to him from her side of the great adolescent divide, and his in-laws seemed to agree he was making a mess of things.

"Maybe I'm the one who's overstepping." Maybe, deep down, he'd come for more than a thank-you. He'd come for his own information, but he'd discovered too much. Finding out what had hurt her enough to teach her how to reach his daughter required a commitment he had no time to make. "I'd better get home before Nettie sets the kitchen on fire and Colleen decides it's already too late to start her homework. Thanks again, India." He stepped onto the sidewalk. "Good night."

CHAPTER FIVE

SATURDAY MORNING, India haunted the clock, anxious to do her own kind of work. Showered and dressed too early for the toddler's reading group, she made herself sit with a cup of coffee until it was time to go.

Finally she ran down the quivering stairs outside her room. Pursing her lips, she tried to whistle as she strode toward the library. Managing only to blow air, she allowed herself a furtive skip over the curbs at the street corners, until she reached the library building.

"No! I'm tired of lying to my father to be with you, Chris."

India stumbled over the completely level sidewalk. Colleen. India turned slowly to her right, hoping she'd be wrong, that he'd have found some other child to pick on.

No. Once again gripping Colleen's arm, Chris tried to pull her away from her two friends. India hesitated, shaking with rage even more intense than the last time. She couldn't let this happen, not to anyone, not to *her* child.

With one clenched fist, she pushed aside strands of hair that brushed her face. She searched for the candy-apple lovemobile. Chris hadn't parked his car on the street, but as attached as he was, he must have left it close by. She couldn't let him take Colleen to it, especially if Colleen didn't want to go.

"Your father never has to know." Yards that felt like miles away, Chris yanked Colleen behind him and eyed the other girls. "Marcy? Leah? Do you think Jack Stephens has to know I'm taking Colleen with me?"

His plain threat fired a shudder through India. Affection played no part in Chris's need for her child today.

"Leave her alone." Colleen's blond friend launched herself at Chris's chest, but he brushed her off like a fly.

India took flight. *Be calm. Be smart. Don't let him see you'd like to take him apart.* But before she reached the four teenagers, Viveca Henderson stepped out of an alley, a blue-uniformed policeman in tow.

"Here he is, Ted. I'm tired of Chris running amok in our streets, and with our young girls. You take him with you, and keep him away from these children."

Ted, the policeman, hooked his arm through Chris's and jerked his head toward the small square red granite building behind him. "I've been waiting for you to mess up, kid. I just didn't know you'd oblige me at my own back door."

India took a few more steps into the street. A white sign nailed to the wide oak door at the center of the building read Official Parking Only. Arran Island Police Headquarters.

"Are you arresting me?" Chris demanded belligerently.

Ted shrugged. "You and I are long overdue for a chat. We'll go from there." He tipped his hat to Viveca. "Thank you, Mrs. Henderson. I'll take over now."

"Goodbye, Chris," Colleen said, apparently unable to welcome the sight of him going to jail. He didn't even look back as Ted took him away. "Do you want me to call your mom?"

"Don't bother. This is your fault, Colleen. Leave me alone."

Disillusionment bunched Colleen's fragile features. India ached for her. Suddenly she understood parents who wanted to give their children anything and everything. What wouldn't she do to make Colleen's trouble better?

But Viveca nodded, completely satisfied, as she turned to Colleen and her friends. "As for you girls—"

"Colleen?" Her name burbled out of India's mouth. "Are you and your friends busy? I need some help."

All three girls started, surprised to see India. Colleen's two friends gaped as if she'd risen from the bay. Colleen's smile looked dazed, and Viveca grimaced at the interruption.

India threaded her voice with sugary enthusiasm. "I'm helping out at the library this morning, and the toddler's story group is making lion puppets. I don't have enough parents." Astounded at the lie that came out of nowhere, she steamed ahead. Colleen and her friends looked as if they'd already got the point of Viveca's lecture. "I need someone to cut, someone to glue and someone else to braid yarn into manes. What do you say?"

"I think we should talk to your parents," Viveca suggested with relish.

"Do you?" India wanted to go to Colleen, but she'd already done far more than she should have. What she'd do for any child in trouble, she could not do for her own daughter.

Colleen's eyes looked too wide. Her skin gleamed too pale. Could she be in shock?

"Will you help me?" Unable to bear Colleen's lack of any other response, India was afraid to leave her out here in the cool morning air.

"Colleen!" Elbowing her, the girl on Colleen's left pushed her lovely pale blond hair away from her forehead and revealed an earring fastened distractingly to her right eyebrow.

India stared. Was this Marcy or Leah? She snapped her mouth shut. So what if Colleen's friend had pinned an earring through her eyebrow? She'd also tried to come to Colleen's rescue. Twice.

"We'll help." As Colleen took stock of the back of the police station and Viveca Henderson's eagerness, her frown hardened into disdain.

India swallowed a victorious whoop. She'd half feared Colleen would worry he wouldn't want to see her again.

Colleen shifted her whole body, firmly turning her back on the station. "India, this is Marcy." She flapped her hand at the one with the eyebrow ring before she waved at the other girl. "And this is Leah."

"Marcy." India shook their hands in turn. "Leah." She turned to Mrs. Henderson. "Don't you think they were trying to help Colleen?"

"Yes, but Colleen's the one that worries me."

"Don't worry, Mrs. Henderson. I know what you want to say to me. I guess you wouldn't be the first, but I've finally heard what everyone else said before you," Colleen said.

"Are you sure?"

Her concern looked even stronger than her love of gossip. India stayed out of the argument. At last, Viveca seemed satisfied with what she read in Colleen's eyes, as the girl nodded. "All right, but remember, I'll be watching you girls."

India joined them to watch Viveca stroll away, tucking her big white purse beneath her elbow. India smiled. She'd underestimated her landlady.

"Marcy, Leah, this is India Stuart."

"You're the one who helped us before." Marcy apparently did all the talking. Leah just stared as she redid her long auburn ponytail with shaking fingers.

India nodded. "I'd be grateful for your help now." Ignoring Marcy and Leah's identical doubts, she started toward the library. "Normally, I cut out felt and sew the pieces together for the bodies, but I don't have my sewing machine with me, so we'll have to improvise with glue." Babbling, she tried to give the girls time to recover.

Colleen lagged behind the others, who seemed anxious to look as if they were on their own. Colleen caught India's arm.

"Are you going to tell my dad?"

India hesitated. "Mrs. Henderson may. I'm not sure someone shouldn't."

Colleen tightened her grip. "I wasn't going with Chris. I thought you understood me, India. I thought I might be able to trust you."

Joy and dismay sweeping simultaneously over her, India shook her head. "You need to trust Jack. He's your father."

"He worries too much, and I'm half-afraid of what he'd do to Chris. Dad still thinks of me as a child."

India knew the story. During her father's business crisis, her parents had directed their energy toward saving the family's livelihood. They'd ignored her efforts to help and assumed she was too young to trust with their financial straits. But Gabe, Colleen's natural father, had treated her like the adult she'd thought herself.

"Chris considers you grown-up?"

"No." In her impatience, Colleen looked more than ever like India's mom. "I wonder if he sees me as a point he has to make. Everyone on this island thinks he's a troublemaker, but they all respect my dad. They consider me a 'good girl.' Maybe Chris hoped I'd clean up his image. Instead, I think his reputation started to spread to me."

Colleen's maturity startled India. "But you aren't excusing him?"

Colleen shook her head so hard her mature bearing nearly flew off her. "I won't forgive and forget. He scared me. One thing my mom and dad always told me was never to go with anyone who made me feel funny. Stark, raving terror probably counts as funny.''

India let her hair cover her face. Now that was good judgment. She sent up silent gratitude to Jack and Mary for the way they'd raised Colleen. Could she have done as well?

At the library's wide doors, Marcy turned around. Sunlight glinted off her gold eyebrow ring.

''Are you sure we want to do this, Colleen? Everything's okay now.''

Colleen only laughed, and India grinned in relief. A girl couldn't sound as if she'd just discovered the keys to her freedom if her heart were breaking. In some dismay, Marcy rubbed her ring thoughtfully between her index finger and thumb.

How many toddlers would go home this afternoon and beg their parents for eyebrow hoops? *If only I'd planned a pirate story for today.*

''COLLEEN?'' JACK CALLED his daughter's name as he opened his front door. All morning long, as he'd finally begun to repaint the boat, thoughts of her had barged between him and his work. He'd found himself smiling at remembered Saturdays in the park with a Frisbee and a cooler of sandwiches. Those Saturdays seemed far away, but his hard work pulled them closer every day.

As he opened his mouth to call Colleen's name again, Nettie came out of the kitchen, twisting her hands in a dish towel.

''She's not here, Jack. She just called me from the library.''

''The library?''

Nettie glowered at his surprise, as if to say he didn't give his own daughter enough credit. ''I didn't say she'd joined the space program.''

Jack shrugged with a rueful grin. "Sorry. She doesn't spend a lot of time at the library these days."

"I told her she could go downtown with her friends, but she said they've decided to help India Stuart instead."

Silky straight golden hair and lithe legs flitted distractingly through Jack's mind. "Did you know she works at the library at home?"

"Really?" Nettie dropped that incidental thread that seemed much more important to Jack. "You notice Colleen called to tell us where she'd be? I told you Hayden and I could make a difference."

"No," Jack teased, "Hayden actually told me, but I'm sure you helped him rehearse his speech."

Nettie waggled a finger. "Nevertheless, we have helped you."

Jack wrapped his arm around her shoulders. "Yes, you have. You always make a difference, and Colleen and I need you anytime you can come. What's that you're burning in the kitchen?"

"Oh, my pies!" Bustling out, she glanced over her shoulder. "What are you doing home anyway? Didn't you say you had to work on the *Mary* today?"

Jack tossed his jacket on the living room sofa. "I decided to take the day off. I thought Colleen and I could do something."

"Go on over to the library, but first come look at these pies. I don't think they're too bad."

"Did she say how long she'd be?"

As he entered the kitchen, Nettie looked up from waving smoke out of the open stove. "I didn't ask. What do you think of my pies?"

Gingerly Jack broke off a piece of dark brown crust and popped it into his mouth. As he chewed, he grinned. "Mmm. Looks aren't everything."

Grinning approval, Nettie still flapped her towel at him.

"Get out of here, and let me know if you two plan to be late for dinner. You know, I wonder if that India isn't good for Colleen."

Uncomfortable enough with his own thoughts of India, which had nothing to do with whether she was good for his daughter, Jack attempted a dignified escape.

Driving to the library, he tried to pinpoint the exact moment he'd lost control of his priorities. Colleen should be his first concern, but a strange, almost unfamiliar warmth unfurled in his body as he anticipated seeing India. Almost unfamiliar, but no matter how harried his life had been for the past three years, he remembered desire.

As if he had time to indulge in lust for India. Where would he work that in, between repairing his own boat, eight hours a day or more on Tim Byar's boat, and most important of all, riding herd on Colleen? Where would he find the hours to make up for time off today?

At the library, he pushed through the glass doors into a din of childish voices. Infectious peals of laughter led him to the story room where Mary had helped out when Colleen was little.

He found his daughter, a maypole in a group of grabbing three-year-olds who jumped at the bright yellow yarn she dangled above their heads. To her right, Marcy Shipp knelt between two little boys who both seemed desperate to engage her in serious conversation—possibly about her eyebrow ring. Jack blinked. Nell Fisher ought to know the kind of havoc Marcy Shipp could wreak with that pair of scissors.

At a table behind Marcy, Leah twisted like a pretzel as she tried to pick several small paper circles from her elbow while the toddlers helped her. She seemed to have glued tiny homemade animal eyes to her skin.

"Once they forgot how cool they are, they started to have fun." India's breathy voice at his side startled Jack.

Off balance, he turned. "How'd you do this?" His hungry sense of recognition surprised him as he absorbed the delicate contours of her face. She wasn't beautiful like the models on magazine covers, but her discerning eyes and vulnerable mouth made him want to know her better. Compulsively he followed her soft sweater's deep plunge into the hollow of luscious, rounded breasts her turtleneck shirts had not displayed and then tried to look away. A decent man would.

Blushing, India bunched the sides of her sweater. "I asked them to help."

Heat spread over Jack's face. *Busted. And either my skin is on fire, or I'm actually blushing.* Dumbfounded, he turned back to the children.

"What magic do you know?"

"No magic, just a need for helping hands."

"You underestimate yourself if you can persuade Colleen and her friends to do good works and look as if they're having fun. Completely against the teenager's code."

As she laughed, Jack faced the unsettling possibility she had awakened him and Colleen from a dark time. He ought to be grateful, but he wanted to be the one to provide emotional and physical sustenance for his daughter. He didn't want to fail her.

Colleen's sudden laughter drew him. He hadn't heard such joy from her in too long. He smiled as she tested a hank of yarn against a little boy's nose. Would she turn back into an adolescent the moment she noticed him?

"I'll get her," India said. As she leaned around him, her scent lingered. Jack shifted, utterly uncomfortable with erotic fantasies that spun through his mind. How long since he'd wanted a woman? And why now of all inconvenient moments?

He followed the curve of India's jaw, the sensitive rise

of her cheekbones. Mesmerized, he studied the pale peach tint of skin he suddenly and desperately longed to taste. Why this woman, who would leave town as soon as she and her father ran out of houses to paint?

How many more friends could he hit up to find work for her?

"Colleen?" India looked different today, lit by happiness, sure of herself as he'd never seen her.

I'm a single father. I have to set an example for my daughter. He turned from India for a last look at the little girl who'd once thought he and Mary were gods.

And the moment Colleen saw him she put on her best beyond-bored expression and swung back to the other children. That was the Colleen who lived in his house. Mystifying child.

India glanced back at Jack. "Nell didn't feel well. After I read, the girls took over for me, so I could finish out here. Nell may offer us all jobs by Monday."

"Why do you paint houses with your father?"

"He needed help, and I was already on a leave of absence." The explanation tumbled out of her. "I had an accident."

Jack knew accidents. Freezing, he searched her healthy body, her long legs and sweetly curved waist, distracting full breasts and soft shoulders. He pictured Mary, still and pale in her hospital bed, gone before he could try one more time to love her better.

"What, Jack?" India took a step toward him, but he backed away before she could offer comfort, and she clamped her mouth shut.

Images of Mary washed him in remembered guilt that made him reject India, because he wanted her with an elemental need he wasn't sure he'd ever felt for his wife. Thoughts of Mary faded as India slipped her hands into the pockets of her tartan skirt, a skirt just like the one

Colleen had bought for the festival. It looked different on India. Jack skimmed a glance over her taut, smooth thighs.

"Do you work in a school?" Trying to sound normal, he nodded toward his daughter and her friends and the story group. "You're obviously good with children."

India nodded briefly, still upset. "Sometimes." She leaned around the door again, all legs and graceful temptation. "Colleen, I can take over."

Jack gritted his teeth so tightly his jaws ached. *I'm sorry* wouldn't come. Maybe once he found time for regular dinners with his own daughter, he could deal with the possibility of caring for a woman again.

Colleen parceled out the last of the yarn to her charges. Jack stared at her, bemused. Though he should be glad he hadn't found her with Chris, or piercing some part of her body, he hoped she hadn't been so willing to help India because she needed a woman's influence.

He was all Colleen had, and he'd have to find a way to be the parent she needed. He'd thought they were managing until he'd grounded the boat, but their problems had grown over time, over the past three years.

He'd reach his daughter. He had to.

Colleen startled him with a slow grin as she patted the last child and started across the room. "I thought you were busy all day, Dad."

He shrugged, pretending indifference so he didn't scare her back into hers. "I thought you might like to see a movie. Invite your friends if you like." He looked at Marcy in particular with doubt. Exactly why would a young girl want to look like a pincushion?

"You liked them when we were younger, Dad," Colleen whispered.

"That was before Marcy turned herself into a pirate."

"It's jewelry—a fashion statement."

Jack dropped his arm around her shoulders. "Yeah.

Some kind of statement anyway." He let her go at the exact moment he estimated she'd pull away. "Go ask them if they want to come with us."

Marcy and Leah abandoned their jobs immediately. India laughed as they rushed for the door.

"Thanks, girls." Her rueful, pensive smile went to Jack's head. He reached for the doorframe, a nice, solid object.

"It was fun, India." Colleen nudged Marcy, who suddenly slapped her palm to her forehead.

"I know where I've heard your name." She turned to Jack. "She's the one you told my dad about. I thought she painted houses."

Pinned by India's almost comical look of horror, Jack tried to laugh. It came out more like a death rattle.

CHAPTER SIX

HUDDLED BY THE PHONE in her hotel room, India poured out her troubles to her mother again. "Colleen's father found a job for Dad and me. He thinks we're desperate for work."

"How compassionate of him. A good sign, don't you think?"

India sputtered. "We're taking advantage of the Shipps. What if they didn't want their house painted?"

"Your dad says their paint's in terrible shape. Don't feel guilty. Just count your blessings and consider what kind of man is so kind to strangers."

India tilted the phone away to stare at the receiver. "So this is the *Twilight Zone.*" Cautiously she rested the receiver against her ear. "You're not seeing this straight, Mom. You and Dad don't seem to understand we're being dishonest."

"No, you're finding out what you need to know to make peace with yourself." Rachel's voice gave absolution and asked for some, too. "I knew the day we left your baby with Mother Angelica we'd let you make a mistake. I thought you should find her, but I was never brave enough to tell you."

"Mom." India pressed the heel of her hand over the ache in her chest.

"Oh no, I don't mean you did wrong. You couldn't have made a better choice for Colleen, but we should have known you better. We should have seen you couldn't turn your back on her and pretend she never existed.''

''Why didn't you talk to me like this then?''

''I didn't know how. We were young when we had you, and I bought all that self-determination stuff that went around in the sixties, so that's how we parented you. Then, you went away to college, and you always pretended you were just fine when you came home. When you decided to live near us, and we saw you on holidays and at family things, I figured you must be all right or you'd have stayed away.''

''I tried to make a family picture, because I knew I'd broken the real one.''

''But that wasn't your responsibility. I wanted to be your mother, make up for not taking hold when you needed me most, but every time I tried to bring up the subject of the baby, you shut me out. How could I force you to talk about what hurt you, when our silence seemed to keep you close? I was afraid you'd leave, and we'd never see you again.''

''I needed to talk to you.'' Dryness scratched India's throat. She couldn't find words to describe what she needed from her own mom now.

''I didn't want to lose you *and* your child.''

India lowered her forehead into her palm. ''I've hurt you and Dad, too.''

''That's not your problem, either. We were your parents, and we tried to let you make your own decisions when maybe you weren't able. Then we pressured you into the one that we should have listened to you for.'' Rachel cleared her throat. ''Tell me, what does she look like?'' She glossed over all talk of guilt, as if she couldn't take any more truth.

India followed her lead, though tears burned her eyes. ''Like you, in those pictures from when you were little.''

Silence came through the phone. "Maybe you shouldn't tell me." Her mother's voice cracked. "I'm strong, but I'm not an iron woman." When she sniffed, India pictured the big square hankie her mother carried in her pocket.

"And she's a thinker, Mom. Jack said she decided not to see Chris on her own anymore."

Her intense pride in Colleen's choice frightened India. "I think we'd better finish the Shipps' house and get out of here. I don't know what's been wrong with her and Jack, but they seem to be coming around to each other."

"And you're falling for her."

"I can't help it."

"JUST FINISH THE TRIM and go back to the hotel." Mick leaned against the ladder. "You know, I may try to turn you into a permanent painter. How many windows do you think you've painted today?"

"You don't have time for me to guess." India turned her aching wrist to check her watch. The motion sprayed paint off her brush, but she ducked just in time. "You'd better go if you plan to beat the D.C. traffic."

Her father didn't answer. In the lengthening hush, India lifted her head. "Dad?" She looked down to find she'd speckled his face with colonial blue paint.

"I don't think this is as funny as it was when you sprayed me."

India tried hard to swallow a giggle. He hauled his hankie out of his pocket to scrub the paint off his forehead.

"Is it all gone?" he asked.

"Hand me your handkerchief." She shook it out. Looking more like a tablecloth for one, it made India homesick for her mother. "Mom will be glad to see you this weekend."

Mick snatched the white square of linen away from her.

"Oh, yeah? First thing she'll want is a good cry. Did you have to talk to her?"

"I guess I could have hung up the second I heard her voice."

He patted her shoulder and backed down a couple of steps. "I'm teasing because I hate to leave you alone. Why don't you come home with me?"

"Work with me, Dad. I'm trying to give you and Mom time alone—as a thank-you."

"Do you know how long we've been married? We've done alone time."

"You'd be afraid to say that if Mom were here. Uh-oh." Catching movement over her father's shoulder, India sank against the ladder and nodded toward the street. "Look who's coming."

"I was afraid she'd turn up here when we took this job." Mick slid down the rest of the ladder as Colleen and her two friends strolled into the Shipps' yard. "You can't let her get too close to you, India."

"I know where we stand." This time when she left, she'd know Colleen was with a good father, in a safe home. Breathing deeply as she felt how much more it would hurt to leave Colleen behind again, India tried to learn to live with it.

"Hi, India." All three young girls spoke at once.

She waggled blue-flecked fingers at them. "Have you met my father, Leah?"

"No." Leah turned to Mick and shook his hand, with more aplomb than she'd ever exhibited before. "Monsieur Stuart."

Mick clicked his heels, a faux French waiter in a bad, old movie. India laughed at him in surprise.

"We're studying together for our French test." Colleen twisted a wry face. "Of course, my dad didn't believe me at first when I told him."

India laughed, just because it felt so good to talk to her without a crisis over their heads. *"Bonne chance,"* she wished them heartily.

Colleen and Marcy and Leah leaned into each other, giggling as they disappeared into the house. India grinned at her father.

"I didn't think it was that funny," she admitted.

"Neither did I. All right, honey," He started toward the car he'd rented that morning. "I've cleaned all my tools except your brush, and I put everything in the truck. Make sure you lock up when you finish."

"I'll remember." She indulged his need to father her. For the first time, she truly understood. "By the way, do you talk to your other employees this way?"

"Hardly ever," he growled.

Happily, she didn't mind. "Say hi to Mom for me."

"I will. Stay out of trouble this weekend." Waving, he slid into the small car's driver seat.

As he steered out of the driveway, India lifted her shoulders to stem a sudden wave of loneliness. She'd miss him. "I should have said so." She contented herself with a cheery, non-Granny Clampett wave. He and her mother had never been apart so long before. Maybe they'd make a second honeymoon out of their reunion.

Trying unsuccessfully again to whistle, India finished the window frame and moved her ladder to start the last one. She hardly ever succumbed to vertigo anymore. She must be improving.

The last window went fast. She was cleaning her brush when Colleen stole out of the house and through the shrubbery.

"India," Colleen whispered with more enthusiasm than care.

India laughed.

Colleen crept closer. "Leah is staying with Marcy tonight, and they're all about to eat dinner. I was supposed to call my dad when I wanted to go home, but I phoned and Grandma says he fell asleep after work. I saw you out here, packing up.''

Understanding Colleen's non sequitur, India glanced toward the darkened windows. She ought to turn Colleen down. Even a ride home was off-limits.

"Could you give me a ride, so I don't have to ask Grandma to wake Dad? You wouldn't believe the hours he works.''

Her concern for her father was progress, not a land mine waiting to go off. India opened her mouth, but ''no'' stuck in her throat. How could she explain it? How could she pass up one small, inconsequential ride home?

"Sure.'' Guiltily she flapped her wet brush on the palm of her hand. ''Are you ready?''

"I left Grandma on the phone inside. Let me tell her we're on our way.''

India finished packing the van. Shivering in the early spring chill, she climbed into the cab and pushed her arms into the sleeves of an old pink sweater. What would she say to Colleen?

Appearing first as a bobbing head at the passenger window, Colleen opened the door and clambered inside. ''Hmm.'' She stretched out her legs and leaned her back to the window, to gaze at India as if from the other end of a football field. ''This is bigger than I thought.'' She bounced on the seat. ''And more comfortable.''

India smothered a grin. ''Thanks. Put on your seat belt?''

Colleen dragged it over her shoulder. ''I've meant to tell you I really enjoyed helping the kids at the library.'' She sounded surprised. ''I think Marcy liked it, too. Leah might have liked it more, but she's still peeling paste off her elbows.''

With gratitude, India took Colleen's conversational cue. "I was glad Marcy didn't pierce anything for the children."

"Uh, her mom hates that ring in her eyebrow. Even Marcy says it's a pain. She can't take it out yet, but she likes to sleep on her stomach."

"She wears it for her mother, then?"

"You don't know, India. Parents can be so unreasonable. You and Mick treat each other like equals, but sometimes I swear Dad *drives* me to do stuff I know I shouldn't do. I can't figure out half his rules."

On uncharted ground, India remembered the worry that so often creased Jack's forehead, uncertainty she sensed was foreign to him. She tried to keep her glance at Colleen casual.

"You know, I wonder if a father and daughter are supposed to be equals? Maybe that comes with adulthood?" No need to spell out her mistakes again. "As you said, Jack works hard for all of you. When he finishes the boat, your lives will go back to normal."

Colleen tucked her knees up. "That's supposed to make me feel better? Dad was strict before he grounded the boat."

India almost lifted her hands to ward off Colleen's confidences. Fortunately, she had to steer. "If you don't understand his rules, why not ask him to explain them?"

"Now you sound like my dad."

India concentrated on the road, swallowing unexpected tears. Colleen couldn't know, but she'd just paid her own mother a compliment. More than anything, India longed to sound like a parent.

THAT RINGING NOISE. The phone. He'd better answer it. He couldn't move. Jack tried to raise his hand to signal he'd be along in a minute, but the phone rang again. As-

suming he was in his own bed, he rolled over and fell off
the sofa with an eye-opening thud.

Nettie, in the kitchen, spoke softly. His name came up
in her conversation, and then the receiver banged to the
hardwood floor, and Nettie swore with astounding skill.

"Jack?" Immediately, she checked to see if he'd heard
her. The most endearing old-fashioned guilt always led her
to do that when she swore in his kitchen. He had to
chuckle.

She came around the living room door. "Sorry about
that. I tried to be quiet, but I dropped the phone. You didn't
happen to hear…"

"Have you thought of taking up mule skinning?" She
was easy to tease. In her consternation, she frowned just
the way Mary used to. He tugged at his filthy T-shirt. "I
smell awful, Nettie. I think I sat down here to pay a few
bills."

"You must have been tired. By the time I brought you
a cup of coffee, you'd already fallen asleep."

"So you left me stinking up the place?" He nodded
toward the kitchen. "Who was on the phone? Has Colleen
called yet?"

"Yes, she called, but that was Tim saying you should
be at his slip at four forty-five tomorrow."

He rubbed his eyes. "When did Colleen call?"

"A while ago. I told her you were asleep, so she asked
India for a ride home."

"India?" His blood raced to keep up with his body's
heightened awareness. "I forgot she was painting Leon
Shipp's house." As he twisted his stiff neck, his fishy
aroma wafted past his own nose again. "Did you say she's
bringing Colleen home?"

Nettie tossed an innocent smile over her shoulder as she
strolled back to the kitchen. "Maybe you should take a
shower."

Her matchmaking gleam troubled him, but he shot up the stairs. After a record-breaking shower, he rummaged through a pile of clean laundry in the corner of his bedroom. Folding and ironing had fallen to the bottom of his priorities.

He yanked on jeans and a creased white shirt and hurried into the narrow hall. No voices from downstairs. Would Colleen invite India in? Somehow, he suspected she would.

"They're not here yet," Nettie called as he stepped onto the hardwood floor in the downstairs hall.

Motion in the small square of glass in the door caught Jack's eye. India's van slid smoothly to a halt beneath the curtain of bare-limbed willows at the end of his walk. "Yes, they are. Should we ask her in for coffee?"

"If you make it. I just poured out the last of this afternoon's."

"I'll make it, if Colleen brings her to the door." He said it more to himself than to Nettie, negotiating a dangerous bargain. He wouldn't go out of his way to get to know India better, but if his daughter brought her in, he'd allow himself to share one cup of coffee that could never mean anything to anyone.

He wrapped his hand around the cool brass doorknob as India climbed out of the truck. In worn jeans and a misshapen sweater, she looked young and sexy and carefree. Jack just stared.

He pictured her, hair mussed, her mouth sweetly swollen from his kisses. Would she share passion or wreak havoc with it? His pulse ripped through his chest. The sun turned her hair to spun gold that drifted over her shoulders to splay across her breasts.

He opened the door and stepped onto his brick porch.

"India." Great icebreaker.

"I've brought Colleen." She tilted her mouth in a lop-sided smile. Jack almost felt her lips against his.

"Dad?" Colleen's voice sounded odd.

He'd better be more careful. At fifteen, she probably saw more than he could guess. "Are you going to ace that French test?" he teased, taking her hand. As soon as he pulled her into the house, she tugged away and lifted her nose toward the kitchen.

"Is that *pain?* Grandma's baking?"

"You mean bread? I don't know," Jack admitted. "I fell asleep."

"Grandma told me, so I asked India for a ride." She sniffed again, a little girl with good things to eat on her mind. "We haven't had fresh bread since..." Colleen's voice dwindled. She stared at him.

He looked back at her just as carefully. The aroma of fresh-baked bread had once wafted through their open, sunny windows into the streets outside. He looped his arm around his daughter's shoulders.

"I know. Smells good, doesn't it?"

He had to convince her she could talk about her mother. He tightened his arm. This girl of his. Too young and too old, all at the same time. They'd both be better off when he began to understand her.

"Come in, India." Colleen pulled away from him, her independent self again. "Dad makes great coffee, and I'll bet Grandma will let us sample the bread. I can't wait."

India lingered on the doorstep until her reluctance stood between her and them like an invisible wall.

What held her back? Her reluctance seemed concentrated on Colleen, like the small frown that wrinkled her forehead. Jack's urge to protect wakened. He might choose to pursue India and hurt himself when she and her father left, but he'd protect Colleen from even the hint of another abandonment, no matter that Mary hadn't chosen to leave her.

Colleen applied a stiff elbow to his ribs. Coughing from the impact, he tried to frown at her, but she only shook her head in disgust. "Dad." She nodded at India. "Ask her to stay."

A cup of coffee wasn't a commitment.

He pushed the door wider. "I brew an impressive pot of coffee."

Still, India faltered.

Colleen grinned. "We don't have a watchdog or anything. Come on in."

She shivered. The Maryland weather could have caused it. But, as Jack watched, mesmerized, she sucked in her bottom lip and then rolled it through her teeth. His legs rocked. He pushed his hands into his pockets to keep from touching her tortured mouth.

"Maybe just one cup of coffee." Her shaking voice found an answering resonance in his heartbeat. She crossed the threshold.

And his home would never again be empty of India. Rooted to the floor, he stared at her as his nostrils filled with her exotic scent. Having decided to enter, she floated past, completely unaware of his physical response.

With appealing curiosity, she studied the pictures Mary had hung on the uneven plaster walls. Pictures of the long-ago women of his family and the men and children they'd loved. Always, the women seemed to burn bright, filling the photos with their passion for hearth and home and life. His home had long been bereft of a woman's passion.

She turned back to him, her glance intense, anxious, defiant. And passionate. A fire burned inside India, closely banked, but sparking ever so unexpectedly behind her eyes.

When she'd danced his daughter away from Chris at the

festival, he'd read the flame in her body. When she'd eased away from him on the steps outside her hotel room, he'd glimpsed a low glow in her eyes. He coveted India's passion.

"The coffee, Dad?"

India stiffened. Jack envied her ability to hide her feelings so quickly. Shutting down was supposed to be his strong suit.

He focused on his daughter. "Suddenly, I'm not sure we have enough clean cups." Nettie tended to break them when she washed the dishes. "Why don't you show India through to the living room?"

"The living room?" From Colleen's tone, he might have suggested she lead India on a brisk tour of Jupiter and all its moons. "What happened to the kitchen table, Dad?"

He flicked her an impatient glance. He'd have to read up on how to offer a woman a caffeinated beverage without looking like a fool in his daughter's eyes.

"The living room, Colleen?"

"I've picked a bad time, haven't I?" India shrugged her long blond hair over her shoulder. "I can go."

Now that she was here, he wanted her to stay. Decisively he closed the door and stepped away, careful not to touch her, because wanting to touch her so badly worried him. "I'm sorry you always see us at our worst, but maybe we can remember our manners for an hour or so. I'll start the coffee."

CHAPTER SEVEN

ONE MORE MOMENT in that hall with Jack in his endearingly creased jeans and shirt, his thick, dark hair standing on end, his eyes as hot as an incinerator, and India would have run screaming.

Which might have been a wiser strategy.

He strode away with loose-hipped elegance. His mixture of rugged independence and lean grace compromised her good intentions. Flattening one hand on the cool wall, she fought to compose herself.

Already stationed at the first room along the hall, Colleen beckoned. "In here."

India followed her through a tall, narrow doorway. A piano reigned beneath the window in the small, boxy room. Massive, it dwarfed even the heavy Victorian sofa and love seat nestled before a hearth that looked as old as the town of Arran Island.

Photos of Mary and Jack and Colleen stood on the shining expanse of the piano lid. Their perfect, artistic placement reminded India of how Jack and Colleen treated the subject of Mary. Both pretended they'd recovered from losing her, and both tiptoed warily around any talk of her.

"India?" Colleen sounded hesitant. "Are you all right?"

Anything but. In too deep. Drowning. "I don't want to intrude."

Colleen's hair hugged her face as she shook her head. "Oh no. I could tell if Dad was just being polite."

India moved restlessly to the piano. "Do you play this gorgeous thing?"

"Mom did." Colleen slid her fingertips along its gleaming lid. "I'd like to learn. Maybe after Dad finishes the boat, I'll ask him if I can take lessons."

Colleen's wistful tone matched her quick glance at Mary's picture. She didn't want to remind her father of the woman they'd both lost. India longed to wrap her arms around the child she'd given up. She could provide comfort if Colleen would accept it.

Dismayed at her own impulse, she clenched her hands and her teeth. She shouldn't have come here. She'd lied to her daughter, lied to the man who'd raised her daughter. She had no place in this house. If they knew the truth about her, Colleen and Jack wouldn't want her here.

"I hope you don't mind caffeine, India. We're out of the unleaded stuff."

India whirled. She stared at Jack, masculine and solid, as he carried a tray laden with a ceramic coffee urn and four sturdy mugs. Behind him, Nettie beamed over another tray full of aromatic, newly sliced, steaming bread.

Their open welcome made her feel more guilty. She wanted her dad back again. She wanted to run from Jack and Nettie's generosity.

She was taking advantage of their trust. India eased in a deep breath and tried to breathe out her panic. She ran her hand beneath her ponytail. Suddenly this little room felt hotter than the hinges of hell.

She'd made enough mistakes. If she skipped out of here now, she'd only create a mystery for a bright, curious girl like Colleen to solve. But Colleen was too concerned with Jack's tray to notice India's silence.

"Not those cups, Dad."

Lifting the tray over her head, he maneuvered it to the small table between the sofa and the love seat. He'd tucked his shirt into the loose waistband of the jeans that fit snugly over his narrow hips and powerful thighs.

India blushed. Something had changed her that day in the drugstore. Jack had made her more aware—of herself, of him, of how quickly time was passing. For so long, she'd lived almost outside of time, focused on the wrong she'd done in the past. Much safer than snatching at unnecessary risks with both hands.

She smoothed her hair away from her face. She had the rest of forever to be sorry. For tonight, she'd be with her daughter. For tonight, she'd sop up each moment of the present.

"Dad." Colleen brandished a mug at her father. "Did you read this?"

"None of our cups match, honey." He zapped India with a faintly uncomfortable, totally charming smile.

"They don't have to match." Colleen turned it for Nettie to read. "What do you think, Grandma? 'Bay Fishermen Do It in Traps.' That's nice for company."

"Oh." Nettie looked anxious as India had begun to realize only Nettie could. "I didn't see that, actually."

Barely swallowing a laugh, India ducked Jack's flailing elbow as he snatched the mug from his daughter and set it back on the tray. "Is that your union credo, Jack?"

"One of the local guys sold these when he broke his leg and couldn't work for six months." He nodded at the plate of bread Nettie offered. "Go ahead, and eat before it cools. I sampled it in the kitchen, and I'm still healthy."

Nettie bumped him with her elbow this time, but Colleen took her father's comment in stride. "Mmm." Her mouth full, she flopped onto the sofa. "Grandma, you didn't even have to call the fire department."

"Don't compliment me with your mouth full." Nettie joined her granddaughter and waved India toward the love seat. "I'd be glad to teach you at any time."

India balanced her mug and plate on her knees. "It smells delicious. I can only bake like this with a machine that does all the work for me."

Jack sank into a spot beside Colleen. "A machine?"

India arched her brows, assuming he disapproved of the mod cons. "A woman has to eat."

Jack straightened. "I guess I pictured you as a home-making kind of woman."

"A woman makes a home with more than her bare hands," Nettie observed mildly. "I don't see you repairing your boat with nineteenth-century tools."

India broke in. "What exactly happened to your boat, Jack?"

"I grounded it a couple of months ago." His self-deprecating tone drew her closer than she wanted to be. "I sprang an oil leak in the path of a storm, so I headed for a cove. But I didn't know the rocks, and I tore the hull."

"My grandfather built the boat." Colleen sounded proud. "The hull is made of wood. It's the oldest working boat around here."

Jack topped off his cup of strong, black coffee. "I almost retired the *Mary,* but after all this work, she should be good as new in another four weeks or so."

"What do you fish for?"

Jack bit into another piece of bread before he answered. "Crabs, clams, oysters, some bass and bluefish, whatever I can find." He glanced toward the window. Did he feel the pull of the water from where he sat? "The bay isn't as generous as it used to be."

"But it's getting better," Colleen defended stoutly.

Jack turned a fond glance on her. "You don't have to comfort me. You can help by being where you're supposed to be when I expect you to be there."

She colored. "I don't try to make trouble, Dad."

He gave her a brief hug. "I know, and I shouldn't have brought it up in front of company."

Over Colleen's head, he smiled at India. She stopped breathing. For a moment, she could almost pretend she really was Colleen's mother, sharing love for her with her father. No. Jack would always be Colleen's father. Her daughter's father. Nothing more to her, and she couldn't even maintain the tentative friendship she'd accidentally built with this family.

Nettie lifted the coffee carafe. "More, India?"

"No, thanks." In no hurry to finish the cup she still held, or the delicious bread, India bargained for time. She promised she wouldn't find a way to come back here, but couldn't she stay for one small visit? The telephone's jangle jarred her from her silent negotiations, and Jack set his plate and cup on the table.

"I'll take it in the kitchen," he said. "Excuse me, ladies."

Nodding, Nettie turned to her granddaughter. "Did you finish your homework?"

"All but my report." Colleen reached for her mug. "I have all night."

"You can start when you finish eating that. You don't need to ruin your supper entirely."

India stood in case Nettie was dropping a hint for her, too. She felt in the way. "I'm interrupting your evening routine. Thank you for everything."

Colleen rose. "Thank you for the ride home."

Nettie stood, also, tiny beside her granddaughter. "I didn't mean to push you out. Quite the contrary. Why don't you call your father and ask him to join us for dinner, as well?"

"India's dad went home for the weekend."

"Oh."

Nettie sounded sorry for her, but India wasn't some little

lost girl. "Thank you, Nettie, but Viveca Henderson told me about a place called the Crab Trap on the other side of the Island. I thought I'd go over there."

She ducked out before anyone could try to persuade her to stay. She'd be such easy pickings if they applied even the smallest pressure.

JACK STARED AT THE YELLOW light that pulsed out the Crab Trap's name above its door. He must be out of his mind, but tonight she'd be alone. He liked India's father and his in-laws, and he loved his daughter to distraction, but tonight, he'd like to see India alone.

Jack gripped the wooden door handle. He should have called her, asked if he could take her out. But arranging a date might have scared her off, and it bothered him a little, too. They could only have a temporary relationship, because she was eventually going back to Virginia to continue her house-painting and librarian careers.

"Damn it, I'm a grown man." Jack shoved the door open. He often sold some of his catch to Bob Davies, who owned the place. Bob's wife, Milly, came around the counter, wiping her hands on tight jeans.

"Jack, haven't seen you in a while. What brings you out tonight?"

"I'm looking for a friend. Kind of medium height. Blond hair…" A face that reminded him of old paintings in well-guarded museums. A smile that squeezed his heart.

"The new girl in town. Oh, yeah. She'd make quite a hit if she'd encourage any of these randy sailors to take a chance on her."

"You've got a way with words, Milly."

"I know. Come with me."

She led him through the pulsing music and loud voices, past a couple of backslapping friends to India's table where he stood, like a stanchion, sticking out of the plank floor. Intent on a novel, India took a few seconds to look up.

"Jack." Her distant tone chilled him.

"You okay if he sits with you?" Milly asked.

India stared. Jack waited, and Milly looked at him strangely until India managed a garbled yes and an unenthusiastic nod.

"I'll get you a beer, Jack."

Milly's doubt echoed his own, but he slid into the booth across from India. Could he be any less assured? He'd never felt like this with any other woman. Not even with Mary. Dear God, why couldn't he have felt this for Mary?

India shrugged her slight shoulders. Jack tried not to notice how the movement lifted her full breasts. "What are you doing here?"

"Nettie said you were alone tonight." Lame. He stared at the pulse that throbbed in her throat. "I wanted to talk to you." And learn about her, about the spirit she tried to hide behind her calm blue gaze.

A muscle jerked in her jaw. She tilted her chin. Light from a converted oil lamp on a chain above their booth emphasized the tremble in her lips. She opened her hand on the table. "Don't take this badly, but you shouldn't have come."

He covered her palm with his, and they brushed their fingers against each other. It felt like trying to catch a lightning bolt, the painful charge, the hint of heat in the air. He couldn't think beyond the tension that flowed between them, thick with wanting.

"I've got to go," she said, taking money out of her shirt pocket. She dropped the bills on her check and scrambled out of her seat. Against his better judgment, he followed her, not thinking till they'd both pushed through the door. Jack caught her wrists. His heart clamored a warning as his body stirred for her.

"You feel the same draw I do." Emotion hardened his voice.

"You're wrong."

"Then pull back." So many reasons he should pull back—Colleen, the boat. The example he should be setting for Colleen. Her feelings for Chris, and their shared horror at watching Mary leave them both. The sure knowledge that everything that had gone wrong in his life with Mary could happen with anyone.

Too aware of why he should back away, Jack slid his hands down India's wrists and twined his fingers through hers. Staring straight into his eyes with her own direct gaze, she trembled, her fear pushing him away as her want drew him.

He breathed her in. Standing so close, he saw her as if for the first time. Her warm skin, glowing with life. Pain that darkened her eyes and made him want to hold her tighter.

He freed one hand to curl his palm around her throat, uttering a small groan as her pulse struck against his skin. She opened her mouth, but couldn't seem to find words. Jack waited for her. He traced the sweet curve of her chin with his index finger. Her breath fanned his face.

"What?" His own heart pounded in his throat. "What scares *you*?"

She shook her head and wrapped her fingers around his wrist, holding on, as if she wouldn't let go. But that wasn't true, and he knew it. Still he massaged the velvet fullness of her lower lip with his thumb, and his body roared with need he didn't know how to slake.

He was teetering on the edge of a precipice. Touching her was crazy. She meant too much to his daughter. And she would leave him alone again, no matter where they took this moment. She would hold him as Mary had when she'd needed him, but India's eyes promised she'd let him go.

Jack cupped her face. Wanting her so badly, he felt naked. He didn't want to stand alone on this cliff.

"I want you." He lowered his mouth almost to hers. The promise of her firm lips shook him. "I've warned my daughter against the only kind of relationship you and I can have. How can I want to make love to you when I absolutely don't want her to do as I do?"

She took his words—errant thoughts he'd never meant to speak—like blows to her body. "Jack, we can't."

He meant to pull away, but her scent spun a sensual cocoon around him that closed off the rest of the world. As if he held a work of delicate art in his hands, he splayed his fingers against her cheekbones. Her breathing shallowed to a short pant that tightened his body, engorged his desire.

Jack lowered his face, just to feel the heat of her against his skin, but it wasn't enough. He had to taste her. He had to know her. He covered her mouth with his and tested the seductive heat of her lips, wary, needing her more each moment. India curled her hands into his shirt. Each one of her fingers burned through the thin, worn cotton.

Her mouth was heaven and earth and an end to loneliness. She opened to him with a surprised cry of pleasure that fueled his desperate hunger.

He plunged his hands into her hair, moaning as the silky strands slid through his fingers. He tried to gentle the kiss, to restrain his need before it licked out of control. But India pulled away first.

"I didn't know," she whispered, "I had no idea you could be so..."

Jack dragged his hands over his face, but his skin was not as pleasant to touch as India's. He shook his head. "I'm sorry."

"Don't say that." India's shaky voice confused him.

He stared at her. "You never answered me. What are you afraid of? I'm the one with the adolescent daughter."

Her expression closed. "I'll stay away from both of you from now on." She opened the van door and jumped in. A moment later, the engine roared to life and she spun out of the parking lot, as if hounds of hell nipped at her heels. He stood in her dust.

Holding her, he'd felt alive. So much generous passion made him want more of her, but why had she pulled away? She'd wanted him as much as he'd wanted her. He shuddered. Did it really matter why she'd rejected him? He had too many reasons of his own not to touch her again. When he closed his eyes, India's kiss, all fire and promise, still throbbed in his body. Cataclysmic timing.

"Jack?"

He turned. "Milly."

"Come back inside. The boys are starting a game of darts. You used to like to play."

"I don't have time."

"Make time. We're your friends. Remember us?"

Grinning tiredly, he patted her shoulder. "Yeah, I remember."

"Good." She pushed through the door, pulling him behind her. "All right, Tim. I caught up with Jack. I believe when last we looked in on the never-ending Arran Island dart tournament of the stars, he was on your team."

"Make it quick, Jack." Tim handed him the darts. "You and I have to be up early tomorrow."

Jack ignored the masculine voices raised in good-natured ribbing and aimed at the board. Months of frustration and doubt, of hard work and climbing straight uphill every day steadied his hand. He threw, and the dart sought cork like a pigeon going home.

"Bull's-eye," Milly called out.

"That was quick," Tim said.

And more like it.

INDIA HUNCHED HER SHOULDERS beneath the hot shower spray. No matter how hard she rubbed the back of her hand over her mouth, she couldn't erase Jack's taste. Hot with need, cold with fear, she wrapped her arms beneath her breasts. Water pooled and spilled down the length of her body.

Desire racked her. With one kiss, Jack had wakened her from sixteen years of dreamless sleep. For sixteen years, she'd believed she was building a life the child she'd given up could be proud of. The truth was she'd only run from life.

She'd pasted trappings of success over empty days and nights. She'd made sure no one ever hurt her again, by not letting anyone in. She'd coasted on the fringes of intimacy.

Until tonight. Until Jack had taken her in his arms and toppled her defenses. The one man she could never be with had taught her to want again.

For Colleen's sake, she had to make sure tonight never repeated itself. India covered her eyes with her hands. Her palms still seemed to smell of Jack's skin. She shook her head.

"Jack—Colleen—what have I done?"

CHAPTER EIGHT

INDIA CIRCLED from the back of the Shipps' house, balancing two cans of paint in her hands. She almost dropped them when she spied her father in raucous conversation with Colleen and her friends at the back of his truck.

What could he be thinking? But then she had to smile. Their time here was growing short, and she valued the moments she and her dad could chat with Colleen, passing inconsequential nothings they would remember all their lives. Finally the girls trooped past Mick, and he started across the lawn.

"I wish you'd let your mother come." In the surprisingly cool, midafternoon sun, Mick tightened his painter's cap on his head. From the top of the Shipps' driveway, Colleen and Leah waved goodbye to Marcy as they continued down the shell road. Mick turned his back on them and lowered his voice. "Your mother's so envious I get to see Colleen, she probably won't let me back in my own home."

India wasn't sure how to answer. It would be easy to dream they could make some sort of life that included Colleen. Her face warmed as she remembered the invitation in Jack's kiss.

She held out the paint cans. "Colleen looks too much like Mom. You know we can't let them meet each other."

"You're already thinking how hard it will be to leave, but shh—here comes Marcy." With a glance over her shoulder, Mick set both cans on the grass while he unlocked the truck door.

"Hi, India." Marcy waved as she shot up the steps to her kitchen door.

India waved back. Good Lord. Not even the glint of Marcy's eyebrow ring shocked her anymore. She'd settled too well on this little island.

"I'm trying to get ready, Dad. I store up memories—the way strands of her hair lift in the breeze, the sunburn on the bridge of her nose, the way she stands with one hand on her hip when she's serious, just like Mom."

Mick's knowing gaze made her uncomfortable. "Should we have come?"

His ragged tone hurt. "I had to. I believe I can say goodbye and mean it this time."

He shook his head. "How? You know her. You love her."

India lifted her shoulders, trying to prove she was strong. "Let's not turn maudlin. I always loved her in an 'I know she's out there' kind of way, and yes, I do know what she's like now, but I also know Jack and Mary raised her well. Pretty soon we'll have to leave."

"When we make sure about Chris. I haven't seen him around." Mick shoved the first can of paint into the back of his truck. "But he'll try again with her."

"What are you talking about? Have you heard something?"

Mick put the other paint can away. "No, but I was a boy a long time ago. Even good guys don't believe the first 'no' when they want the girl. Hell, I remember Colleen's father begging you for another chance."

India twisted her mouth. "Only after you dragged him back, and I turned him down. He felt safe asking to make me an honest woman when he knew I didn't want a captive husband."

"I should have told you years ago, but I finally saw you were right. I can't believe I tried to force you into marrying so young."

"That's one grudge I never held. It was a different time, and I embarrassed you and Mom." She patted her father's hand. "I'm so sorry for all the notoriety I brought you."

Mick lifted one of the paint sprayers off the tarp they'd spread on the grass. "We were not conventional people, but I truly thought you'd be better off with a husband if you wanted to have the baby. I didn't believe you could give her up, and I didn't want you to take all the responsibility alone." He stowed the sprayer and the tarp and shut the van door. "On the other hand, I don't know how many jobs I got because the neighbors wanted to see how deep the family breakdown went."

"EXCUSE ME."

Colleen's voice brought India's head up from her post behind the desk where she was checking books out to the library's patrons. She blew her hair out of her eyes and watched Colleen sidle around a woman at the microfiche machine to stake out a position at the back of the line.

India tried hard to focus on the three people before Colleen. She'd clung to her good intentions and maintained her distance from Jack and his daughter for over a week.

Absence most assuredly made the heart grow fonder. Hers beat a rapid tattoo in anticipation. She treasured these random moments with her daughter, but she glanced over Colleen's shoulder. Only to herself could she admit she was also looking for Jack.

Colleen smiled shyly when her turn came. India almost laughed aloud with happiness that bubbled inside her.

Colleen drew herself up on an apparently important mission. "I liked helping you the other day."

The last gambit India expected. Colleen had already told

her she'd liked helping. She went along with Colleen's formal tone. "You were a big help, and so were your friends."

"They may be too cool to come back." Colleen's grimace signaled disapproval at their reluctance. "Can I help you today?"

A yes leaped to India's lips, but she held it back. "Does your father know you're here?"

"He said I could come. He's going to pick me up." Colleen grinned. "Maybe he's finally convinced me I'll have more freedom if I play by the rules."

India never knew what to expect. "Fathers do know best sometimes, huh?"

"He won't hear that from me." Widening her mischievous smile, Colleen slid her hands into her pockets. "So, what can I do?"

For the first time, India avoided her gaze.

"You don't want me to help, India?"

Why did she want to help? What did she really want? India had worked around children long enough to know when one reached out for her. How foolish she'd been to think she could stumble across this girl and not get involved. She had to discourage Colleen.

"You might find work here monotonous. We don't make puppets all the time." Weak, but this was terribly short notice.

Colleen only lifted her shoulders, unconvinced.

Sudden inspiration struck. Shelving. India'd never met an adolescent who liked to shelve. They didn't seem to realize the treasures that waited for them in the bulging stacks.

India headed for the cart of books beyond the counter. "How about shelving these?" Colleen's expectant smile chipped at her nobler intentions. How was she supposed to turn down a chance to share work she loved with the

child she longed to love by right as well as by instinct?
She told Colleen the truth. "You may find books you
never knew existed. You may need all night to finish this
cart."

"Why?" Colleen tilted her head with endearing curiosity.

India ran her hand over the spines. "You just can't resist
some stories. You may have to sit right down and take a
read."

Colleen's soft giggle wrapped itself around India's
heart, a warm small, incredibly strong fist.

"Yes, this is the job for you." India moved away from
Colleen, because she seriously wanted to hug her in this
softer guise. "Colleen?"

Though she'd already plucked one of the books from
the cart, she looked up. "Hmm?"

"I'm glad you came back." A masterful understate-
ment. She headed back onto the trite and narrow. "Li-
braries always welcome friends."

Colleen laughed. "You sound like my dad again."

Still laughing, she bent over the books, and India turned
away. Jack. She let herself imagine how it would feel to
wait for Jack to come for both of them this evening. No.
She grabbed a stack of books. Dreams like that could only
lead to nightmares.

Quiet sank into the library as early evening lengthened
into night. Colleen proved India right. She spent much of
the few hours with her back to a shelf, cushioning a book
on her knees. Another memory to press and keep safe.

Outside the wide windows, streetlights flickered on. India tidied up the signs of use the day's visitors had left
behind. She looked up as the front doors swished open.

A jolt of awareness caught her by surprise. Jack's red
plaid flannel shirt flapped open to reveal a white tee
stretched across his finely muscled chest. India imagined

his textures beneath her palms—hard body, soft material, strength and tenderness she already knew from the one kiss they'd shared. Her body had seemed to recognize the touch of a long-lost lover.

She clasped her hands behind her back.

She'd cared only once before for a man—for a boy who'd thought he was a man. Nothing and no one had prepared her for Jack. She licked her lips, remembering the firm strength of his. She wanted more.

His dark chocolate gaze slid over her shoulder as he looked for Colleen. He searched the bookshelves, his mouth straight and thin, exposing his discomfort. "Did Colleen come in?"

She nodded toward the back. "She's over there, behind the shelves." She searched his closed gaze. Something else was on his mind. His tension was strong enough to inhale. "You expected her to be here, didn't you?"

He nodded in an obvious effort to relax. "She told me. She even asked if she could come. How are you?"

"Fine." Colleen, so close by, made her afraid to ask what was really bothering him.

"Your father's back in town?" Jack asked.

She nodded.

"Colleen said he was." Half a smile softened his features. "He told Colleen some wild story about painting Thomas Jefferson's outhouse pink."

"He tends to stretch the truth for a good story. It was a chicken house, and no one ever confirmed Thomas Jefferson built it, but it's in the right neighborhood, and someone carved the initials T. J. into a rather frivolous molding near the roof."

"Frivolous? And that was before your father painted it pink?"

"He took the job as a favor, but he used some old paint that was supposed to be white. When the sun hit it just right, it glowed kind of pink.'' She couldn't ignore the tension he radiated. She lowered her voice. ''What's wrong, Jack?''

His smile hid whatever the truth might be. As he leaned across the desk, a pesky lock of hair fell onto his forehead. He didn't notice.

''I've meant to talk to you.'' His breath fanned warmth and spice across her forehead.

''About?''

He shrugged, but not as if he didn't care, more as if he cared too much. ''About what happened. That night—at the Crab Trap.''

India glanced warily toward the stacks. ''She may hear you.''

''I'll be careful.'' A mouse under the desk could hardly have heard his whisper. India had to lean closer. Close enough to drown in his nearness. ''I know you've stayed away, but I don't want you to feel you have to avoid Colleen, because of what I did.''

She backed off. ''I leave here soon, and I don't play at relationships well.'' Great. Could she sound any stiffer? ''I just don't want to make anything worse for Colleen.''

He scrubbed his knuckles over his chin, and dark brown stubble crackled like the sound of his restlessness. India flattened her palm against a low ache in her belly.

His gaze dropped to her hand, but he looked up again. ''You don't understand me. I know she likes you, and I like you too much. I have to set a good example for her. I want her to trust me. I don't know why I can't persuade Colleen to come home after school, but she wants your approval.''

''India doesn't treat me like an infant, Dad.'' Colleen popped up from the back of the fiction rows.

India closed her eyes and tried to replay her and Jack's cryptic conversation.

"We don't need to include India in any more of our quarrels, Colleen. Are you ready to go home?"

Colleen glanced back at the shelf. "Actually, I didn't finish all these."

"I'll take care of the rest." Unsure what Colleen might have heard, India moved in front of the desk. How long until Colleen noticed the fire between her father and her new friend?

"No, I'll do the books." Colleen ducked away, an astute grin lighting her eyes. "I only have a few more."

India froze. Had she already deciphered the atmosphere?

Jack covered India's hand. "Don't panic. She tried this once with her history teacher, but she let it pass when she realized we weren't interested in each other. All she heard was the tone, not the conversation. We just have to watch what we say in front of her."

As if India needed another secret to keep.

THAT NIGHT, AFTER DINNER, Jack carried the recycling bins to the curb in time to see India, strolling home along the sidewalk. In the dim glow of the streetlamps, she looked as cold as the night, deserted by early spring.

He knew the moment she saw him. She froze and stumbled, but she kept on coming. He wanted to protect her. Who had hurt her enough to frighten her away from the possibility of love? Why hadn't he been able to match her casual attitude in the library? Because her casual attitude was no more real than his.

He wanted to comfort her worries away. He'd like to stroke her sweet body in all its secret places until she rose to his touch. Instead, he had to make conversation. He had to play by her rules.

"Car trouble?" he said in a gruff tone.

Her hair floated in a corn-silk curtain around her shaking

head, tendrils lifting in the cool air. "No, I decided to walk. I love these clear nights."

A ridiculous lie. She'd come here for a reason. "Did you leave your father's truck at the library?"

"Uh-uh. I walked over there this afternoon, too." A nervous smile betrayed her. "Did you know this was a shortcut back to the hotel?"

"A shortcut?" He felt strange, as if he'd put his skin on sideways, as if his body no longer belonged to him. As if his whole life were in an uproar.

Too bad he couldn't sand down his life, the way he sanded the boat. Apply a new paint job. Polish up the brightwork. Inform loan officers they'd get their money when he scraped it up. Pursue this woman until she told him why he shouldn't.

"Jack, are you all right?"

"Is that the question you came to ask? This isn't a shortcut."

"I was concerned. I hoped you'd be outside, away from Colleen, because I didn't want her to see us together."

"Who are you really, India?"

She blanched. Jack closed his hand around her forearm. "What are you afraid of?" he demanded for the third time, more fiercely than he meant to.

She flinched. "I think the weather's turned colder since I left the library, and I can't convince my father to stop waiting up for me. I'd better go."

Jack turned with her. "I want to know you. Is that so wrong?"

"Good night, Jack. See you around." She paused. "I hope you're all right."

"Tell me why you won't let me get close to you."

"I live in Charlottesville. You live here. You have Colleen. I have a life at home."

"Can't we find out if what we feel is real? Are you seeing someone else?"

She hesitated, but finally she shook her head. "I have to go now. Dad will wonder where I am."

"Listen to me. I have a daughter and a business. One of my best friends called me from the bank today to apply pressure for my loan. This is the worst time for me, but I'm not sure when a good time will come. Do you think you can pick and choose your time to care for someone?"

India whirled away. "I can't trust this feeling. It's too strong to be real."

He didn't try to stop her. He didn't have the guts to lay himself open and admit he felt more than mere passion for her. Sadness wrapped around her slender shoulders. He'd known enough grief to recognize hers. He hoped he hadn't caused it.

SOMEONE BASHED AT THE DOOR with a heavy fist. Reluctantly India uncurled from the warm nest of her bedclothes and stared at the pale blue morning light coming through the curtains. She hadn't had a decent night's sleep since Jack had kissed her.

Still half-unconscious, she stumbled across the room. "Dad?" No. He was behind the other door. Opening the one to the street before her caller actually woke her father, she blearily met Colleen's flustered gaze.

"Hi." India lifted her brows at Colleen's many-colored, oddly draped ensemble. Jeans on bottom and bits of silk on top. "Where's Jack?"

"Why do you always ask me that?" Colleen eased inside, out of spitting snow, and undraped her wrappings to reveal a kind of quilted garment sewn to her sweatshirt. "Dad's working on the boat, but don't worry. Grandma knows I'm here. I need help, India."

"Is it snowing?" India drifted through the door, lifting her face to the slate-colored sky. "It's snowing."

"Come on, India. I have a problem."

"Okay, but I don't get this weather. It warms up, and then it snows." Coming back inside, India reached instinctively for the silk. "Is this a quilt?"

"No." Colleen's voice dripped pique. "It's supposed to be a dress."

"A dress." She twisted the material in her hands.

"I'm going to a costume party." Colleen narrowed her eyes, and India sobered as tears shone in them. "This is my costume."

"This?"

"I'm supposed to be Cinderella, before the Fairy Godmother got to her." Colleen stopped unwinding at the last uneven, garnet square firmly attached to her sweatshirt. "I wanted to make this pattern, but I couldn't afford enough material, so Grandma and I came up with the pre-godmother idea."

"How creative, and the pieces are lovely, like gemstones."

"They aren't real silk." Colleen nudged the door shut with her foot. "These were all remnants on sale. See? None of them is big enough to make anything more than a handkerchief, but I sewed them all together, and then I cut out the dress."

India lifted her end into the air. "So you did." The squares draped themselves into a bodice and a skirt, though the bodice dragged at Colleen's shirt. Some of the seams bunched and some drifted strings, but they absolutely formed the shape of a dress. India eyed Colleen with awe. "I'm amazed. I never would have thought of it."

"I've clumped up the seams, and the shoulders don't work at all."

"Do you have a seam ripper?"

"No." Colleen looked away. "And this was the final straw. The rest, I can manage, but I can't go with this sweatshirt hanging off me, like a train." She looked up, and a plea curved her mouth. "I remembered what you said that day we helped you make puppets. You said you would have sewn the bodies together if you'd had your sewing machine."

India already dreaded what came next.

"Grandma tried to help me..." Colleen trailed off, obviously hoping she wouldn't have to ask. "She's not much of a seamstress, though."

India gritted her teeth. She couldn't volunteer. She'd promised to stay out of Colleen's life, not keep wading back in every chance she got.

"I wouldn't ask you, but the party *is* tonight." With every passing second, Colleen became more reluctant—and confused.

India wrapped her arms around her own waist. How could Colleen begin to understand why she wanted to say no? How could she hurt this child when she'd never get another chance to do anything for her?

Reckless and desperate herself, she nodded. Not that she was sure she could save this day, but she'd choke before she'd admit doubts to Colleen. She draped the dress back over the girl's shoulder and hurried to her closet.

"Don't worry." Her daughter had come to her for help. Now was not the time to cogitate. "We'll fix it."

"By tonight?"

India snatched a pair of jeans off a hanger and yanked a sweater from a dresser drawer. "You've done the hardest part. We just need to trim here and there." And there and here, maybe. "Let me get dressed, and we'll go back to your house."

Shifting one foot on top of the other, Colleen looked much younger than she was. "Grandma's waiting outside in the car. I don't know if she thought I'd get lost in snow flurries or run away so I wouldn't have to face my friends.''

India lingered at the bathroom door. ''Go ahead, then. I'll drive myself.''

''No. Grandma can drop you when she takes me to the party. We may need that long.''

India couldn't disagree. She jumped into her jeans, wrestled the sweater over her head and swept her hair into a ponytail. She didn't worry about running into Jack. His Saturdays belonged to the boat.

Colleen waited where she'd left her. India leaned down to peer through the window. ''Still snowing? Better take a jacket. Want one?''

Colleen shook her head sadly, holding up her costume. ''No, I'll just wrap up in this.''

India tried to hide her inadvertent smile. She wrote a quick note to Mick explaining where she was and slipped it under his door. Outside, she clattered down the stairs behind Colleen, a length of the dress gathered in her hands. Nettie revved the engine in a kind of funny welcome for an older, extremely ladylike woman. Laughing, India slid into the back seat. ''Morning, Nettie. How long have you all been up working on this?''

''Since last night, I believe. Can you really sew, India?''

''I'll fix this or die trying.'' She meant it, too. ''Can we stop at the drugstore for a seam ripper?''

When they reached Jack's house, India and Colleen hurried over to the sewing machine in the living room. With every sign of marked relief, Nettie retreated to the kitchen to make coffee and burn some scrambled eggs.

India fished the seam ripper from its package. ''Let's start with that decorative sweatshirt.''

''I started to clip the seam, but I lost my nerve. I don't have enough scraps to make mistakes.''

India leaned over her. "Your father knows about this party?"

Colleen took an impatient breath and then burst out, "You don't have to worry. I broke up with Chris, once and for all."

Ah, relief. "Did you?"

"He came by at school the other day with the same old story. You heard it that morning outside the library. He told me to choose. Dad or him." Colleen shifted the seam. "So I chose. Sheesh—I'm only fifteen."

India longed to dance her around the room, but Colleen wouldn't understand. Safer for everyone if she remained in character. Interested, friendly librarian and housepainter.

"So your dad doesn't mind about the party?"

Dropping Chris easily, Colleen leaned on the table. "No, but he tried to talk me out of making the costume. You know, dads don't want you to be disappointed if you can't do something you really want to, but I also don't want to be the only one who doesn't wear a costume. My friend's parents are chaperoning. Like I told my dad, they won't leave us alone for a second."

India leaned over the seam between a turquoise and purple square. Unfortunately, when her parents had tried to overprotect her, they'd been right. Her conscience smarted. Instead of delving deeper into Colleen's life, she should be backing away. She'd meant to check on her daughter from afar. Instead, here she was, making a dress with Colleen and wondering how best to put in a good word for Jack.

"Your father probably can't help himself." Neither could she.

Colleen's laugh almost put India off her stride. Amusement was not the effect she'd tried for. Maybe she should concentrate on the dress.

One crisis at a time.

With care and a series of earnest prayers, she managed to remove the dress from Colleen's sweatshirt. Redoing the squares that needed adjustment proved more complicated, though Nettie saved the day with refreshment intervals.

"I still can't believe you did this." After a hasty bite of lunchtime chicken pita, India began to pin a seam back together. "I wouldn't have dared."

"I couldn't ask Dad for a costume. I even decided not to go, but then I saw the remnants on sale, and Grandma and I had this brilliant Cinderella idea, but my sewing class at school didn't cover everything."

"And I'm completely hopeless at household chores," Nettie put in.

India looked up, her gaze sweeping the cozy room. "Not completely."

The older woman actually blushed. "Thank you, but my daughter made this a home. I just follow in her footsteps and try not to muck anything up."

"Grandma, you've got to stop being such a Southern lady and take more credit."

India stared at Colleen. She was a distinct person, with her own thoughts and beliefs, clever thoughts, heartfelt beliefs. Maybe mothers who got to raise their children reached this epiphany early. To India, it was a whole new gift.

Nettie patted Colleen's hand. "If I were a Southern lady my grandmother could be proud of, I'd have learned how to sew a fine seam."

Glancing at the older woman, India felt comforted, as if they were all just friends, gathered to get a girl ready for a dance.

"My mother taught me to sew," she said without thinking. She bit her lip, not wanting to bruise Colleen with reminders of her mother. But curiosity gleamed in Colleen's eyes.

"Why doesn't your mom come to visit you and your dad? Isn't she curious about where you're working?"

India couldn't possibly say that the more she knew Colleen, the more she was reminded of Rachel. "I'm all grown up, you know. She doesn't look after me the way she used to." Colleen didn't seem to think that enough explanation. While she waited, India floundered around in her imagination. "She's taking care of the business at home." India hit the pedal on the sewing machine. It roared to life, loud enough to cut off conversation.

Colleen only lifted her voice. "Do you have any brothers or sisters?"

"No." She couldn't discuss her family. She couldn't even ask if Colleen ever wondered about her birth mother and the family she would never know.

"I always wanted a brother," Colleen remarked. "Mom and Dad said adopting me was so difficult, they didn't have the courage to try again. So many people only want babies—but you know, I've always kind of wondered if maybe my mom just didn't want to take more than her fair share."

India gazed at her in surprise. "Did she tell you that?"

Colleen shook her head. "No, and I could be wrong, but it would be like Mom. She cared so much. She couldn't let a stray cat or a dog pass our door unfed." Colleen swapped a laughing look with Nettie. "Sometimes, we had more pets than animal control. And Mom was always first in line to volunteer. She helped start a kitchen for homeless people next to the church. She said we shouldn't go in to services on Sunday mornings feeling satisfied with ourselves when others didn't have a place to go on Sunday or any other day."

India lifted her foot from the pedal. "I like your mother."

Colleen's smile looked broken, drawing Nettie to stroke her hand. "It doesn't make sense, honey. It never will."

The corner of Colleen's mouth quivered for a moment, but she ducked and pretended extreme interest in the worn knee of her jeans.

India and Nettie shared a glance, but they left her alone. No matter what problems she had with Jack, Colleen never seemed reluctant to voice her opinion or her needs to her grandmother, and India did what Nettie did.

Abruptly Colleen straightened. "What about you, India? Do you have any causes?"

India considered her response. She'd practiced a "no-harm" policy after Colleen's birth.

She'd hurt her parents enough, getting into "trouble" in the first place. They'd made no secret of their concern for her, but India hadn't known then how to tell them how deeply she loved them back. She'd tried to make up for the loss of their grandchild by ensuring she caused them no more pain.

"When you talk about your mother, I think I've missed opportunities I should have taken." She felt their increased interest, but she looked away in case Colleen and Nettie might see too much truth on her face. "You'd better let me concentrate on this dress," she said. "I wonder how we'll manage the hem."

They hemmed the dress by consensus, and when they finished, Colleen tried it on. The jewel-toned colors suited her beautiful young skin. She twirled as she came out of the bathroom, swirling to a lovely halt in front of India and Nettie with a satisfied air of joy.

"I'll bet Dad will make me wear shoes, though."

India widened her eyes. "You don't think you should?"

she demanded at the same time, in the same words as Nettie.

The front door suddenly flew open, and Jack sailed into the room, brandishing a large flat box. India smiled at the inexplicable triumph in his dark gaze. He halted when he saw her.

"What are you doing here?" he asked.

"Jack!" Nettie protested.

"I didn't mean it like that." He lowered the box. "I'm just surprised to see you."

As she realized she was standing in front of his daughter, she took a proud step to the left. "Wait until you see Colleen."

At first he widened his gaze. Maybe he hadn't realized she'd grown into such a lovely young woman. A battle of emotions played across his face, a mixture of wonder and disappointment that made no sense, especially when he glanced India's way with a hint of accusation.

"What's the matter, Daddy?"

He shifted the box at his hip, and India saw the truth. He didn't even have to say what he'd brought home.

"You look beautiful," he told his daughter.

"But what?" Colleen jabbed her index finger in the air. "What's in the box?"

He tucked it behind his back. "A costume. They didn't have Cinderella in rags, but they let me rent a ball gown." With a will that reached across the room, he smiled, pretending it didn't matter he hadn't been the one to save the day. "I don't believe the store-bought dress compares."

Colleen threw her arms around his neck. Nettie leaned into India, tightening her arm at her waist.

"Thank you," Colleen's grandma whispered. "I don't know if you're aware, but you've helped them."

India searched her gaze. She wanted to believe, and yet

nothing could be worse for Colleen. Colleen couldn't need her.

"Thank you, Dad." Colleen twirled away from her father. "You couldn't have done anything nicer, but let's take it back now."

"You don't even want to look at it?"

India held herself motionless. Colleen could have no idea how much the costume had truly cost Jack, with the threat of a bank loan over his head.

"I don't need to open the box," Colleen replied. "I want you to take it back and get a refund. I like this dress. India and Grandma helped me with it, so it's special. Besides, all the other girls will be dressed up. I'll stand out."

"You look like a treasure chest of jewels," India said. Jack's eyes reddened as he tried to reconcile himself to his suddenly responsible child.

Colleen tiptoed to kiss his cheek. "Lighten up, and put the money toward mending the nets. We've got to get the *Sweet Mary* back in the water."

Jack hugged her again, pride curving his mouth. "You amaze me." He tugged at her hair, a single father, strong and vulnerable all at the same time, unafraid to show his daughter how much he loved her. "If only you didn't manage to keep me hopping."

India's heart thudded. This afternoon felt like a miracle. She'd shared conversation and feelings, some truth she hadn't meant to tell, and best of all, her intense joy at being able to help.

And Colleen had shared a new side, her concern for Jack's situation, even her need of India's help. She hadn't displayed one moment of adolescent angst, not to India, not to Nettie, or to her father. Colleen had dropped her teenager's guard, even around Jack. She'd turned down a fairy princess's costume in favor of nets for the family boat.

So, why, wrapped in the affection that flowed between father and daughter, did India feel more than ever, like the interloper she was?

COLLEEN HARDLY LOOKED BACK as she ran up the walk to her friend's house. The door opened to girlish squeals. Jack waited until her friends herded her inside before he pulled into the street. He drove home slowly, wishing India could have seen the way the other girls greeted Colleen.

The thought dragged him upright in the truck. How could he consider sharing Colleen with India, even in so small a way? India lived in a hotel. She wanted her life back.

The deep breath he exhaled smoked up the windshield. He turned on the defroster, but snow had begun to fall again, in quiet flakes that skittered across the glass and the road. He didn't want to go home. Hayden had arrived in time to share a quick meal with Nettie. Jack felt like the odd man out.

He felt lonely.

Though India had refused to let him drive her home, he hadn't believed her when she'd said she'd rather walk. Watching her in his rearview mirror as he'd driven Colleen in the opposite direction, he'd seen India glance back more than once. She would have liked sharing Colleen's entrance.

Making a sudden decision, he turned down India's street. Looking at her window as he parked, he locked his truck and stepped onto the curb. A golden glow flickered on, silhouetting India as she turned away from the lamp behind the glass.

Something made her pause. The same innate awareness that had brought him here? His breath caught as she widened the part in the heavy drapes and lifted her hand in recognition.

Her hair floated like a soft curtain around her face, shining in the lamplight behind her. Jack lifted his own hand, flexing his fingers, as if he could touch hers, as if he could communicate this longing he didn't begin to trust to a woman who went out of her way to avoid him.

She turned away, and he pushed his hands down the legs of his jeans. Had he ever felt so much longing? Or did India mean something different to his life? Something not even Mary could mean to him? Could he trust her? Could she care enough to love him through thick and thin?

She opened her door and stepped onto the small porch, framed in a halo of light. Jack's heart leaped to his throat, a sensation he'd never before experienced and one that only weakened his grasp of rational behavior.

"What's up?" she called.

"I delivered Colleen, and Nettie and Hayden don't seem to need me tonight."

She didn't answer. Starting up the stairs, he didn't wait for an invitation. He just wanted to see her.

"I have pizza," she finally said. Not an offer, certainly not an invitation.

Halfway up the long stairs, Jack stared at her. The wind painted her snowy shirt over her breasts, delineating every lush curve. He didn't want pizza.

"No?" She sounded unsure.

"Where's your dad?" Oh, now that was subtle. He shoved his hands into his pockets. He wanted India, plainly, desperately, foolishly. Pizza would be safer.

"He's at the Fish Market with Leo Shipp." She lifted her brows. Funny. Colleen had the same gesture. "Not hungry?" India asked.

"Starving." He hoped the wind carried his voice's telltale gruffness out to sea. India only cared about the hunger that made his belly growl, not the kind that raged and ached in more vulnerable areas of his body.

As he drew level with her knees, her shirttails curved lovingly around the lithe muscles of her thighs and then flew up, tantalizing him with a glimpse of rounded hip. He swallowed hard and started climbing again. Coming here might have been more mistake than decision.

"What did Colleen's friends think of her dress?"

"They dragged her inside to show her to everyone else. She loved it. Thank you again."

She shook her head. "I didn't do much. She and Nettie just panicked when she sewed it to her sweatshirt."

She stopped as he halted on the step below her, his mouth even with hers. He loved the full, enticing shape of her lips. He couldn't look away.

"She needed you," he said. The words surprised him as much as they did India.

Even her mouth tensed. He could kiss away the anxiety that quirked the corners of her lips.

"She needed someone," India rasped.

Puzzled, he brushed his index finger across the curve of her lower lip. "What's wrong?"

She caught his hand. For a moment, she let her fingers slide over his, testing his skin, loitering deliciously over the back of his hand. Abruptly she pushed his hand away.

"Don't." She lowered her head.

He scooped her hair over her shoulder, but suddenly he remembered where they were, on the steps outside her room, in full view of some of the most capable gossips Arran Island had to offer.

Taking her hands, he turned her toward the door.

"Let's go inside," he said. "You'll be the talk of the town tomorrow."

"I'm not already?"

At her wry tone, Jack realized he already expected the dry humor she used to defuse tension. He enjoyed it. "Up till now, you've been famous because you persuaded

Marcy Shipp to make puppets with preschool toddlers. I don't want to ruin your reputation."

She shuttered her gaze. Her generous smile thinned. "I don't think that's funny, Jack."

He tightened his hand on hers. "I was only joking." She offered no response. "India?"

Digging her heels into the wooden landing, she pulled her hands from his. "You can't afford to play with your reputation. You know what small towns are like."

"It was a joke." He pulled her through the door. "If we argue out there, Colleen will hear about it before she gets home."

He shut the door behind them. The intimacy of the situation, their privacy, and the newness of his feelings changed into desire. If she couldn't feel it, she wasn't the sensitive woman he believed her to be.

If he didn't get out of here, he might just do something about it.

"Maybe you think I overreacted." Her eyes glowed deeper than the bay on its bluest day even as her low voice seduced him. Jack raked his hands through his hair. Get a grip.

"I didn't mean to insult you, India."

She turned away from him to fiddle with the lampshade. "I know all about small-town reputations."

He wondered at the bitterness that wasn't like her. Who had made her so defensive about her reputation? And how?

More important, who was he to set himself up as her protector? Didn't he have enough to worry about? A daughter who preferred India's rags to his hard-won fancy costume, a boat and business that both looked to be on the edge of sinking. Where could India fit?

Her spirit, so all her own, made him wary. She held herself apart, even as she seemed to take life in her arms. She might be attracted to him today. She might care for

Colleen right now, but she could decide to leave tomorrow morning and erase all traces of herself by lunchtime. He dragged his hand over his mouth, amazed at his own shaking fingers.

"What?" she asked.

Her concern compromised her ability to keep her distance. Beneath her iron will lay a heart that had no time for pride. She cared too much.

But how long would her caring last? Could she commit to day-in-and-day-out life and stick? How did a single father of a fifteen-year-old girl find out without compromising his own family?

CHAPTER NINE

JACK'S STRICKEN LOOK MADE India forget she should send him home, back to his family. Whatever was hurting him, she wanted to fix. She curled her fingers into fists. Completely apart from her feelings for Colleen, she didn't want to hurt Jack. She didn't want anything to hurt Jack.

"Has something happened with the boat? Did your friend from the bank call about your note again?"

"No, India. You're my problem."

"I can't be anything to you." She tried to back away from him, but he caught her hands. "Go home," she suggested gently.

Shaking his head, he ran his palms down her arms and she couldn't stop herself from shivering. Arousal followed the burning path his fingertips left behind. Her nerves jumped as he slid his hands around her hips and pulled her against him. Her traitorous heart sang with the heavy beat of his pulse.

Her body, on hiatus from Colleen's birth until now, ached for Jack. Mindlessly she met his planes and angles with her curves and need.

He leaned toward her, and she traced the line from his nose to the corner of his mouth. With the assurance of a lover, he touched his tongue to her skin. Heat burned deep inside her. As if he knew, he tightened his arms, causing her to tilt her head back. Anything to avoid taking. Still, he held her.

He wanted her, and she was capable of wanting him

back. She hadn't killed desire in herself when she'd given up her child. She half sighed, half smiled. She'd stood alone for so long.

"What's so funny?" His low growl of need reminded her how empty her life had felt.

She clenched her fingers in the silk of his hair. Did he lower his head? Maybe she stretched to meet his kiss? She didn't want to know which was true.

His mouth was hot and carnal. She strained to meet him, craving his life-giving kiss. His yearning consumed the last of her reticence.

She couldn't fight life itself.

His kisses burned her cheek as he dragged his hands down her back. She arched against him, unable to resist the demands he conveyed with touch alone. She tucked her face against his throat so she couldn't see, couldn't acknowledge the mutual passion spiraling between them, but his earthy scent was a feast she couldn't deny herself. She opened her mouth against his skin and tasted salt and male. His groan reverberated inside her body, and a voice she didn't know whispered through her mind, *This man knows how to care. I would be safe trusting him.*

Such a dangerous thought brought a hard dose of reality. She couldn't make love to Jack Stephens. Never to Jack Stephens.

"Wait," she gasped.

He didn't seem to hear. He lifted his head from her hair and kissed her again. India whimpered a protest that lost itself in his mouth. Trying to push away, she shifted her hands to his chest, but she lost her way, relishing his lean body, all this want just for her.

Reaching for sense, she pushed as hard as she could. "Stop, Jack, please."

He staggered backward, but she couldn't meet his hollow eyes. Turning from him, she wiped the back of her hand against her mouth.

"Don't do that." He strode back to her, harsh and virile, vulnerable and male. He caught her hand. "You don't mean it. Don't pretend you can undo what just happened. You want me, India."

"I can't." Nor could she explain. He might have the right to know, but he wouldn't have the strength to forgive. She couldn't change his and Colleen's lives forever. They deserved so much better than the consequences she forgot the moment he touched her.

He dragged her hand to his chest and flattened her palm against the rapid beat of his heart. She could drown in the heady power he gave her.

"Why, India? How am I supposed to understand? Who did you leave behind in Charlottesville?"

"No one," she said. "This just isn't right. Colleen—"

"Colleen is my concern. I take care of Colleen."

"I know." India lifted her hand to his jaw. Tight as a drum, he looked ready to explode. She'd foolishly hurt him. For nothing. She stroked his skin in a silent plea for him to try to understand. "Colleen likes me. If you and I become more than friends, we might hurt her. I won't hurt Colleen."

"You mean when you leave?"

"Yes." If only she'd been able to forget her child. If only she'd been able to give Colleen up in her heart.

"You won't stay? What we feel isn't worth a few more weeks?"

"I can't stay. My life isn't here, but yours is."

He released her so abruptly she stumbled. Catching the chair again, she stood by as he put on his coat.

"You're lying. I can see you're trying to hide something," he said.

"If I could explain myself, I would."

"I don't know why women skew their priorities and throw away the important things." Tension radiated from him, as cold and fierce as the strengthening wind that rattled the windows.

His direct hit chilled her. She gripped the chair back hard. "Are we still talking about me? You don't know me well enough to make that judgment."

He didn't look at her again until he reached the door. He turned around with his hand on the knob. "I don't understand you."

Who else had skewed her priorities? Surely not Mary. India hardly remembered when her plan to come to Arran Island had seemed sound. She should have realized how much she could love Colleen, but she couldn't possibly have anticipated Jack or how much he would matter to her.

She lifted her head slightly. "I'm trying not to hurt you, Jack. Please believe me."

"I'm not angry because you said no. I'm angry you don't trust me enough to tell me why." Hardening his gaze, he said coldly, "You've probably guessed you're not the first woman who's hidden important secrets, but at least she came clean. You—you'll do anything to protect your secret, won't you?"

Without waiting for her to answer, he yanked the door open and stalked through, slamming it behind him.

At his angry footsteps on the wooden stairs, India nodded her head. "Yes." The word hissed in the echoing, empty room.

COLLEEN TOUCHED the white tablecloth to make sure the table was solid before she set down her glass. "I feel funny."

"Huh?" Marcy's voice said.

Colleen jumped. "Where'd you come from?" Even

though she stopped turning her head as soon as her friend's face came into view, the room continued to spin. She grabbed Marcy's arm for balance.

"I've been right here," Marcy said. "Whattsa matter with you? Are you hot? I'm so hot."

"Marce, I don't feel good. Where's Leah?"

"I don't know. She's spending the night, remember?"

"Oh, yeah. I think I'd better go home. Let's call my dad now."

"My knees are tingly. Do you think we have the flu?"

Colleen ran her hand over her forehead. "Can't tell. Wait. You feel strange, too?"

Marcy set her own punch on the table, carefully, though she didn't test to make sure it was there first. Colleen admired her courage. Marcy licked her lips.

"Yeah, I feel odd," she finally pronounced. "Like I can't keep up. Like everything's happening too fast. What do you think is wrong?"

"What'd you eat? Could it be salma—saspa—salmonella?"

"Naaah." Marcy dragged it out. "Nobody else is clinging to the table. Why don't you let go? You won't fall."

Colleen stared at her foreign-looking fingers wrapped around the table's edge. "Oh. I'm holding on, but the floor looks so close. I wanna go home."

"We'd better wait. You know my mom. Don't eat or drink anything else. After an hour, we'll see how we feel."

"An hour?"

"Yes." Marcy pushed up her sleeve. "Where's my watch?"

"I have mine. I'll time us."

"'Kay. Do you think Ned Lambert will ask me to dance?"

Colleen spied him over her friend's shoulder, draped

around their school's head cheerleader. "He'd have to get off Kim Dunlop first."

Marcy followed Colleen's gaze. "What does she have that I don't?"

Colleen studied Kim, who'd dressed up as herself. "Take a look at her sweater."

Marcy looked from Kim's chest to her own. "Oh. Men are so shallow."

"Men? Ned Lambert?" Something about that struck Colleen as too funny. She tried not to laugh, because she didn't want to hurt Marcy's feelings, but laughter kind of spilled out of her, around her hands, even though she tried to hold it in. After a startled moment, Marcy joined her.

"What do I care?" She fingered her eyebrow ring. "I need a man who looks beyond my bra size."

Dimly Colleen realized that wasn't funny, but she had to laugh again, and Marcy seemed unable to resist joining her. After a while, they both just stopped. Colleen pulled out a chair for her friend and another for herself.

"Let's sit down. One hour. Marcy?"

"Yeah?" She turned her back firmly on Ned and his curvy Kim.

"How much punch did you drink?"

"Two glasses. How about you?"

"One and most of another. You don't think?"

Marcy blinked, three times in slow motion. "My mom will kill me."

"My dad won't stop at murder."

They sat quietly for almost twenty minutes.

"I wanna go home, too," Marcy finally said as Ned and Kim started their fifth slow dance.

"I don't. My dad'll never believe we didn't know."

"Why? You haven't done anything like this before. Can you feel your knees at all?"

"Forget my knees, Marce. I've done enough. I'm afraid to go home until I'm okay."

"What if we're sick?"

"At the same time?"

"You don't sound right."

"Let's go to India's."

"What?"

"She'll take us home. Maybe we won't have to tell Dad or your parents. Come on. We won't even wait."

"You like her, don't you? Do you think your dad does? My mom says he must, or he wouldn't have told us she and Mick needed work."

"He doesn't tell me how he feels about anything. He thinks he's protecting me." Colleen eased carefully to her feet and pointed herself toward the room where they'd stowed their coats. "I might start hoping they like each other."

INDIA STARED INTO the pitch dark, restless, her mind spinning overtime, while Viveca Henderson's furnace had apparently retired once and for all. Just when Viveca had retired to Atlantic City to "invest" her Bingo winnings. India rolled to her side, yanking the bedclothes more closely about her shoulders.

Jack. She couldn't evict him from her mind. Hunched against the cold, head bent against the gusting, mounting snow, he'd blown out of her room and down her stairs as if he couldn't escape fast enough.

She didn't blame him. Her behavior baffled her, too. Before she'd come to Arran Island, she'd kept such a firm hand on her life.

After Colleen's birth, she'd sworn she'd never need help from anyone else again. She'd finished her last year of high school and applied for college. She found enough work to pay most of her own way. Though Mick's business had begun to improve, she'd rejected her parents' offers of financial aid. She'd made herself an adult at sixteen when she'd given birth to a child she couldn't keep.

At least she thought she'd behaved maturely. Tonight she looked backward through new eyes and admitted she'd been an adult about material things, but, emotionally, she'd refused to take even one frightening step forward until she'd ridden a ball of flames down a runway.

Maybe these weeks on Arran Island would teach her how to start looking at a free future, one where she determined her own next step, where risk wasn't a bogeyman. But first, she had to finish painting Leon Shipp's house and stop interfering with Colleen's and Jack's lives.

She took a deep, frosty breath and curled her legs into a ball, groping for warmth. A knock on the door that connected her room to her father's had her lifting her head. "Dad?"

"Are you awake?"

Dragging herself out of the bedclothes, she tried to put on her best face. An effort that grew harder with each passing day. "I'm afraid to go to sleep, in case I freeze to death." She jumped up and flew to the door to unlock it. "Come on in." Whirling, she hurled herself back to the bed, but she wasn't sure her cold didn't come from inside. She hadn't felt warm since she'd pushed Jack away.

Her father came in, immediately banging into the dresser that stood beside the doorway. "Ouch." A shadow of Mick's size hopped across the room, spewing more forceful dismay. "I stubbed my toe, damn it."

"Turn on a light."

"They're all off."

"What?" She clambered out of bed for a look out the window.

The street stood empty, except for ghostly lumps where the snow had long since covered the cars. Blue-gray flakes swirled in the moonlit air. No streetlights burned. No light shone anywhere.

"We'll be ice cubes before morning, Dad. Do you have your coat?"

"Good idea. I'll be right back." He ran into something else. "India?"

"Yes?"

"I just wanted to hear your voice. I'm trying to find my bearings."

"Me, too," she muttered. She'd made a mess. Jack wouldn't accept her presence from now on without some sort of explanation. No matter how decent he was, he couldn't forgive her for coming here. He'd think she'd come to take Colleen from him. She'd believe the same thing, in his place. If she could imagine she might salvage some happiness for all of them from such a disaster, maybe she'd be willing to attempt the truth. But she refused to hurt Colleen and Jack—and Nettie and Hayden and her own parents—for nothing.

"I found my closet, India. Do you want another pair of socks?"

"When we finish painting the Shipps' house, we have to go home."

Silence. Finally he said, "How about those socks?"

"Yes, please, but did you hear me?"

"I heard. What's happened? I saw Jack's truck down-stairs earlier." A crash from his room near their shared door saved India from deciding whether to increase her sins by lying to her father about Jack's visit. "Damn it," Mick groused, "another toe. I think I may have shattered it. At what temperature do toes freeze?"

A sudden thud on the outer door saved India again.

"Who's there?" Mick called.

"India, is that you?" Saying India's name, Colleen sounded odd. "You don't sound like you."

India stared at her father's shadow. "Oh, no."

Another thud on the door preceded Marcy Shipp's demand, "We need to come in. Now. We need to come in right now."

Mick reached the door first and flung it wide. "Marcy, what's wrong with you two?"

The young girl merely shoved Colleen at him. "You have to take care of her. My parents are going to kill me." She turned unsteadily to go and slid into the doorframe on one of Viveca's handmade rugs. "Oops!"

She and Colleen, who clung to Mick, burst into laughter. India's stomach clenched. "You've been drinking."

"No." Marcy's face, completely in shadows, was unreadable. "At least, if we have, we didn't mean to."

"That would really explain a lot though." Colleen spoke too crisply, as if she had to concentrate on forming each word. She looked at her friend. "We wondered about that, but hoped not. Right, Marcy?"

"I don't know—gotta go." But Marcy paused again, long enough for India to grab her. "What's wrong with you?" Marcy demanded. "Take Colleen home, okay? She felt too funny to face her dad, so we thought you'd help her."

India held on to her. "You can't go back out there."

"My dress and coat aren't that warm," Colleen announced from inside the room. "Can I borrow your coat, Mick?"

Mick had already hauled the comforter and blankets off India's bed. India helped him wrap the girls.

"Listen to me, Marcy, and you, too, Colleen. Don't ever do something like this again. You could have gotten lost in the snow. You could have— Something horrible might have happened to you."

"We know about staying put in the snow, India." Colleen sounded terribly patient. "We just didn't realize how bad it was until we had to decide whether to go back or come on. We couldn't see the yellow lines sometimes.''

"You're probably both frostbitten," Mick said.

"Nope." Marcy flung her coat and her blanket wide, apparently to show off her costume.

India didn't know how to respond. "I can't see a thing."

"I'm the Easter Bunny!" Marcy dropped her arms. "The only costume they had left after Mr. Stephens rented the ball gown."

"She has a pink eyebrow ring to match her bunny ears." Colleen's awe struck India as the crowning point of this debacle.

"Wonder what happened to my ears? Colleen, do you remember my ears?"

"I bet they blew off."

India shucked off her coat and tucked it around Marcy while Mick rewrapped Colleen.

"We have to call your parents," India warned the girls.

"No." Marcy lowered her voice. "I left the kitchen window open. I just climb into the sink, use it as a step to the floor, and they never know I've been gone."

"This is what my students back home called too much 4-1-1," India said with an eye on the shadow of Colleen's best friend.

"Oops," Marcy said again, turning to Colleen. "Maybe I shouldn't have told her that?"

"No, India's cool." She turned her in India's direction. "Just let us stay here until we don't sound like we drank funny punch."

"Where's Leah?" India asked, hardly ever having seen one of the girls without the other two.

"She's spending the night. You know, her parents let her stay the night anywhere." Colleen dropped so suddenly to the floor, she scared India. "Here, sit down, Marcy. Let's wait until we feel better."

Marcy took her friend's advice. Mick stood over her, a blanket stretched in his arms, as if transfixed.

"I have to call your parents now, girls." Filled with dread, India twisted her hands together, but she continued. "They'll be worried about you."

"No." Marcy tried unsuccessfully to stand, but she gave up, even though India was already on her way to the phone. "India's not *that* cool."

"We're grounded forever." Colleen flourished one arm dramatically in the air. "I've never been grounded forever before."

"I don't think I'm going to like it."

"Maybe the phones won't work," Colleen suggested.

India didn't report on the dial tone in her ear, or on the fact that Jack answered the phone before it completed its first ring.

"Colleen?"

"No, but she's all right. She and Marcy are here with me."

"Thank God. I'm going to kill them both."

"Do you want me to bring her to you?"

"No, I'll come get them. Just let me call Leon. They're as frantic as we've been."

"Jack, wait—"

"Yeah, tell him on the phone—by the time he gets here, he'll chill out," Colleen suggested hopefully.

Afraid Jack would hear the state of Colleen's voice, India turned her back on her. "She came here because she felt too funny to go home."

"Funny?"

"Someone spiked the punch."

"We didn't know, Mr. Stephens," Marcy shouted. "Boy, I really don't like spiked punch."

"She says they didn't know?"

"I don't think they did. Surely they would have tried to cover better."

"Let me call Leon. How bad are they?"

India contemplated the question. "Tipsy?"

"Great."

India hung up and looked to her father. Mick dropped the last blanket around her shoulders.

"How'd he take it?" Mick asked.

"To paraphrase Marcy, I don't think he liked it."

ONE OF LEON'S MONSTER TRUCKS was already parked in front of India's building by the time Jack slid his to the curb. He scrambled out of the cab, armed with blankets and a thermos of bad coffee Nettie and Hayden had pressed into his hands.

Once again, Colleen had gone to India first. Despite being so damned glad she was safe, Jack found a trace of resentment for India. Must be nice to lack any responsibility for the teenager who worshiped you.

He skidded through the snow toward the stairs, knowing how unfair his feelings were. Colleen's willingness to confide in India first frustrated his idea of being a good father to his own daughter. And he wanted India, too. He had to admit it. The fact Colleen liked her only strengthened India's doubts about a relationship with him.

The door opened as he charged up the stairs. Leon Shipp and Marcy spilled into the night. At least he thought he recognized them.

"Don't even think about seeing the light of day until you're twenty-five. Your mother and I searched all over town for you," Leon said.

Jack had performed two such searches himself.

"When we saw car lights we got scared, so we hid behind fences. It's really late, Dad, and nobody's supposed to be out." Marcy spoke too distinctly.

"Leon." Jack squeezed past him on the stairs. Leon hardly even grunted. Focused on getting to Colleen, Jack forgot him and Marcy immediately.

As India's door almost closed in his face, he thrust it back open. "Colleen?"

"Dad, nice to see you. I guess you heard? Oh, yeah, India told you." Colleen's voice issued from a lump on the floor. She scooted toward India. "I wish you hadn't. I did promise Marcy you were cool."

India lifted her hands in submission. "I gave them both water, Jack. I read somewhere that helps ease a hangover."

"Hangover?" Colleen rocked to her knees. "I don't want one of those. India, why don't you turn on your lights?"

"I can't, honey. Power's out."

Jack appreciated her gentle tone. As angry and anxious as he was about Colleen, as deeply as he wished she'd come to him first, India's unquestioning acceptance somehow softened his heart toward his own daughter. He wanted to believe she hadn't known about the alcohol in the punch.

"Give me your hand, Dad." With his help, Colleen managed to stand. "I wondered why it was so dark. It's really cold in here, too."

"Let's get you home. Hayden was building a fire in your bedroom when I left. Thank India and Mick for taking you in and calling me."

"We can't leave them here." Colleen let go of his hand and backed away from him. "They'll freeze to death."

"We're fine," India said quickly.

"Dad, we have fireplaces in every room."

Jack held his silence, unable to think of an answer. His heart raced ridiculously at the idea of India sleeping under his roof, but he'd bet she didn't feel the same.

"We have plenty of blankets." Mick scooped up the

ones Marcy must have left behind, next to Colleen's spot on the floor. "And in the morning, I'll trek over to the market for supplies."

Jack spoke to Mick. "We have plenty of room and a gas stove, and Nettie stocked the pantry when she heard the forecast yesterday. We won't even run out of firewood."

"Thanks anyway." With a firm tone, India tried to end the discussion. "We couldn't impose. They'll turn the power back on anytime now."

"No, Dad. I won't let them die after they saved me."

Jack stared at Colleen. "You don't think you're being overly dramatic?"

"No." She faltered. "Why should India and Mick freeze to death? I'll bet Mrs. Henderson's other guests already ran back to the mainland."

"I suspect only fathers of teenage daughters are out driving in this storm." He pulled Colleen into the circle of his arm, but when she shivered, he turned to India for assistance. "I know you don't want to come, but I'd like to get her out of this cold and into her warm bed. I'll bring you back tomorrow if they restore the power."

"Jack—" India broke off, but he didn't need the rest of her protest. He knew it by heart.

"I understand, but help me out here, please."

Not even a please that cost him dearly counted with her. "You aren't being fair."

"Good." Colleen somehow thought India had agreed.

"India, you're safer at our house." He'd hardly attack her in front of both their families.

"All right." India turned to her father, "But I want to go home tomorrow if they don't get the power back up."

"Home? What about the Shipps' house?" Mick asked.

"We can't finish it anyway until the weather turns. We'll come back then."

"Agreed."

Jack searched the darkness, wishing he could see Mick's face. He must know India's secret.

They packed quickly. Colleen started down the stairs first, but Mick caught up with her, throwing Jack a don't-worry look over his shoulder. Jack waited for India, sheltering her from the storm with his body so she could lock her door. He slid his arm around her waist and helped her turn toward the stairs, though she stiffened in reaction to his touch.

He tried to let her go. She had her own life, as she kept telling him. And she clearly knew how to take care of herself, but longing kept his arm firmly curled around her waist.

"The steps are slippery," he said in a hoarse tone. He couldn't think of an any more plausible reason for holding her. She wouldn't accept "I need you tonight." Tendrils of her hair blew back into his face, stinging him.

Maybe she didn't care for him. Maybe she cared too much for his daughter to think of him as more than Colleen's father. He smiled wryly, finding little humor in the situation. If not for Colleen, who'd brought them together, India might be willing to look at him the way he wanted.

As they reached the frozen sidewalk, India hovered near her father. Jack guided Colleen to the back seat of his truck's extended cab.

"The doors are unlocked," he shouted over the wind.

India took the other side of the back seat.

He turned his key in the ignition and patted the reluctant truck's dashboard. "Come on, baby. We're headed for the barn."

Mick rubbed his hands together. "My engine feels about the same as this truck's."

"Me, too." Colleen blew on her hands. "Hit the gas, Dad."

He pressed his foot to the pedal. "Keep an eye out for the edge of the road." He started home. "You sure you're okay, Colleen?"

"Fine. I feel much better after the walk in the snow." Her hand floated toward India in the rearview mirror. "Thank you for letting Marcy and me in."

India smiled a wary "you're welcome." Jack held back his own smile. Ridiculously, he wanted India in his house tonight. The cold gave him an excuse to steal a few hours with her.

After stopping to scrape piling snow off the windshield twice, he finally found his own door. He parked half on the sidewalk to leave more room for the plows when they showed up. Without waiting for Mick and India, he led Colleen, slipping and sliding down the cobbled path, to their gate.

Hayden must have watched for them. He opened the front door and lit their way to the end of the walk with a flashlight. Snow danced around their legs and through the beam of Hayden's light.

Colleen ran into the house. She straightened and opened her arms. "Feel how warm it is." Even in the dim hall, her eyes shone. She reached for India's arm and clung. "I knew you'd be better off here with Dad and me."

Jack stared at the two of them—good friends—a mother and daughter to anyone who didn't know them. With uncomfortable clarity, he understood India's point about Colleen.

CHAPTER TEN

"WE'LL USE THOSE MUGS on the drainer, India." Nettie set a pot of hot cocoa in the center of a heavy tray. "Do you think you could eat anything?"

India turned the face of her watch to catch the flickering candlelight. "It's almost midnight."

"I know. I always get my second appetite about now if I manage to stay up this late. It's murder on the figure." Nettie uncovered a basket of sweet rolls. "How do these look?"

India smiled at the diminutive woman. "Delicious. Why does everyone tease you about your cooking?"

"I'm not good at it, but I've practiced a lot lately, and I'm improving."

Smiling at her, India began to stack mugs on the tray. "What do you suppose Jack is saying to Colleen?"

"We'll see. I hope Hayden manages to stay out of it. He thinks Jack should ground her for the next year, but I believe what she said. Mind you, I still don't want her to go to bed until she's completely—sober."

India nodded. "I don't much like that word, either. Who'd spike a punch bowl at a teenager's party?" She read cynicism in Nettie's pursed lips. "Dumb question, huh?"

She picked up the tray, but Nettie reached for it, protesting. "Put that down. I overloaded it. I'll carry it."

"I'm fine." India grinned over her shoulder. Nettie made her miss her mother.

Scrapes and groans issued from the living room before the kitchen door had time to swing shut. She hurried down the hall to find chaos reigned as Mick and Jack and Hayden tried to shift the Victorian furniture and Colleen all at the same time.

They'd moved a bookcase to make room to pull the sofa farther away from the hearth. Books and magazines tilted at crazy angles on the shelves. Being men, India thought, they hadn't bothered to unload the books first. Now they staggered under the sofa, and Colleen added to their problems by leaning across the couch to reach for a book.

"What are you doing?" India hovered out of range as the men tried to turn.

"We're moving furniture so your dad and I can sleep down here in sleeping bags. Hey, Colleen, get off. No, don't slide under there." Holding one end of the sofa while her father and Hayden strained beneath the other end, Jack couldn't grab Colleen as she tried to crawl beneath it.

"Wait," she said breathlessly. "I'm trying to get something."

The men set the sofa down away from the fire. India reached for Colleen, who still rocked on unsteady legs.

"Why would you sleep down here, Jack?" If he planned to give her his room, he had a different think coming.

As if he read the challenge in her voice, his only answer was a grim look. Colleen flitted out of India's hands to sprawl on the couch. "Dad's a gentleman, and you're supposed to take his room. I told them you wouldn't."

"You were right. I'll use the sleeping bag down here."

"The thing is, Dad won't give in, so you might as well." Waving one arm, Colleen managed to knock off every book on the shelf behind her head.

"Whoa!" She scrambled down the cushions, amid the fallen books, trying to avoid them, but she only managed to make a bigger mess. "This is what I was after. I knew I saw it."

"Are you all right?" Leaping to her rescue, Jack took her arm and tried to help her over the heap. Colleen was so focused on something at her feet, she dangled from his hand to reach for a large red leather-bound volume.

"I'm fine, Dad, but look, it's the photo album." Colleen juggled the book between them.

Jack nodded, doubtfully implying he didn't trust her high spirits. "I'm glad you found it, but let's look at it later."

"No, it has my baby pictures. I've searched the house for this one." She held it toward Jack. "Hold it for me, while I put the others away."

India froze. In her imagination, she saw a picture of herself bolting across the room to snatch the album from Jack's hands. Colleen wouldn't understand. Jack wouldn't understand. They'd both think she'd lost her mind. She might if she had to pretend she wouldn't sell her soul for a peek at those early photos of Colleen.

"Why isn't it with the others in Mom's sewing room?" Colleen hopped over the couch again to sit on the hearth.

Her father's expression softened. "It was your mother's favorite. She kept it down here where she could get to it whenever she wanted to."

Colleen looked up at him, her eyes watery in the firelight. Two involuntary steps led India toward her, but Mick pulled her to his side.

Colleen turned her face to the flames, away from company and her father. Jack didn't push. He stood at her side and rubbed her shoulders. No one spoke. Silently cursing, India held on to her lie. If only the truth wouldn't hurt Colleen and Jack so much more. She was an intruder in her own child's life.

Colleen suddenly swung around, her eyes bright but her

grief under control. "Hey, how about some of that cocoa?"

Nettie poured, her hands shaking as she passed the cups to India. Grateful to have anything at all to do, India served the others, but Nettie turned away once everyone else had a cup and a sweet roll.

"I think I'll see if I have any more rolls in the kitchen," she said, her voice trembling.

"Let me help you." Hayden followed, his shoulders hunched protectively over her.

Their granddaughter stared, crestfallen. "Did I make Grandma cry?"

"No." Her father patted her one last time on the back. "They miss Mary, too, and tonight has been tough for all of us. Let's give them a minute or two."

"Jack, do you mind if I use your phone?" Mick set his cup back on the tray. "I've suddenly realized India's mother may hear about this weather on the news and try to call us at the hotel."

Jack nodded toward the hall. "You'll find some privacy in my office. Opposite the kitchen."

Mick went. Like a huge sore thumb, India stood alone with her daughter and her daughter's father.

Jack didn't notice her discomfort, but he looked at her over Colleen's head as she carefully opened the photo album. "Do you want to see my kid when she was bald and lumpy? I don't think we have a choice."

He didn't have to ask twice. She dropped beside Colleen. "I'll bet she was never bald or lumpy."

Colleen traced her index finger over her name in gilt on the first leaf. With a quick smile at India, she turned to the next page, where the pictures began. "You know, I did look kinda like Derek Gibson."

India raised her eyebrows as Colleen turned to her, sliding the book across both their laps.

"Lead singer for Off Ramp. He shaves his head. You and Mom didn't shave my head, did you, Dad?"

"We might have, to improve your looks," he teased.

India's soft laughter died as she saw the first picture, of Mother Angelica with Colleen in her arms. Mere seconds after she'd taken her out of India's room.

Jack pushed Colleen's side of the book down so he could see, as well. "Where are we, here? Oh, you hadn't grown the lumps yet."

She elbowed him. "Do you mind, Dad? India's interested if you're not."

"What was her name?" Jack tapped Mother Angelica's picture. "We were so excited that day I didn't quite catch it. Mary always had to remind me."

"That day?" Colleen looked at him, completely content.

"That was the day you came to us." Jack's slow, fond, heartrendingly proud smile was a gift India never expected to match again in her life. She looked at Colleen as he went on. "She ran the home where you were born."

"I wasn't born in a hospital?"

"They had doctors and nurses. I guess it was a clinic, too."

Colleen turned to India. "I do know. I just love to hear this story."

Had she ever asked about her birth mother? India forced a smile to her lips and stilled a terrifying urge to blurt out her own questions. Fortunately, she couldn't fool herself with the mistaken thought they'd be glad to know who she really was. She'd only hurt them, and that was one mistake she refused to make.

"Let's look at the rest." Colleen flipped the pages with a bit of story for each photo. India drank them all in, careful to hide her true interest. She hated lying, but it was becoming her worst habit.

Before very long, Colleen began to yawn. After all, she'd had the biggest day, working on her dress, getting tipsy for the first time and fighting snow to reach India's hotel.

Jack stroked the back of her head as she lowered her face to hide a jaw-breaking specimen. "Put the album away for now, and help me take these cups to the kitchen. It's late."

On cue, Mick appeared in the doorway. How long had he waited there? His concern for her matched Jack's for Colleen. India tried to tell him she was all right with the expression in her eyes.

Between them, Colleen shut the album and stretched to her feet. "I'll wash dishes, Dad. Why don't you start setting up the sleeping bags?"

India followed the photo album with a longing gaze, but Colleen set it on top of the mantel. India hoped for a chance to look at it again before the power came back on. She'd love to take her time with it.

"Let me help you with that tray, Colleen." Mick took it for her.

"India?"

She turned. Jack looked serious.

"Are you all right?" he asked. "You're tense."

"I love to look at photos, like the ones at the library display, but I always want to know the stories behind them." On shaky ground, India bit back her questions about Colleen's first days with him and Mary.

"Colleen is like that, too. I guess all children like to hear how they were born. Unfortunately, Mary and I could never tell her too much. Sister—no, Mother Angelica— that was her name—only told us Colleen had a normal delivery. You don't seem surprised that Mary and I adopted Colleen. Has she already told you?"

India nodded in time to the beat of her own heart. Such

a question tempted her again to enter a dreamworld, where Colleen would get used to the idea of her true identity, and Jack would find forgiveness for her lies. India breathed slowly, aware of the breadth of his shoulders, of his strength.

"J-Jack," she stuttered, "Colleen's birth mother could tell you all about her birth. Have you never wondered about her?"

He shook his head. His vehemence gave away the depth of his feelings for the birth mother.

"No." His frown hit her like a blunt instrument. "Mary was Colleen's mother. That's all I need to know. For years, Mary and I dreaded the idea of some woman trying to take Colleen away from us. I still think about it when I hear one of those stories on the news."

His voice trailed off, and India tried to hide her utter dismay. Averting her face, she scrambled for composure. He'd given her a swift, detailed answer. He'd think she'd come for his child if she tried to tell him the truth.

"WAIT, JACK. I need to talk to you." Hayden caught up with Jack as he went to the kitchen to take fresh batteries from a drawer beside the sink. "What did you say to Colleen about the party?"

Jack resisted looking at Hayden. Colleen was his daughter. No one else's. Not the mysterious birth mother India had accidentally reminded him of, not Hayden's and Nettie's. "I haven't talked to her alone yet, but she says she didn't know someone spiked the punch."

Hayden began to open a package of batteries. "You believe her?"

"I have to. I don't think she'd lie about something so important."

"In my experience, the important matters drive children

Colleen's age to lie. She knows the kind of trouble she'd bring on herself for underage drinking.''

"Look, Hayden, she's my daughter. I've lived with her night and day for fifteen years. I usually know when she's lying. That's why she disappears rather than facing me."

"Don't get so defensive. She's our granddaughter. You and she are all we have left of our Mary. I have a right to worry about Colleen."

Jack handed his former father-in-law a flashlight. "Here, change the batteries in this, too. I understand how you feel, and you know I'm grateful you and Nettie make so much effort with Colleen, but if we don't try to trust her, we may drive her to do the things we want her to avoid."

"What do you plan to do about this party?"

"I've talked to her, and I'll make sure she understands she's not to risk drinking at her age." Feeling disloyal, Jack realized that as Colleen grew older he'd have to watch Hayden's tendency to overprotect—even out of love. The last thing he needed was to make Colleen feel she had nothing to lose. "How about the flashlight?"

Hayden unscrewed the top to replace the batteries. "I don't think you understand—"

"I do understand. I'm as worried as you, but instinct tells me she didn't know about the punch. I'm going to trust her, but I'll talk to her again."

"Jack—" Mick Stuart broke off as if he sensed the thick disapproval in the air as he came in. "Am I interrupting?"

"No. We're just about to hunt down the sleeping bags. You can join us."

"I don't think you need me." Hayden nodded at Mick as he walked, stiff-backed, out of the kitchen. Jack looked after him, worried, but he knew he was making the right decision for Colleen. He'd talk to Hayden again, too, as soon as the older man had time to cool off.

"I did interrupt."

"No." Jack felt strangely at ease with India's father. "Raising Colleen has turned into something of a community project, and sometimes the committee doesn't agree on direction."

Mick jerked his chin out, looking like India in a defiant mood. "I've been there. He's just worried. I always wished we'd had parents when India was born. Rachel's mother, Jenny—she was a steady influence. Responsible, riddled with common sense, but unconditional with her love. A special woman—you knew she had a wise soul the moment you met her."

Jack waited for more, half holding his breath to keep from stopping Mick.

"Rachel and I lived in a commune the first year we were married. Jenny never said a word. Just sneaked food into the communal kitchen and gas money into this big old macramé purse Rachel kept. Then, we decided to go to India—you know, for kids in the late sixties, with the Beatles and all, it was a pilgrimage. Rachel had some money her father left her. Jenny let us use it. She thought we needed to make our own mistakes, but when we came back, Rachel was expecting our India.

"Well, Jenny pulled us out of that commune and into her house. She told me I could paint on something other than cheap canvas. I had a wife and child to support, and she was right. She died in a car accident just a month or so before India came. I believe India's life might have been different if Jenny had lived. She was old-school where we believed freedom showed you the right road to take. Jenny loved unselfishly enough to let us resent her when she set us straight, and we had the good sense to listen."

"Are you telling me I should listen to Hayden?"

"I don't know you well enough to tell you that, but I remember a time in our family when a loving arbitrator like Jenny would have been a gift—'' Clearing his throat, Mick stopped abruptly. "I've said too much and stepped in where I have no business. What about those sleeping bags?"

"In the linen closet. Upstairs." What time in their family? Was this India's secret? What had happened to her? He led the way. "Is that why you called her India? The pilgrimage?"

"Yeah. India Jennifer. After the two parts of our life we loved best until she came along."

"She told me she'd had some problems at Colleen's age."

"Did she tell you?" Mick might have blown with the wind in his youth, but as a man in his fifties, he'd learned to erect defenses Jack recognized in his sharpened tone.

"She didn't offer any particulars." Jack opened the linen closet door. "I guess you won't, either?"

Mick shook his head. "Her stories to tell."

"What if I told you I care about her?"

"I'd tell you I'm still smart enough to know I'll only make things worse for my daughter if I interfere in her life."

Jack studied the older man. Soon the day would come when he had to back out of Colleen's life. Why that time came just after you had to take the most control was a little joke he'd never understand, but he admired Mick, even though he'd rather get a handle on India's secrets.

He turned back to the closet and passed the flashlight over the contents. "Will you hold this? I know the sleeping bags are in here." He tugged a stack of sheets out of the way, agreeing to close the subject. "Point the light toward that right corner."

The light tilted over his shoulder and picked out more blankets. This linen cupboard might have been someone's bedroom when his family had built the house. The shelves

were deep enough to sleep on if they didn't find the sleeping bags.

"We haven't used them in a couple of years, but I
thought they were here."

"Dad?" Colleen's voice ricocheted up the narrow stair-
well. "Dad, the flashlight's dying down here."

Jack backed out of the cupboard. "I just used the last
batteries." He leaned around the closet door. "Hayden has
fresh ones."

"He's outside bringing in more wood."

"How long will the power stay off?" Mick asked.

"I don't know. Could be as long as a few days."

"Dad!" Colleen called more urgently.

"I'm coming." Jack negotiated the stairs ahead of
Mick. In the kitchen, they found India and Colleen and
Nettie clustered around their flickering light. "You could
have lit a candle until we got back."

"I'm not supposed to mess with fire," Colleen replied
in a fed-up-teenager's tone.

India slid away from the group and him. She almost
equaled Colleen in moods. They all increased his curiosity
about her, because they made him see how she tried to
take life on the chin even when it hit her hard. India obviously cared for his daughter, but was she afraid of being
hurt, herself?

The other light went dark. Jack offered his. "You finished the dishes already?"

"People clean fast when they're about to do it in the
dark." Colleen dried her hands on a towel. "What about
the sleeping bags?"

He glanced at her, torn between her needs and India's.
He owed his first thought to his daughter, who probably
didn't realize the woman she admired so much was already
planning to leave.

"I don't think they're in the cupboard. Maybe they're

in the attic. Come with me, India. You're thin enough I can push you through the opening if I can't make it."

With annoyance in her posture, she followed him down the hall. He felt her back there, her warmth as well as her unwillingness. His body had attuned itself to hers. At the top of the stairs, he lifted the light to look into her face.

"Are you all right?"

"I'm fine." She smiled. Brittlely.

Her pulse beat away, in the hollow of her throat. Following his glance, she covered it with her hand.

"Don't look at me like that. We can't say anything to change the difficulties between us. You and tonight complicate an impossible situation."

Jack lowered his voice. "I don't expect payment for offering you a spot in front of my fire. I want you, but I won't attack you because you're handy."

India widened her eyes. Maybe she hadn't considered he might have an ulterior motive. Sheesh—he'd probably put a new bad idea in her head.

She pressed her fingertips to his shoulder, a whisper of touch that made him want to cover her hand and hold her closer, seduce the common sense out of her. "I shouldn't be here," she said. "I don't want to give Colleen any false hopes about us or even about me. She came to me when she needed help. You don't want her to depend on me, instead of on you."

"Just don't make promises you can't keep." He glanced at the stairs, half-expecting Colleen to peek up at them. "She knows you're temporary here."

"I *have* to leave." Misery deepened her voice and her eyes.

"Can't you try to trust me, India? Tell me what's wrong. Maybe I can fix it."

"You can't fix everything on earth. If I could find a fix for my problem I'd have done it myself."

"You can't do it all yourself."

"And who am I supposed to lean on? You?"

He stared at her in the semidarkness. They didn't know enough about each other or their feelings to make an offer either of them might regret, but India smiled at his hesitance, as if it pleased her.

"Case closed. Now, where is this attic of yours?"

"Damn my attic." He set the flashlight on the floor. Catching her by surprise, he ran his hands up her arms and pulled her against his body, no plan in mind, just a need to hold her. She muttered a startled complaint as he pressed his lips to her forehead, counting each silky strand of hair that slid against his lips. "Give me a chance. I want to help you," he said. "I'm willing to take a chance. We just have to be careful about Colleen."

"No." India held herself stiff. "What do you think this grope in the hall accomplishes?"

"Hold me." His voice broke as he spilled words that made him vulnerable. "Just be with me for a second. Feel how we are together."

Not even the darkness could hide her dismay. "Men aren't supposed to think like you, are they?"

She moved her hands over his chest and locked them behind his neck. She felt so good—so right in his arms. He loved the thrust of her breasts against his chest.

"You make me think differently," he admitted. "I won't judge what you tell me."

"I wish I could tell you." Her voice wrapped him in velvet. "But this is *my* problem—and only mine. I can't involve you and Colleen. I don't even want to, and I shouldn't let you touch me. I shouldn't let Colleen care for me, because I absolutely cannot stay here."

Jack tangled the fingers of one hand in her hair, as he caressed the long sweep of her waist with the other. It would be so easy to make love to her. So right, and yet, he was a man, stronger physically, aware of his ability to intimidate a smaller person, especially a woman who didn't know where to turn. He had to take her word about how they could go wrong.

"All right," he said reluctantly, his body stirring as he compulsively stroked the warm skin beneath the hem of her short sweatshirt.

Even as he tried to stop, India arched to his touch.

"Jack." Her protest at her own response whispered against his throat.

The delicate frame of her rib cage felt fragile. He swept his hand slowly upward, until the tips of his fingers brushed the smooth edges of her satin bra, the delicious swell of her breast.

Closing his eyes, he pushed her away. Unsure whose breath filled the silence between them, Jack tried not to hear the tortured sound. He reached uncomfortably for the flashlight and turned away from the woman he wanted enough to release because she'd asked him to.

"The attic is over here." He pulled the cord and unfolded the ladder. "We'll have to air the sleeping bags out before we can use them. I'd like to get Colleen to bed soon, but I doubt she'll go until you and your father are settled."

India caught his hand as he climbed the ladder's first rung. "Let me take the sleeping bag. Please don't make me put you out."

"You aren't imposing." Stepping down again, he looped her hair behind her ear. "How am I supposed to sleep in comfort while you tough it out on my living room floor?"

India ran a restless hand under her sweatshirt, across her own belly. "I can't sleep in your bed."

Her strangled tone stopped Jack's breath like a lump in

his throat. "Any chance you'll let me show you what ideas you just put in my head?"

Instantly she retreated. "I knew I shouldn't be honest."

With an iron force of will, Jack began to climb away from her. "I like honesty." He tried to clear the huskiness from his voice. "Come up behind me, and hold the flashlight while I search."

"I thought I was supposed to go first."

"No." He grinned down at her. "I just wanted you all to myself."

She shook her head, endearingly solemn. "Neither of us can want that."

"I'll try," he promised dryly.

He found the sleeping bags on top of a chest of Mary's things. He pulled the two bags off and hurried back to the opening in the floor where India waited.

Back downstairs, Mick took one of the bags and India took the other. As they shook them out, Jack sensed Colleen's intent gaze. He lifted his eyebrows, unsurprised to find her sizing him up.

"You're letting India sleep down here?" She sounded curious. His little girl had grown up enough to recognize undercurrents.

He avoided a telltale glance at India. "She talked me into it. What do you say you start getting ready for bed? I'll put more wood on the fire in your room."

Yawning mightily, she became his child again. "I'm ready for bed now. Do I have to brush my teeth, Dad?"

"Tonight of all nights, I can't believe you have to ask."

"What do you suppose they put in the punch?" She frowned convincingly. "We could have been sick or worse."

Jack ruffled her hair. "Keep that in mind for future reference, but I'm still going to have to talk to the kid's parents."

"Okay, but you'll turn me into a social nothing." She yawned again. "Will you pass me that light?"

Light. They needed more. Light in the house, a break in the snow clouds, and a spotlight on India's baffling motives.

SHE COULDN'T SLEEP. The grandfather clock in the corner ticked on, inexorably counting the seconds until morning came. She shifted in the attic-smelling, toasty warm sleeping bag. On the other side of the hearth, her father snored on, oblivious to the astounding reality of spending a night in her daughter's house.

Add to that Jack asleep just up the stairs. Did he wear pyjamas? Did he sleep on one side of the bed rather than the other? Did he sprawl across white sheets, his skin bare to the soft caress of cotton and the cold air's harsh breath. She imagined wrapping herself around his body to warm him.

India scrambled to her feet. She stared at her father, but he only grunted and snored on. Water. She was dying of thirst.

Picking up the flashlight Jack had left them, she made her way to the kitchen. She eased her hand into the freezer to extract a couple of ice cubes and shouldered it shut again. Over the low flow of water from the tap, footsteps startled her.

She expected Jack even before she turned the flashlight toward him. He blinked against the light, and she answered her own inappropriate question.

He didn't wear pyjamas.

His tousled hair fell to the collar of a dark T-shirt. Sweatpants hung low on his hips, the drawstring falling in a suggestive trail. India swallowed.

His grin chipped at her will to do right by him. She lifted the water glass to her lips.

"Couldn't sleep?" he asked in a low voice.

Her legs trembled. She shook her head. He reached around her for a glass. Shivering in reaction to his own ease with his big body, she slid away from him.

"Me, either," he said. "Is that water? Want something stronger?"

"No. Water's fine."

"I'll join you, then. Sit down, and we'll wait for morning together."

She turned the light to her watch. "It's not that long to wait." Thank heavens. If she were smart, she'd sacrifice one of Jack's glasses to wake her father, but she didn't have the nerve. She took a seat across the table from Jack instead.

"I haven't thanked you for taking Colleen in." He eased his own chair out and sprawled, his long legs pushing dangerously to either side of India's.

"You don't have to. What did you— Oh, that's none of my business."

"What did I say to her?"

"It's none of my business, Jack."

"We talked while I built up the fire in her room. I told her I was glad she hadn't tried to get a ride with another punch victim, and I asked her to drink only unopened soda at parties from now on."

"You don't think she knew, then?"

"You sound as worried as I was, but she's my daughter. I'll take care of her."

She wanted to take his slightly edgy hint, but she couldn't help herself. "I just wish you could be sure she wasn't experimenting."

"Didn't you believe her?"

"Yes, I did, then, but she's safe now—and I don't know. Marcy strikes me as being more streetwise than Colleen."

"Meaning they might have cooked up this spiked-punch story?"

The idea repelled India. "No—well, maybe—no, I don't think so. They both seemed confused and worried, but what if they talk about it with their friends, and drinking looks harmless in retrospect?"

Jack considered. "Sometimes you have to take your child's word."

How did he know when to trust? Maybe because he'd known Colleen all her life. India turned her face to the darkness. "I guess."

"Have I hit a nerve again?" Jack pushed his glass aside.

After fifteen years of silence, she couldn't admit he'd sawed at her exposed feelings. She loved Colleen, and she cared for Jack, the one man in all the world she would have chosen to be Colleen's father.

"I think I'd better go home," she said.

He frowned. "Don't be crazy. Colleen was right. You'd freeze, and no matter how strong he is, your father is not a young man."

India bit her lip and released it. "We can't stay here indefinitely. We're all just taking a break from real life."

Jack leaned across the table to stroke her stinging lip with his thumb. "Don't hurt yourself."

Averting her head, she pushed his hand away. "Stop. I've told you before, I won't risk hurting Colleen."

"You won't even look at me?"

Got that in one. Every time she looked at him, she lost all sense of right and wrong. "You know why I'm not comfortable with you."

"Because you want me as much as I want you."

"Because of Colleen. Pick on someone she doesn't like."

"Someone who can leave and not hurt her?" With one phrase his tone shifted from teasing to taut. "Colleen has a parent. She likes you, but she's not in the market for a new mother. You don't have to be her mother.''

His fierceness shorted out India's rigid nerves. Why not tell him the truth? She *was* Colleen's mother. She wanted to yell it. She'd give anything for the right to call her daughter her own.

But she couldn't. In that moment, she understood the finality of her fifteen-year-old decision better than she ever had. Jack couldn't possibly understand, but she had to make him stop throwing rocks at a minefield.

''Maybe I'm not worried about Colleen,'' she lashed out. ''Maybe I'm worried about how I'll feel when I have to leave her.''

Jack stared at her, puzzled. ''What are you talking about?''

She knew her answer. She could tell half the truth and change the way he felt without hurting Colleen. Now that she'd made the unthinkable mistake of letting him get close to her, she had to destroy his feelings for her without hurting anyone else.

He could get over her as a person he couldn't respect. He might not be able to forget she was his daughter's birth mother.

''I had a child once, Jack, a baby girl, and I gave her up. I gave my daughter to strangers, and I don't know how to survive loving another child and giving her up, too.''

CHAPTER ELEVEN

TURNING THE FLASHLIGHT toward her ravaged face, Jack searched India's wet eyes. "What did you say? I can't believe you."

Her confession echoed in the silent room. This woman who'd become his daughter's friend, whose concern for Colleen he didn't doubt for a moment, had given up her own child.

Memories flooded him, razor sharp. The tests he and Mary had undergone, their pain and humiliation, Mary's final betrayal when they'd realized they couldn't hope any longer for a child of their own. Jack brushed his hand over his forehead.

How easily had India become pregnant? How thoughtlessly had she turned her child over to strangers?

"No," he muttered, more inside his past than in the present.

"Jack?"

He saw her through a haze of grief. He'd struggled to be happy when his friends had children. He'd tried to love his wife again when she'd told him she'd used another man to forget their problems.

He'd tried to love her despite the fact she'd used him to keep Colleen. He'd agreed to give his marriage a second chance, because another woman had given birth to Colleen and given her up.

"Was it easy for you?" he choked out.

India stared at him, openmouthed and angry. Past

blended with present. In his mind, Mary answered. *I wanted to see what love felt like without a purpose.* As if he'd caused their infertility. As if she blamed him. No matter that he could have had children with another woman. He'd wanted only her until she'd tried love with someone else and then settled for him, like a meal that keeps you healthy but doesn't satisfy.

"Jack?" When India reached for him, he moved so her hand fell to the table between them. "Say something," she pleaded.

She'd given *her* daughter away. Like clothes that didn't fit, like shoes she'd worn out. Furniture she didn't want.

"You got pregnant, and then you gave your child away?"

India flinched from his harsh voice, but she brought up her chin. She tried unsuccessfully to hide her sadness.

"I gave my daughter a future." Her intensity cut through his shock. "I made sure she had everything I couldn't give her."

"You gave her to strangers," Jack retorted, too angry to care that he was taking his past with Mary out on her, or that his words would hurt.

India stood, flattening her palms on the table. "You obviously think it's like closing a door you're glad you won't have to open. You're wrong. I tear out a piece of myself every day of my life." Her voice caught on a sob, but she straightened. "I won't discuss this again. I'm going back to my sleeping bag, and we'll pretend nothing's happened. When Dad wakes up, he and I'll go home."

God help him, Jack let her go.

A SOLID KNOCK SOUNDED at the door. Still wide-awake, aware of Jack as silent as death in the kitchen, India jumped at the sound. A few feet away, Mick fought free of his sleeping bag, rubbing his face.

"Someone's up and about early," he muttered. Peering around, he pushed the sleeping bag off his legs. "Is the power back on?"

A man's voice shouted Jack's name from outside. Swift footsteps preceded a brief glimpse of Jack loping to the door. The hinges protested loudly as he hauled it open and closed it behind himself.

"...boat sinking..." said an unfamiliar voice.

India's heart thudded in response to urgency in the man's tone.

Colleen and Nettie, followed by Hayden, appeared on the stairs.

"What?" Colleen leaned over the balustrade, worry shortening her tone. "Did you hear what he said?"

India struggled out of her sleeping bag. "Something about someone's boat." She hurried to the hall, praying for a break for Jack and Colleen. The boat in question couldn't be theirs. "It's sinking."

"India, Colleen—" Jack opened the door and slammed it shut again "—get blankets, all you can carry. Nettie, Hayden, Mick, take food to the community center. You may have to walk, because the snow's deep, but bring what you can. Colleen, take the blankets to Mr. Pearson's slip."

He ran up the stairs, and they all sprang to follow his orders. Colleen's grandparents rushed Mick toward the kitchen. Colleen led India up the stairs to the linen cupboard.

"We have two comforters in here," she said. "And we'll take the ones off the beds." She turned a chilled gaze on India. "Mr. Pearson has three kids. Did you hear that man say whether he was on the boat?"

"Don't borrow trouble, sweetie. Let's just do what your father said." She noted Colleen's flimsy pyjamas. "Put on jeans and a heavy coat. And two pairs of socks."

Colleen ran into her room as Jack came out of his, pulling a sweatshirt over his head. His eyes burned holes in India's soul as he hurried down the hall. Stopping beside her, he wrapped one hand around her forearm.

"Keep your eye on Colleen." His haggard face frightened her. "If you have to, send her to the community center. Everyone else will end up there."

India nodded. Silently she begged him to be careful. She had no right to caution him aloud.

Staring at her, he lifted his voice. "Colleen, listen to India. Do what she tells you."

"What will happen, Jack?" India asked. "Are you in danger?"

"Just get there. Colleen knows the way."

He left, his footsteps pounding down the stairs. Without listening for the door, India gathered up her own clothes and changed in the bathroom. Back upstairs, she threw blankets and the comforters over the railing and then hurried down to snatch coats from the hall closet. Colleen turned up behind her, shoving a pair of gloves into her hands. India put them on, and they divided up all the bedding they could carry and ran from the house.

"Which way?" India asked as they skidded through the snow on the porch. She grabbed the tails of Colleen's blankets and tucked them over the girl's shoulder.

"Toward the bay." Colleen's young voice stretched thinly over her anxiety. "Mr. Pearson's mooring is one of the farthest out on the dock."

India slogged silently through the snow by her daughter's side. As they turned the curve toward the docks, they met another woman bearing similar burdens. She smiled nervously and matched Colleen's and India's pace.

India turned a worried glance on Colleen. Was she thinking of her father? Was she worried he'd do something foolish—like climb onto a sinking boat? India worried, too.

Colleen strode, with the silent maturity of a grown woman, a member of a fishing community to whom disaster was nothing new. India tried to breathe. Disaster was not a sinking boat. The cataclysm would be anything that happened to Jack or Mr. Pearson or any of the other helpers.

But especially, please don't let anything happen to Jack.

They came to a finger of the dock that reached for the sea. "Down there," Colleen gasped.

India put on a troubled burst of speed that drove her into the crowd milling on the narrow dock. She glanced back at Colleen, but the girl waved her on.

People took blankets and wrapped them around the wet men who stood shivering in puddles on the frozen planking. She found herself at the stern of a listing boat with nothing more in her hands.

"Four feet of water below deck," said a gruff voice behind India.

She turned. Where was Jack?

"Jack Stephens," she said to a bearded man huddled in one of the blankets she'd brought. "Have you seen him?"

The man pointed with his blanket-covered hand. "He's on board. They'd better get out of there soon. I feel bad for Pearson. He's got half his life down there."

Another man spoke in a hushed tone. "I heard he and the wife were having some trouble. He's been living on board."

India's heart contracted as she searched among the line of men passing personal belongings toward the dock. She took a place in the line. She had to obey a physical need to be as close to Jack as she could. She knew about being alone. What did this stuff matter? A CD player, a television. What about the men who stood to lose their lives?

What about Colleen, who craned her head over the

crowd but kept mercifully back? How could Jack risk leaving her alone?

A sharp crack rang out in the thin air. The boat tilted more swiftly toward the icy harbor water. India cut off a cry of despair. *Jack!* She rushed toward the boat, but strange, grasping hands dragged her back.

"Out of the way, miss! You men, get off there, now."

The men still on board struggled over the side. Two fell into the water, but the crowd hauled them out quickly and passed them blankets. Still Jack didn't appear. Finally a tall, blond man climbed over the listing deck and jumped to the dock, his face pale, his eyes staring.

"Pearson and Jack Stephens and Lem Burke are still in there. Get me an ax. The door shut on them, but I can go through the deck."

India searched frantically for Colleen, but the crowd had closed around her. India prayed the man would get to Jack before Colleen heard the desperate whispers about her father.

Three other men came forward with axes, but the blond man shook his head. "She won't take much more weight."

He struggled back onto the boat, scrambling over the tilting deck that slipped ever closer to the water. He swung the ax frantically, again and again. Wood splintered. He shouted, and a man appeared, soaked, gasping for air.

India lowered her head in shame. With all her heart she wished he'd been Jack. A shout from the crowd made her look again. Jack and the blond man were on deck, carrying something heavy between them. *Someone* heavy.

They struggled to lower the unconscious man over the side, clutching him until India and several others on the dock managed to drag him to safety. India turned back to the boat as the blond man leaped off. Jack followed, wet, his face pale with cold and shock, his eyes almost black in contrast.

He landed on the dock with both feet, but his legs wobbled. India threw herself into his arms, grateful and horrified and furious all at the same time.

The idiot only laughed as he pulled her close. His body trembled with the cold, but he held her so tight she felt his fear in her bones. Strangely, pictures of Colleen shot through India's mind, as if Jack put them there.

Unable to stop herself, she sobbed into his already soaked shirt. She clutched at him, trying to infuse her warmth into his shivering body, grateful beyond belief for the hard reality of his arms around her. Someone threw a quilt over his shoulders. He pulled it around them both.

"It's all right." His frozen voice, hoarse, spoke close to her ear, only for her. "I'm all right."

"What were you thinking? What about Colleen?" She cupped his face to rub his chilled skin, but Jack caught her hands. He touched her tentatively, his fingers unsteady as he turned her palm to his mouth.

"You probably have frostbite," she accused, her fear grinding out hostility.

"Daddy!"

India broke away just as Colleen skidded into him. He bent to pull his daughter into his arms, murmuring soothingly, as he would to a small child, not a fifteen-year-old young woman who had done her share in the rescue.

India tucked his quilt around him and Colleen, patting gently at her daughter's back. Though Colleen had worked as an adult in the rescue, she'd become a little girl who'd suddenly heard her father was trapped in a sinking boat.

Another man approached behind them. With his hands on Jack's shoulders, he pushed Jack and Colleen and even India toward land.

"Come on, now, Colleen, India. Let's get Jack to a dry, warm spot before he loses any of his extremities."

India stared at him. Al, from the drugstore. She turned

around. Most of the people in the crowd behind her looked
absorbed in their own families. Hardly anyone bothered to
look their way.

Who had seen her throw herself upon Jack as if he belonged to her?

JACK TOOK A STEAMING CUP of milk from India and allowed Colleen to tuck one more blanket around his feet.
He followed India's stiff progress around the bed they'd
made for him on the huge old sofa. Outrage sparkled in
her eyes. She was mad, but she'd say nothing in front of
Colleen or the rest of their families. The knowledge made
him smile. All in all, he felt pretty confident right now.

Whether she ever admitted it or not, after he'd jumped
over the side of Pearson's boat, India had been plainly,
blazingly elated to see him, crying hot tears into his frozen
shirt, oblivious to the crowds around them.

She wasn't so glad now.

"Are you warm enough, Dad? Can you feel your toes?"

Jack nodded at Colleen. "I'm fine. I won't lose anything. Al is a pharmacist, not a licensed doctor, and you've
restored me to warmth and health."

She retucked the blanket around his feet. "I wish I could
restore you to good sense. When will you learn? You jump
into every disaster around here." She glanced at India,
who'd stopped pacing to hover on the wings of outrage.
"Last September, Dad walked into Mrs. Hollings's house
just in time for it to explode because of a gas leak."

"I'm part of the volunteer fire department." Jack tried
to make light of his actions. "Brett and Lisa Hollings were
trapped in their mudroom. I couldn't leave them there.
Thank God, the furnace was at the other end of the house."

Colleen stared at him. "I know you couldn't leave them,
but I'm starting to wonder if you're some calamity mag-
net."

Jack pushed a breath through his teeth, but he understood. "Maybe you could get me a rabbit's foot for Father's Day." He tousled Colleen's hair. "Don't worry
about me. I promise, I won't go to any more fires unless
I'm invited. If I ground my own boat in another storm, I'll
stay on board until she sinks, and if I see someone else's
boat sinking, I'll just toss a life jacket at the wreckage."

"You aren't the only volunteer." Colleen stood and
took his glass. "I'll freshen this. India, don't let him up."

Jack laughed out loud. His laughter faded as India
leaned over the back of the couch, her gaze restless as the
sea but hard as stone.

"What would Colleen have done if you hadn't made it
off the boat, Jack? Just answer me that, and I won't say
another word."

Her accusation hit him square in the chest. His parents
were gone. Nettie and Hayden would give Colleen anything she ever asked for. Hayden might overdiscipline.
She'd be spoiled and nuts by the time she turned twenty.

"I'd fight heaven and earth for my daughter."

India clenched her fingers on the back of the couch so
hard her knuckles shone white. "Not good enough. How
can you take chances like that? You scared the hell out of
me. What do you think it did to her?"

Jack stared at her flushed face and diamond-hard eyes.
She was a tigress, protecting his young. "You're so
damned beautiful."

"Concentrate on Colleen."

"I didn't think I was taking a chance. Bill Pearson is
like the rest of us here. We have enough to get by, but we
don't have more. His wife decided she preferred their tax
man to a fisherman, so she suggested Pearson live on the
boat. She doesn't let him see his children unless she wants
to go out of town with her lover. Those 'things' are all
Pearson has. That boat and his few material possessions

may be all that's left between him and the last of his self-respect. I'm not the only man who knows about his problems, and I wasn't the only man down there.''

''Here's your milk, Dad.'' Colleen came back, carefully balancing the brimming glass.

Jack took it, but he was tired and his patience began to slip. ''You know, Colleen, I don't really like warm milk.''

''Drink it anyway.'' She set the glass beside him and sent India a shrewd glance. ''I think I'll wash those wet clothes. Grandma asked me to do them before the house stank of bay water.'' She paused, flouncing to the door. ''By the way, they'll be at the community center for most of the afternoon, and I'll be busy upstairs.''

India dropped like a stone to the coffee table's edge. Jack caught her hands. A landing like that had to hurt, but he looked over his shoulder.

''Colleen?''

''Yes, Dad.'' Already halfway up the stairs, the little matchmaker didn't bother to stop.

''I didn't mean to scare you.''

''Prove it. Don't do that stuff anymore.''

India tried to pull away as Colleen slammed her bedroom door. ''See? She already knows.''

He laughed. ''What's she supposed to think after the way you wrapped yourself around me?''

''Funny. I didn't think—my God, I sound just like you.''

''Don't think. Come here.''

He pulled her, but she held back. ''You know who I am now. Stay away from me,'' she said.

''You thought I would if you told me about your child, didn't you?'' Old anger flickered deep in his heart, but it couldn't find fuel to burn now. He just wanted to hold India. He wanted to feel alive as he'd been in her arms.

''I made a bad decision. Maybe I've made a couple, but

don't you ever jump on another sinking boat. I wanted to kill you myself.''

He laced his fingers through her hair. "I saw." He lifted himself to brush her mouth with his lips. "Come show me.''

She spun away from him. "I have to go home. As soon as Dad gets back, we're leaving.''

"And Leon Shipp's house?''

"We'll paint it when the weather breaks. If I stay here much longer, I'll—''

"You'll make love with me. I say, move right in.''

"I can't be as reckless as you.''

"You've brought Colleen and me a sense of life we haven't known in three years. I dream of you at night. Hell, I fantasize about you damned near all day. You're walking, breathing temptation. I dream of loving every sweet curve I see, but I want your spirit, too. You're tough. Look at Colleen's costume. Look at the way you handled her trip to the punch bowl. You rescued my daughter as surely as we rescued Bill Pearson today.''

"And what I did with my daughter?''

He looked inside himself. "I want to be honest with you. I resent that you could get pregnant when trying nearly ruined Mary's and my marriage—''

India's mouth made an O of horror. "What are you talking about?''

He lifted his chin, expecting an emotional punch. He'd never shared his and Mary's secret, but he wanted to tell India. "She found someone—for a little rest from working to have a child of our own—and then we heard about Colleen, so we managed to make a life together and a happy life for our child. But we never would have had Colleen if not for a woman like you. I overreacted this morning. I see why you're afraid to get any closer to Colleen.''

"I care too much for Colleen already." She paced to the fireplace, a huntress, backing off to plan new strategy. He looked forward to the battle, but he didn't want to hurt her.

India didn't seem to know yet that the feelings between them might lead to more than desire. He wanted more, but maybe he'd pushed her hard enough today.

For now, he needed to get his daughter out of her icebox room and back to the one fire still burning in the house. He kicked free of the bedding. With a little time, maybe he could even show India what she was throwing away.

"I care for Colleen, too," he said, "enough to get her back down here where the heat is. What do you say to a harmless game of cards?" He went to the stairs. "Colleen, come play cards with us." Jack turned back. "I vaguely remember Hearts, and I saw some cards in that desk by the window."

India scooped up one of the blankets. Nervously she stroked a satin ribbon that had come loose at one corner through her fingers. "Lie back down. You need to stay warm."

Drawn as much by the pulling motion of her slender fingers as by the troubled note in her voice, he gathered her into his body heat. "I don't want or need mothering from you." He rubbed her hands between his. "See? I'm alive and warm, and I am not going away."

CHAPTER TWELVE

JACK STOOD BACK on the dock. The *Sweet Mary* looked sweeter than ever, freshly painted, whole again, ready to put back to sea. The freak blizzard had given Jack the week he'd hoped for to work on his boat without the distraction of fishing for Tim Byar, who'd docked his fleet until the weather let up.

Jack slapped his gloves against his thigh. *His* boat. Back in the water. His business, back on track. Pride made him smile. It would be perfect if...if he could tell India.

She and her father had packed and gone back to Charlottesville with a polite farewell, as soon as the roads had cleared enough to let them out of town. Colleen had reported they'd come back yesterday, though, to finish Leon's house.

Once India fled, Jack had tried to bury his stray thoughts of her in his work. He hadn't counted on the images he couldn't restrain, the rough texture of her sweater against his hands, the silk of her hair against his lips, the melody her voice played in his head.

He'd listed all the valid reasons to be responsible rather than pursue her, but she'd mauled his priorities, and finally, boat repair was a moot point.

Once he'd realized he could go back to work for himself, he'd known he had to decide what to do about his feelings for India. He tilted his wrist to look at his watch. Colleen still had almost three more hours of school, and the woman he desired, the woman he'd missed for the past seven days, would be at Leon's.

Still running on the high of being somewhat in control of his life again, Jack parked in Leon's driveway. He skidded down the slippery grass slope to the house. From around the corner, India's voice floated back to him, husky, laughing, potently familiar.

"We've got Thomas Jefferson's outhouse all over again." She stood with her father, both of them studying Leon's dormer with their hands braced on their hips. "I swear I see a hint of lavender."

Jack slid the palm of his hand over his jacket. His heartbeat pulsed through the heavy material. Her paint-spattered white overalls bagged around her long legs, and the dark blue turtleneck emphasized her pale hair.

Seeing her after a week away, he experienced an intense relief that silenced him. He almost knew how it would feel to stroke the silky blond strands from her face. His body throbbed in time to the beat of his heart.

"Lavender?" her father growled. "It's purple, okay? I don't know what happened. That paint was white the day I put it in the truck. I don't know how one can out of the lot could be affected." He took off his cap and slapped it against his thigh. "I'll go into town and see if I can match the paint that's left in one of the other cans."

Jack waited in silence, glad he'd have her to himself. India turned as if she felt him there. She curved her mouth in a smile of pure joy, and Jack laughed out loud. By the time Mick turned, her smile had faded, but her blue eyes still sparkled. Secret desire created a bond between them Jack didn't intend to let her deny. He wanted to kiss her again, hear her speak his name in need.

First thing, he'd have to kiss away the frown between her brows. "Where's Colleen?" she asked pointedly.

"School." He wouldn't let her push him away with reminders of his daughter. "She says you always ask her where I am when you see her, too."

Nodding slowly, she edged closer to her father. "Yes, I do."

Jack offered his hand to Mick. "Good to see you again. Colleen said you'd come back."

"Yes." Mick shook Jack's hand. "We just need to finish Leon's house. My wife has managed to scare up some business at home." He turned to India. "The hardware store for me and you?"

A strand of her ponytail flipped around India's neck. Jack tucked it behind her high collar, but then he had to stop himself from stroking the curve of her cheek. India straightened away from him to look at her father.

"I think I'd better take care of this," she said.

Jack narrowed his eyes. What had she told Mick? The older man's expression glinted pure disapproval as he began to climb the hill. His accusing look reminded Jack of how he'd felt seeing Colleen with Chris, but he and India were different. They were adults.

She stepped in front of Jack's gaze the moment her father moved out of earshot. "What are you doing here?"

"I want to show you something."

"What? Is Colleen all right?"

He took her hands. "Once in a while, I wouldn't mind if I was your first thought, but Colleen's fine. Come with me."

"Where?"

"Just come with me, India. I promise, I'll keep you an hour, no more."

She shook her head. "I made a vow."

Her seriousness dragged a reluctant smile from him. "Not to see me? I'm not surprised. Unfortunately, you forgot to account for me."

"Yes, I did." She pulled her hands from his. "Nevertheless, I promised myself I'd stay away from you. You're not good for me. You make me behave in ways completely outside my character.''

''Who gets hurt if we spend one hour together?''

''An hour?'' India slowly wrapped her arms around herself.

Jack envied her hands their slow progress beneath her rib cage.

''No.'' She shook her head restlessly. ''I can't go with you. Dad needs me here.''

''Leave him a note.''

''I can't leave him a note.''

How would she react if he tossed her over his shoulder and hauled her to his truck at top speed? Not well, he suspected.

''This has nothing to do with Colleen.'' He took her hands in his. ''I promise I won't even tell her I saw you. Just give me one hour from this one day.''

At first she didn't answer, but she arched her fingers against his palms. At last, she swallowed as if her mouth were as dry as his. ''Where do you want to go?''

''I finished the boat,'' he admitted. ''Don't you want to see her?''

Maybe he should have been able to hide his pride better, but he'd worked like a dog, and since snow had closed the school, Colleen had worked at the boatyard with him every day. She'd helped him rebuild their family business.

India's caution fell away. A smile lit up her eyes. ''I'm so glad for you. Colleen must be proud.''

Jack's voice felt rusty. ''I couldn't have finished without her. She worked until she couldn't stay awake anymore, and then she fell asleep on the couch inside the shop while I worked.'' Jack took India's arm. ''Come see what we did.''

India looked so deeply into his eyes he wondered if she

could read his mind. If so, she'd realize that vow of hers didn't stand a chance.

He started up the hill, hoping she'd follow. He risked a glance back and smiled. India trod in his footsteps like a sleepwalker. She scooped up her jacket from the ground. As she pushed her arms through the sleeves, he dropped his gaze over the baggy overalls that barely hinted at her so feminine body beneath. Though he'd only dreamed of touching her, he knew every curve of India's body like the back of his own hand.

"One hour, Jack." She lifted her head and looked surprised to find him watching her. "No more than one hour, and the ground rules remain in effect. No touching."

NO TOUCHING. *How naive could I be?* Clinging to the bench seat of Jack's truck as it purred toward the dock, her thighs well over fifteen generous inches away from his, India felt as breathless as when he'd held her in his arms. Talk about close confines. She might have to open the door and jump out of the truck if they didn't reach the dock soon.

She was honored he'd come to her. She hoped she'd hidden her joy from him, but she doubted her ability to act. As soon as he angled the truck into a space, she shot out of the cab.

"This way." He led her down a steep slope of wooden planking. "Be careful. It's damp and slippery."

She took "damp and slippery" as an excuse to cling to his hand, but at the bottom, she gently extricated her fingers from his. Touching him had become an exercise in pleasure and torture. Pleasure to share the heat of his body, to sense his desire for her. Torture to know she could never slake her own.

In all the years since Colleen's birth, she'd known no one like Jack. Maybe the Jacks of the world, loving fathers, responsible men who provided for their families and cared for their communities were too busy to stand out.

Able to smile at the broad unseeing, unknowing expanse of his back, she followed him down the dock. The thud of his boots reminded her of the rescue the morning after the blizzard.

"How is Mr. Pearson?" she asked.

Jack glanced back at her, his dark brown eyes warming. "He'll make it. The boat may not pull through, but we'll find something for him to do before he starves. Tim will need someone to replace me."

The Jacks of the world went about their business in silence without fanfare, taking it for granted they should wade in where their friends and family needed them.

She lowered her gaze to the gleaming white planking. Then there were the Indias of the world. She'd given Colleen up with the best intentions, knowing her mother and father couldn't provide for her daughter, no matter how they'd wanted to try. Her child had not been their responsibility.

She just hadn't known how wrong the right decision would be. She stared at Jack's back again. Why couldn't she see him as a reminder of the risks she was still taking?

She lifted her face to the warm sun. On such a beautiful day, the sky hung over them like a child's drawing of fleecy clouds and deep blue background. A big golden blob of butter bobbed a little west of center. The air bit, cool and crisp, at her lungs.

Maybe it was time to forgive herself for letting Colleen be adopted. All these years, she'd fought to keep from weeping, when maybe she needed a good cry. She shook her head until her ponytail swept her shoulders, stray strands tickling her face.

No crying today. Not in this sunshine, surrounded by Jack's jubilance. What good would crying do? How could she hurt anyone with one hour of happiness at being with Jack?

"There she is," he said suddenly.

India stopped short, so close to his back all she could see was his thick jacket. Her fingers clamored to stroke the soft, fleecy material. Instead, she moved around him, aware of his scent and his heat but unwilling to give in.

The *Sweet Mary* glistened in her spanking new paint. Even the cables and dredges shone, pristine and ready to start their work. The boat rocked in the water, eager to be under way.

"Want a ride?" Jack asked.

India laughed. "And be back in an hour?"

"Look at that sky. Did you ever see clouds like that in your life? Did you ever see the bay so smooth?" Jack started toward the boat's bow. "Not that I've become a fair-weather sailor, but come on."

She hesitated over the small matter of her vow.

He cast off the mooring lines. "I have to be back in two hours. Colleen will be out of school, and I told her I'd meet her at home. Come with me."

She studied the open water. "I'm sorely tempted."

He jumped onto the boat and held out his hand to her. India hesitated only a moment longer. Twining her fingers with his, she promised herself she was only making another memory to treasure, filling an hour she'd remember back in Charlottesville, after she'd given up her daughter for the second time, after she'd given up Jack, as well.

He tugged her onto the deck and turned toward the cabin, pulling her with him. "Come stand behind the wheel. You won't believe the bay on a day like this."

She gazed out at the town, busy and yet silent. She turned to the water. "How can it be so calm after that storm last week?"

He shrugged. "We live in coastal Maryland. Weather, like our guests," he said pointedly, "is changeable."

She laughed. They had an hour, maybe two. Today wouldn't change the future she'd grab in both hands to keep Colleen safe.

Jack started the boat's engine and turned toward open water. The motor purred to life just like his truck. As the prow sliced through the water, Jack pulled her to his side, and she let him.

"I feel small against all this." She waved her hand at the bay's huge expanse as they headed into deeper water.

He leaned close enough to speak against her ear. "Don't worry. I've gone over her with a fine-tooth comb. She's shipshape now. Tomorrow, I start working for myself again." He shrugged wryly. "Well, myself and the bank."

"Do you have regular customers?" Goose bumps rising on her skin made her shiver. She had to concentrate hard just to speak.

"A couple of restaurants on specific days. Mostly, I sell to the suppliers who come to the docks." Jack turned up the throttle, and India glanced back at the marina falling behind them. "Most of the fishermen sell to suppliers." He clanged the silver bell beside him, with so much joy India knew he hadn't heard the sound in too long. "Do you hear that? It's music, the most profound melody I ever heard."

She laughed. Jack lifted her hand to the bell's rope. She tugged gently, but the bell clanged in a deep, melodic voice.

"My father found it in an antique shop. Colleen just polished it up again." His pride warmed India.

She rang the bell again, with more force. "You're right. This is a beautiful day." Turning, she lifted her face to his. Jack's smile started in his eyes. His heat, his certainty, took her breath away, but she didn't want to share it.

"Thank you for coming," he said.

She turned back to the water, knowing he would pull her into his arms. His tenderness, as he slid his hand around her waist, cherished her. She moved with him, leaned back. With a slow, sensuous slide of palm against palm, Jack lifted her hands to the wheel and covered them with his own.

She closed her eyes. She never wanted to forget the strength in his arms, the steady beat of his heart against her back, joining them in the big, wide world that was all their own today.

He pressed his mouth to the curve of her jaw. She breathed in sharply, wanting to be his. He followed the sensitive cord of her throat with his lips. She stirred against him, hungry for his possessive kiss.

"Turn around," he whispered, so softly she should never have been able to hear, but his words were meant for her, and she wanted to turn. She wanted to explore the hard, warm planes of this man's body. She shook her head, and Jack followed the motion with his mouth on her neck. She chuckled, nervousness blending with desire.

"You'll break your boat again."

Laughing, he tilted her face, and his breath whispered over her. "Break it?"

As she met his gaze, he glanced past her at the bay, and India touched the corner of his smile. He moved his head to suckle the tip of her finger. She'd never known such play with a man. She closed her eyes to hide the sharp wave of pleasure that washed over her.

"Give in to me." He leaned his forehead against hers. "Give in to yourself."

"I can't."

"I can convince you."

"I know."

He caught her close with one arm. "We'd both like it

better if you helped me,'' he said against her ear. He pushed her jacket off her shoulders and unzipped his own to curve it around her, sharing his warmth.

Unable to help herself, cautious and curious, India slid her hands over the firm, yielding muscles of his chest. He unbuttoned the top of his shirt and pressed her hand to his skin.

''You're hot.'' She wanted more of his heat. ''You don't have a fever?''

''Oh yes, I do. Find out how much with your mouth.''

Her heart beating like a drum, India held back, but she was no saint. She tried her lips against his skin. The greedy splay of Jack's fingers across her back pleased her. He smelled of sun and salt and sea. He tasted of all three.

He whispered her name as she kissed his skin. She breathed on him, stirring the sparse hairs on his chest. India noticed as if from afar when he stopped the boat's engine. He lowered his head and opened her mouth with his.

His kiss, at first nearly savage, soon gentled into sweet persuasion. Jack teased, pressing for more when India tried to draw away, pulling back himself when she plunged her hands into his hair.

''What are you saying, India?''

''Please don't ask me.''

Dissatisfaction stole into his gaze. He kissed her forehead, and she closed her eyes. Whispering incoherent sounds, he traced the line of her cheekbones and nibbled her lower lip.

''India?''

Why couldn't he let her pretend this didn't matter? She looked at him, wanting him, needing to stop before she hurt him.

With a steady gaze, he unclipped one overall strap and dragged his hand down her shoulder, over the curve of her breast. A groan seeped between his lips as his palm bumped over her nipple.

Shyly, she lifted her arms around his neck. Tentative still, as if he might scare her off, he pushed his free hand beneath her shirt. She sucked in a breath filled with his scent as he found the ridge of her rib cage.

His shirtsleeve scraped sensually over her bare skin. The texture tempted her to touch him the same way, to bring him the same deep pleasure.

"I've dreamed of holding you like this," he said.

India pressed her mouth to his beating heart. "You're getting cold."

He didn't answer, but he unclipped her other strap. The bib of her overalls fell, and Jack slid his other hand beneath her shirt. India arched against his seeking fingers, all thought impossible. She pushed his shirt up, urging him to press his bare skin to hers. He held her fiercely, as if he couldn't get close enough.

When he pulled back, India murmured a protest, but he pressed his mouth to hers. He traced trembling fingers over the thin lace of her bra.

I'm lost. The words whispered in her conscience.

He followed the shape of her chin with his mouth, tilting her head at an angle that exposed the hollow of her throat to him. Flattening his hands on her shoulders again, he watched her expression as he dragged both his palms with exquisite slowness around the curves of her breasts. Too aware of his scrutiny, India gasped as he teased her taut nipples with his fingers. His face tightened, and he lowered his mouth to one thrusting, silk-covered peak.

His mouth touched off fire and delight against her skin. She might have fallen if he hadn't grasped her hips as he moved to her other breast. Time fluttered on, imperfect, because she couldn't lie down on the deck of this boat and make love with him, precious, because his loving touch brought light back into her life.

Groaning, he brought his mouth back to hers. He claimed her in a kiss more intimate than she had ever known. He rocked against her, imitating the love she longed to make. When he broke away, she was still reaching for him. Their hands tangled together, moving of their own volition in a dance of frustrated yearning. Jack kissed her temple, holding unnaturally still.

"I have to stop unless you want to make love here and now."

She shuddered. "I don't know how we'd explain the splinters at the emergency room."

Laughing hoarsely, he freed one hand to twine his fingers in her hair. "Would you regret making love with me?" He moved her gently, regretfully away from him.

She only hesitated because she knew he'd resent her answer. "You won't understand, but yes, I would."

"And you still won't tell me why." His expression sharpened. "You'd better get dressed, and I'll take you back."

India stared at him. Passion continued to stamp his eyes, but he couldn't help being frustrated with her. She turned away and fastened her straps and then began to stuff her shirt back inside her overalls. Her hands trembled, and her knees felt weak. Every muscle, every sinew longed for Jack's touch.

Startling her, he caught her against his chest. "Don't go that far away," he growled.

India sank into him, relieved, though she shouldn't stay. He reached around her to start the boat again, and she turned in his arms, slowly buttoning his shirt and zipping his coat. At last she rested against his long, hard body.

His arms felt right, but she was so wrong for him.

Once the moorings and marina rose out of the shoreline,

India edged away to stand at Jack's side. He looked serious. "There's Colleen."

Her throat tightened. Colleen waved from the dock in a
wide, sweeping gesture. Breathing fast, India waved back.
How lovely to pretend this was real, that she and Jack were
coming home to their daughter.

But today had already been dangerous enough. Soon
she'd have to say goodbye and mean it.

She looked back at Jack. This hour haunted her from
his eyes. A closeness lay between them, a bond they had
formed with their bodies. Today was for magic.

JACK WATCHED INDIA JUMP lightly to the dock. He smiled
as Colleen danced around her. They resembled each other
in their uncertain affection. He twisted his mouth. India's
home in Charlottesville wouldn't be a trip to the moon and
back. They didn't have to say goodbye.

"We've missed you," Colleen confessed with the in-
nocence of youth. "How'd you like the boat?"

"She's a beauty." India averted her head to hide a furious blush.

Jack felt a proprietorial pride in the rush of color that
infused her skin. He'd never felt like this. India was an
emptiness in his heart that only filled when he held her in
his arms. Why couldn't he make her value the fullness
she'd taught him to long for?

He frowned, Mary on his mind. He hadn't felt this even
for her, but he had loved her with all his heart once. A
different kind of love.

"Are we really finished with the boat, Dad?"

He turned to Colleen, a smile at the ready. "We're completely finished. Do you want to go out? You did a great
job."

Colleen shook her head. "No, I'm starving, and I have
too much homework. Actually, India, I meant to ask Dad

whether I could come by the library tonight if it's your night to volunteer. I have to write five paragraphs on Susan B. Anthony, and I have to critique this painting by a guy— I forget his name—but the picture's some alien-looking guy, screaming.''

Teasing laughter spilled first from India's eyes, and then from her luscious mouth. Jack slid his hands into the back pockets of his jeans, drawn to her joy.

"It's not my night to work, but I think I can help you," she said. "What time?"

"Actually, I came down here because I hoped Dad would buy me dinner. I could walk you over to the library after. I haven't caused any problems lately, Dad."

"A strong recommendation," he agreed. He brushed at dirt on his jeans. "I'm not really dressed for dinner." He glanced at India, faintly uncomfortable himself in Colleen's sharp-eyed presence. "Would you care to join us at a drive-through?"

India slapped her hand to her forehead. "I can't! My dad's probably wondering if I've been abducted by aliens."

"Ooh, *X-Files,*" Colleen helpfully chimed in.

Jack tried to quell her with a glance she met laughing. His daughter took his arm and India's.

"We'll drive you. Is Mick at Marcy's?"

"Unless he's called out the FBI."

COLLEEN KEPT UP an undemanding chatter on the drive to her friend's house. India enjoyed the steady, youthful hum, even as she worried her father wouldn't be able to hold his tongue in front of Jack and Colleen. He'd warned her against letting Jack get any closer.

He'd been right.

She peeked at Jack from beneath the fall of her loosened

ponytail. The slow, inexorable pulse of desire still thudded in her veins as he stole a look at her.

Nothing was different. She still couldn't stay. She couldn't tell him the truth. More than ever, she couldn't make herself say the words that would leave him believing she'd come to Arran Island to take her daughter away from him. She couldn't change his and Colleen's life together.

Still, an amazing, completely unlooked-for joy sang inside her, a tune that belonged to her alone, a gift from Jack. Whatever came of the future, she'd always have this afternoon, right down to Colleen's cheerful prattle.

She was almost sorry when Jack turned into the Shipps' street. Her dismay turned real as she recognized the car parked behind her father's truck.

"Mom," she breathed in surprise. Rachel stepped around the side of Leon Shipp's house.

"Who's that woman?" Colleen asked, all unaware.

India stared at her daughter. She must not have said "Mom" out loud. Colleen must be completely oblivious to the painful resemblance between herself and her grandmother. How long would that last with this too-observant girl?

Why on earth would her mother be so reckless?

As Jack parked, India clambered out of the truck. Rachel saw her and opened her arms, and India's anger subsided a fraction. Running ahead of Jack and Colleen, she hugged Rachel tightly, as if she could hide her mother from them with her body.

"I told your father you wouldn't mind."

"I do mind. What are you doing here?"

Rachel wavered. She looked so much like Colleen did whenever she realized she was in trouble, India almost laughed. Sheer terror stopped her. Jack couldn't possibly miss such a clear resemblance.

Before he and Colleen reached them, India dragged her

mother around the side of the house, where her father was mixing a can of paint.

Alarm blended with guilt in his gaze. "Want the bad news? I couldn't find the right paint. We have a faint gray they couldn't match at the hardware store."

"What's that?" India pointed at the paint can between his feet.

"Your mother brought it. That's the good news."

India stared at the lavender dormer and then swung to face her mother. "You added purple to the paint."

Rachel smiled. Nervously.

"Hello, Mick." Colleen stared up at the dormer. "It's like that outhouse story, isn't it? I thought Mr. Shipp was mad when he saw Marcy's eyebrow ring. Wait till he sees this."

Rachel, unfazed, moved to her husband's side. "Please assure me you didn't tell that story?"

"This young lady dragged it out of me. You know how reluctant I am to spread tales." Mick patted Colleen's head. India silently congratulated him on his control. He grinned at his granddaughter. "How's school? Did you have a nice vacation during the snowstorm?"

"Almost a whole week," Colleen said. She turned to Rachel expectantly and then glanced at India.

"This is my mother, Rachel Stuart. Mom, this is Colleen Stephens and Colleen's father, Jack."

They both shook hands politely with Rachel, who raised an eyebrow at her own daughter in silent appreciation of Colleen's manners.

"You look so familiar to me, Mrs. Stuart," Colleen said.

India nearly swallowed her own lungs. Of course Rachel looked familiar. Colleen saw a version of Rachel's face every time she looked at her own reflection. India gaped at her mother, but Rachel never faltered.

"Have you ever been to Charlottesville?" she asked with interest India feared she'd overdone.

Colleen nodded, narrowing her eyes. "Don't you think India's mother looks familiar, Dad?"

He smiled absently at Rachel as he bent a warning glance on Colleen, more interested in those same manners Rachel had admired.

"How was the drive over, Mom?" India might have turned the paint sprayer on herself to change the subject, but she couldn't reach it.

"Have you ever been to Monticello?" Colleen asked Rachel.

Beaming, Rachel clapped her hands together. "That must be it. I work as a docent there." She lied as if she were born to the craft.

India hardly believed her own ears. Where did all this family dishonesty hail from? Rachel was cool as ice and warm as a maternal hug, and Colleen's curiosity faded before India's wary eyes.

"Hey, small world. I went there on a field trip last spring. My dad came along as a chaperon. Remember, Dad?"

Jack eyed Rachel as if to take a closer look. India held her breath.

"I must have been preoccupied," Jack said. "I was busy with that kid who kept ducking under all the ropes."

"Oh, I remember him," Rachel said. "He tried to sit in one or two of the chairs." She paused a world-weary moment. "Thank goodness, we don't get too many of those."

India goggled at her mother. They'd all been irresponsible coming here.

"That's the boy," Jack said. "I can believe you remember him."

"Some young ones just don't realize..." Rachel tapered off in darned sincere regret.

India shook herself from her stupor. "Dad, I'll repaint the dormer. Mom must be tired. Why don't you take her to the hotel and make her rest?"

Even she heard the hysterical note in her rising voice. Mick looked as if he was standing nose to nose with a runaway train. He set the paint can down and took her mother's arm.

"Good idea. Are you hungry, dear?"

India stood between Jack and Colleen as her father hustled her mother away. "I don't mean to be rude," she said, low enough to keep her mother from hearing. "And I'm sorry, but I'm going to have to put you and Susan B. on hold. If you can't wait for me, you could ask Mrs. Fisher. My mom tires easily."

"She looks pretty energetic to me," Colleen said.

India searched for a tactful way to say she had to get her mother out of range before Rachel tripped on the loose weave of her own dramatic tapestry. "She's so tired, she's giddy."

CHAPTER THIRTEEN

"YOU'VE CHANGED YOUR TUNE, India. I can't believe you're so upset with me, because I wanted to see my own granddaughter, same as you did." Rachel carried her mug of coffee to the table and sat with a dejected thud.

India stared at her. "I guess I have changed. I came here to find Colleen, but I found out some things about myself. It was irresponsible of me to come at all." She stroked Rachel's hand, as if she were the mother. "I'm not saying I could have done anything else. I couldn't seem to get past what I'd done all those years ago. I had to know Colleen was all right and happy." She covered her eyes. "I don't want to hurt her, but now that I know her, I've come to love her for herself, not for the baby I left. It's harder than I realized."

Rachel pulled India's hands away from her face. Eyes warm with understanding, she became the mom again. "You should be glad. Her adoptive parents have loved her well."

"They *were* her parents. Jack *is* her father, as if Gabe and I never had anything to do with her." India hugged Rachel. "They were the parents I dreamed she'd have, but I can't help feeling left out." India smiled at her mother as she dug for courage. "I didn't mean to snap at you. I know how you felt, but we can't risk having Colleen find out the truth by accident. What if Jack had figured it out? What if he'd recognized something of her in you? You don't know how much you look like her."

"I didn't realize it before, either." Mick nudged Rachel's shoulder as he set his own mug on the table. "Where did you come up with that docent story on such short notice? I have to admit, you impressed me."

Rachel laughed at Mick's teasing, but her smile faded quickly. "I guess India's right. Maybe I should go home in the morning." She turned to look at her own daughter. "I did so want to talk to her."

"You already talked mighty fancy," Mick said.

Rachel looked embarrassed. "I guess I did. Who can say what came over me?"

India nodded. "I know. I've done things since I've come here I wouldn't have believed I could consider. I'm even more alarmed to find it's genetic."

Mick patted Rachel's back with husbandly affection. "Don't listen to her. She's playing with you, and she doesn't mean it." Rachel aimed a mischievous punch he ducked. Laughing, she leaned into his shoulder. "I didn't mean to stir up trouble, India. But I didn't realize just showing up with my face could let the cat out of the bag."

"It's all right." India rubbed her mother's sleeve with her knuckles. "I'm awfully glad you got to see her."

Rachel's lip quivered. India struggled to hold back her own tears. They had plenty of time to cry later.

Mick stroked his wife's other arm. "I'll drive you back. India won't mind a few more days here, and we'll go back by way of Coopersville. You know how you love to shop in that outlet mall."

Rachel nodded. "I'd like that. Do you mind, India?"

She should say yes, she did mind. She should insist she and her father finish Leon Shipp's house as soon as possible and get out of town for good. But that would mean getting out of Colleen's life. Out of Jack's life. And she just wasn't strong enough not to grab any excuse.

So she shook her head slowly, from side to side. Her

hair fell into her eyes, shielding her from her parents' close examination. She swallowed the lump that rose in her throat. How could she go wrong with just a few more stolen days?

That night, while her father snored volcanically in the other room, India shared a cup of chamomile tea with her mother.

"You know I didn't mean to hurt you or Colleen, don't you?" Rachel asked again.

"I've learned tolerance since I came here."

"What do you mean?"

"I never forgave myself, and I couldn't let you or Dad, either."

"But we loved you. No matter what mistakes you make, you can't keep us from loving you."

"Is that what you thought I was doing?"

"Weren't you?"

India shrugged. "I don't know for sure. It was hard enough to forget for twenty-four hours at a time. Seeing the two of you always brought everything back. Can I be honest with you?"

"I wish you would," Rachel said.

"I wanted her, Mom. She was my baby. I wanted to raise her and teach her about life and give her the kind of unconditional love you and Dad gave me." India remembered, an ache in her heart. "But I could only afford to give her the things I didn't ever want her to know—struggle and need, uncertainty about the future. I made myself believe I was giving her a life, and you and Dad helped me believe that. Unfortunately, my certainty only lasted until Mother Angelica took her away. When I couldn't have my baby, I felt like I didn't deserve to be part of a family anymore."

"You didn't take the easy way out. You worked hard for your degree and for the life you've made."

"I did it all for her. I kept thinking if she ever found me I'd want her to be proud of me."

Rachel froze. "If she found you?"

"Some adopted children search for their birth mothers. It was a false hope I kept."

"And now? Do you want her to know who you are?"

India slipped her hands from beneath her mother's. "For a while, I wondered what it would be like to tell her and Jack. Now it's my worst fear. She'd hate me."

"And how would Jack feel?"

India nodded. "Yes, Mom, he also matters to me." She couldn't find words to say how important he'd become, how she longed for the sound of his voice, the brush of his fingertips.

Rachel measured her with a look. "You can't let yourself care for him."

"I sure do pick 'em, don't I?"

"When this is over, honey, come home to us until you have to go back to work at the school, okay? Just stay with Daddy and me until you feel better about things."

India sprawled in her chair. "Thank you. Since I'm confiding all my secrets tonight, I'd better tell you this, too. Those old bad days between us are over. I don't want any more time to pass in silence between you and Dad and me."

INDIA WAVED HER PARENTS OFF in the morning, on her way to toddler's story time at the library. Rachel blew a kiss through the car window, and India wrapped her arms around herself as if she could hold her mother's embrace a bit longer. This brief visit had gone a long way toward healing the rift that had stood so long between them.

In the past fifteen years, she'd tended to treat family time as penance. She'd participated in activities and holidays, but always, she'd held herself apart, just enough apart that they wouldn't have to share her remorse.

Never again. Coming here, her father had given her this chance to know both him and her daughter. Her mother had made her feel sheltered again. India finally felt she deserved her parents' support.

Mick suddenly stopped the car and leaned out of his window. "Don't finish the house without me. Take a few days off."

India braced her hands on her hips in mock disapproval.

"I mean it!" Mick's voice floated back to her as he turned Rachel's car up the hill.

India stared after them. Cold air feathered through her hair, raising prickles on her scalp. But it felt good. Clean. Fresh.

Her mother had left in such a scattered hurry, she'd swept India along in her wake, a bit early for story time. A hint of salt in the air turned India's head toward the sea. She followed her feet toward the bay road. Yes, it led past Jack and Colleen's house, but she didn't have to stop. She certainly wouldn't go to their door.

She couldn't help laughing as she remembered her mother's inspired expression as she'd reeled off that docent story for Colleen and Jack. What had they thought of Rachel? Had Colleen sensed any sort of connection with her indecently young looking grandmother?

Spiky waves raced over the dark green bay. India stared hard out to sea. She wanted to remember this moment. When she was gone, she wanted to look back on this water that raced to the edge of Colleen's house.

As she reached the bay end of Jack's fence, Colleen burst through their front door as if she'd been waiting. India twisted her mouth. Talk about bad luck. She shouldn't have come this way.

"India," Colleen whispered in a carrying voice. She

waved something in a plastic bag as she ran down the sidewalk.

Overwhelmed by a rush of pure love, India wrapped her hands around a picket. Colleen was dressed in sweats, her honey-colored hair twisted into a micro ponytail that made her look the little girl she seemed so eager to leave behind.

"Look." With a furtive glance around them, Colleen opened her bag. "Dad's already gone out on the boat, but I wanted to show you his birthday present."

"His present?"

Colleen nodded. She pulled a tan hunk of cloth out of the bag. "I've saved for this. What do you think?" She flapped the elongated bill of a fisherman's cap.

India stepped back. A bill a pelican could be proud of. "It's great," she said. Was she allowed to grin? Did fifteen-year-olds accept undeniably indulgent grins?

"I thought 'new boat, new cap,' and anyway, it'll sure keep the sun out of his eyes. I wish I could have given it to him this morning."

"When is his birthday?"

"Well, today, but his party isn't until tonight. If I'd given it to him before he left, I wouldn't have anything when everybody else gives him their presents." Colleen tucked her cap away with the air of a girl caring for a national treasure. "That's why I stopped you, really. Would you like to come? We'll only have a cake, but we can sing 'Happy Birthday' to him—he hates that—I'm not even sure he remembered it was his birthday, he's been so busy. I'm making the cake myself."

India rejected the invitation. "No, I can't come tonight, but thank you."

"You can't?" Colleen's disappointment touched her. "But you have to. I told my grandma you'd come."

"She won't mind if I don't, though." India sucked in a swift breath. "You and your father hardly know me."

"We know you. We just haven't known you long, and I want you to come. I think my dad would, too."

Guilt washed over her. They didn't know the most important thing about her, and she needed to get out of here before they found out. "I don't have a present for him."

"So, help me make the cake." Colleen grinned. "I cook almost as well as I sew."

"I can't, Colleen. Thanks for including me, but I just can't." Wanting nothing so badly as she wanted to give in, India turned to go.

Colleen caught her sweater. "Please." She looked so serious India had to clench her fists to keep from hugging her. Colleen went on, "I really could use the help with Dad's cake. I kind of hoped you'd offer when I told you about it."

India nibbled at the inside of her jaw. She was leaving in a matter of days, a week at the most. How many more celebrations would she share with Jack and Colleen? Yesterday's boat ride and today's birthday party were sure to be her last.

Images of Rachel and the cooking lessons they'd enjoyed together in their large, sunny kitchen passed through India's mind. Another mother-daughter tradition she wouldn't share with Colleen. She glanced over her shoulder, as if she could still see her parents. Would they disapprove? "My mom taught me to bake a mean birthday cake when I was your age."

"Good. Last year I had to glue Dad's cake together with icing." Colleen waved her hands in a "no" gesture. "Before you ask, nobody got sick, but it wasn't a pretty cake." She tucked her bag beneath her arm and rubbed her hands together as she backed toward the house. "What time can you come over?"

"I haven't said yes."

"But you will if I beg, so just give in."

India guessed she was right. Colleen knew her too well. Pressing her cool palms to her own flushed cheeks, India surrendered. "I work at the library until noon, but I can stop by the market on my way home. What time is your party?"

"At six-thirty." Colleen came back to the fence. "Of course, you'll have to make the cake here. I could pick up whatever you need for it. Dad let me stay home alone today. I think he's testing me to see if I run off with Marcy and Leah to find another punch bowl."

India couldn't share her amusement. "Then I'll go by the market alone."

Colleen scoffed. "I told both of you I didn't know about the punch. I'm not sure either of you believes me, but Dad won't mind if I'm doing something with you."

Her expression looked hopeful. Her eyes shone with enthusiasm that curled around India's heart.

"Who else will teach me to bake?" Colleen asked impishly, cementing her argument.

"Nettie?"

Colleen giggled. "Grandma already suggested we hurry out and order a cake this morning. Besides, she and Grandpa still have to get Dad a present. They'll be in Baltimore all day."

India relented. God help her, she couldn't resist a day with Colleen.

"All right," she said. Opening her purse, she took out a small notepad to jot down the ingredients they'd need. She glanced up at Colleen. "Are you sure your father won't mind if you go out to the market? What if he calls you?"

"I'll take the other cell phone with me. If he doesn't get me at home, he'll try that." Colleen flashed a grin. "You're almost as bad as he is. Besides, he told me I could go by the library if I wanted, and he gave me lunch money." She laughed. "As if I were ten, instead of fifteen. Last, but most definitely not least, he told me not to make a nuisance of myself. I think that was to cover all his bases."

India ripped the sheet of paper out of her notepad and handed it over. "So I'll come back when I finish story time?"

Colleen seemed to think the world had fallen in perfectly with her plans, and her happiness tempted India to bask. When Colleen unexpectedly leaned forward to wrap her arms around India's neck, she stiffened.

"I'm glad you're coming," Colleen said briefly. "And thank you for the cake." Turning, she flitted back inside.

India stared after her, astounded as a tear of unbelievable gladness slipped coldly down her cheek. After Colleen closed the door behind herself, India scrubbed her hands over her face and started down the street with a step that grew lighter each second.

All but floating to the library, she began to count down the minutes before her cooking lesson.

JACK TIED THE LAST LINE and jumped down to the dock. He glanced at his watch. When he'd cast off this morning, he'd meant to stay out until the last minute to make the birthday celebration Colleen had planned, but the thought of her at home alone had niggled at him. She'd sworn to abide by his rules, and he'd believed her, but he hadn't been able to stop worrying about her. She'd damn near killed him with good intentions before.

The spiked punch, coming so close on the heels of the Chris situation, made him anxious about her judgment. She'd been too eager to stay home. He could tell himself once or more an hour she was only preparing for his birthday, but how long did it take to bake a cake?

Chuckling to himself, Jack remembered last year's cake,

a monument to the sticking powers of frosting. What tasty treat had Colleen planned for tonight? Maybe he should have suggested burgers at the drive-in.

He pried his truck keys out of his jeans pocket and started up the wooden stairs to the parking lot. A guy should be able to go home early on his birthday without feeling guilty for wasting a few hours of light. He lifted his face to the deepening sky. He'd make up the time later when he could bring Colleen along.

He drove home through the early twilight. Parking in front of his house, he smiled at the lights burning warm yellow through slits in the drapes. How long since his home had seemed to welcome him? It was different these days. Maybe he was different.

He should have asked Colleen to invite India. They'd agreed to keep the party down to a cake with just family. He shied away from the question of how India fit that definition.

Memories of yesterday afternoon on the boat singed him. Her curvy, needful body in his arms. Her hungry response. She didn't kiss like a woman who planned to leave him. Why couldn't she see the plain truth?

He was falling in love with her, and he believed she cared for him more than he'd ever persuade her to admit. Her secret demanded more than she would or could give him. What kind of a secret could destroy his longing for her? She should trust him.

He slid his key into his front door. Could she be married? No. She would have told him. Did someone back home in Charlottesville have a prior claim on her?

Jack shook his head as he stooped to pick up the evening paper. He didn't believe either of the most logical reasons India might have for pushing him away. She had no reason to hide a husband or even a lover from him. She was honest. She would have told him if she cared for someone else.

Squaring his shoulders, Jack reached for the doorknob and tried to put her out of his mind. His daughter deserved his whole attention, if only he could stop thinking of compelling, infuriating, utterly desirable India.

With a decisive twist of the knob, he opened the door and walked into a burst of feminine laughter.

"No, try this red," Colleen's voice suggested, ending on a shriek that implied sharks had invaded the kitchen.

Jack dropped his coat on the hall floor. Not another Marcy- and Leah-inspired makeover? Not after all Colleen's promises to abide by house rules. He strode toward the kitchen, prepared to find his daughter in full Marcy Shipp-coordinated regalia. He just hoped the red wasn't for her hair.

"You try the brown," India's voice proposed suddenly. Giggling, she sounded more like one of Colleen's friends.

Slowing even as his heart rate sped up, Jack eased through the kitchen door. Between the sink and the table, Colleen pushed India's arm away with one hand, while applying red frosting to her chin with the other.

"Nice beard," Colleen crowed.

India ran her finger through the red froth and licked it off with her tongue. Jack reached for the lintel as his body clenched with longing.

"Tastes good, too," she remarked, completely unaware.

Jack stared. Her face anointed with a rainbow of frosting colors, India looked more beautiful than ever. She looked positively edible. She had to be the best birthday cake anyone ever ordered.

Jack fought for sanity as he went through a list of ways he might help India denude herself of frosting. Such plans were completely inappropriate as long as his teenaged daughter was in the room.

He swerved his gaze to Colleen, who'd fared better in the icing wars. Though a slather of brown slashed across her cheekbone, he imagined she must have applied the red mustache herself.

As she turned, Jack hoped his clamoring desire for India was less obvious than it felt. Colleen widened her grin and waved a frosting-covered wooden spoon at him.

He suddenly realized the house smelled of apples and cinnamon. It smelled like home.

"Daddy," Colleen said.

India's silver mixing bowl nearly slipped through her fingers as she whirled. A grin stretched across his mouth. India was here, and the last time Colleen had called him anything more affectionate than a casual "Dad" he'd just emerged from a sinking boat.

"What a great birthday," he said.

"I hope it's a happy one." India's low voice did nothing to cool the fire in his body.

Are you my present? The words echoed in his head as he imagined how she would taste beneath the sweet, colored sugar on her lower lip. A big blue splat of icing perched just above the right eyebrow she tended to quirk when she tried to be subtle. Like the night she'd asked him what he planned to do about Colleen's punch bowl escapade.

Colleen. Jack cleared his throat. He'd better remember himself under his daughter's watchful eye. She looked almost as interested in his response to India as she was in his sudden appearance.

"You're home early," she said. "We aren't finished."

"What exactly are you decorating?"

As if galvanized, woman and girl turned to the cake on the counter between them. They rushed at each other, apparently to hide the cake from him, but they collided and both landed on the floor in another storm of giggles.

Jack made his careful way around them, through a slippery path of icing. He studied the cake of blue-green sea. A slightly squat fishing trawler steamed across its broad waves.

"Dad," Colleen protested, getting lopsidedly to her feet. She turned to help India up as well. Unfortunately, she closed her hand on a glob of the pink icing that perched on India's shoulder like an epaulet. Shrieking as her fingers slid, she fell on top of India, raising another tempest of laughter.

At last, Colleen struggled to sit up. She took off her shoe to flourish a squashed patch of green frosting on the heel. "Look what you did, India."

"No." This time, India managed to stand and pulled Colleen up beside her. "You were in charge of the green."

"Shh," Colleen said to India conspiratorially. "He won't ground you."

"He can try."

The wicked dare in India's eyes took Jack's breath away.

Colleen chortled, as if India's nonsense was perfectly rational to her. Jack stared at them. He envied the bond that flowed between his daughter and the woman who kept insisting she could turn her back on them both in an instant.

Colleen was different since India had somewhat reluctantly become her friend. She'd tried to regain his trust. For that, he had to be grateful, not envious. He advanced on the two cohorts but stopped just short of touching either.

A breathy laugh escaped India's lush lips. Jack seriously wanted to try some of the frosting that clung to the corner of her mouth. He dipped his finger in and tasted it more discreetly than he would have without Colleen's restraining influence.

"It is good," he said. "Piquant, with a full body."

"Just what do you mean by that?" India demanded in mock indignation, as if she'd also forgotten they weren't alone. As if she were including him in the magic that softened the air around her and Colleen.

"Dad, are you making personal remarks about India's figure?"

Taken off guard, Jack stared into India's eyes. "I could not imagine her shape more perfect."

"Oh." Colleen's satisfied tone appreciated the flawless answer. Alarm bells clanged in his head. He backed away from India, but Colleen had already turned from the counter. "Well, then, I think I'll go take a nice, long shower. Leave the mess, India. I'll clean it up."

She darted out of the kitchen. Jack stared after her, the shameless little matchmaker. India moved suddenly, but her foot must have found frosting. She slipped and he jumped to catch her, just in time to keep her off the floor.

"I'm sorry," he said. "I kind of forgot her, and when she asked about your figure, it was like having permission to ogle you."

Her mouth quivered. "You're nuts. It's easy to see where she gets it."

He loved the little twitch at the corners of her lips. "You look delicious."

"Let me go, Jack. You'll get this stuff all over you."

"I kind of have that in mind." He breathed in her sweet scent. "At least I hope you might let me help you get rid of some."

Quick desire darkened her eyes. She lifted her hands between them, but pulled back when she looked at her fingers, still covered in icing.

"Go ahead," he said.

"*Colleen* is upstairs."

"What did you think of her exit line? Did she give us her blessing?"

India stiffened in his arms, but he lowered his head to lick at the frosting on her lip. Her gasp aroused him deeply.

He slanted his mouth over hers to let her taste the icing he had taken from her lip. She reached for him, but again stopped herself from touching him, from smearing him with the frosting they would have to explain to Colleen. Jack took her hand and lifted one delicate finger to his lips.

India closed her eyes as he stroked the pad of her fingertip with his tongue. Carnal yearning licked through his limbs as she groaned. He had to taste her mouth again. She opened to him, seeking as he sought, needing as he needed. He breathed her in, joining himself to her in spirit and heart, as his body surged to complete their union.

"Jack," she gasped, trying to push away, but she only managed to arch against him.

"I see more," he said, reaching for the first fastened button on her denim blouse, the button level with her soft, full breasts. "How did you get it here?"

"Wait." Her voice grated in her effort to catch her breath. Jack caught her gaze with his again, but the smoke in her eyes dazed him.

He worried the button loose, but at his discovery, a breath hissed between his lips. She wasn't wearing a bra. He opened two more buttons and lowered his head to her velvety rose nipple. Mmm, sweeter than life.

"You're killing me." Shifting restlessly, she offered more of herself to his questing mouth.

He smiled against her skin and turned his head to taste the full curve of her breast. Remembering where they were, he held still for a moment. From overhead came the sound of water rushing in the shower.

He gave himself up to the perfume of India's body. He

opened the next button on her shirt and pushed the denim material aside to expose her other taut nipple. It bloomed against his tongue. He felt like the first man who'd ever loved a woman. He did this to her. He made her body swell and want.

He slid his hand between the rough denim and her soft skin to cup her other breast. She whispered incoherently. He met the push of her pelvis with his own. He wrapped his arms around her.

"I want to touch you," she said, hoarse with passion.

He wanted that, too, but she still held off. Enthralled, he molded her breasts to the heat of his mouth. She arched into him, uttering a fierce moan that made his knees tremble. He cupped her bottom and lifted her. Weak with wanting her, he shook as she hooked her legs around his hips. Her giving, woman's body cradled his arousal, but she still wouldn't put her arms around him.

"India," he begged against her mouth, "please touch me."

She stilled, watching him. Lord, he wished she'd stop thinking. In unexpected surrender, she wrapped her arms around his waist and clung as if he were a lifeline. Breathing his name, she worked one hand to his shoulder, testing each muscle along the way, cutting his breath short, making him want more, teaching him how deeply a man could long for one woman to possess him.

She pulled his sweatshirt over his head. "You're going to look like a cake, Jack."

"You can write 'Happy Birthday' anywhere you like." He brushed his nose against hers as she traced every inch of his shoulders with her palms. He looked straight into her eyes, to make sure she knew he was serious. "I want to make love to you, India."

Alarm filtered through her gaze. She bit her lower lip,

but Jack smoothed away the indentation of her teeth with his thumb.

She pulled his face to hers. With her mouth, she brushed his lips. With her tongue, she enticed him to take her. Between them, she caressed the muscles her touch tautened in his chest.

Curving her voluptuous mouth in a slow smile, India leaned back and fingered a dollop of frosting from the bowl Colleen had left behind. She daubed it on his nipple and lowered her head to lick it off. He tensed, pushed by pleasure, lazy with desire. He threaded his fingers through the strands of her hair, easing it away from her face so he could watch her slide her tongue over him.

"We have a whole lot of frosting left," he breathed.

Provocative laughter floated between them in her husky, desirous voice, but she only tightened her legs at his waist and kissed a heart-stopping path to his other nipple. Her body's heat made him dizzy. He shuddered. He'd never look at a birthday cake the same way again.

He pulled her hands up his shoulders and locked his arms around her, groaning as her breasts thrust against his chest. India reached for his mouth with frank hunger, and Jack yanked at her shirt, too hungry to allow any cloth between them. Its metal buttons clanked as they hit the sink, but India froze at the sound, as if a siren had clanged in the heated room.

"No," she muttered, and she twisted to reclaim her shirt. "Good Lord, what are we doing? Have we both lost our minds? Jack, put your clothes back on. What is the matter with me?"

He stared at her, too startled, too near taking her on his own kitchen counter to respond. India pushed him hard enough to free her legs, gently enough, with more than a little regret in her eyes, to make him realize she was as close as he. Dropping off the counter in one movement, she picked up his sweatshirt and tossed it at him.

"Put this back on." She pushed her arms through the sleeves of her own shirt in a sensuous motion that only deepened Jack's desire. Her quirky smile touched his heart. "You'd better hand me that towel, Jack. You have frosting behind your ears."

He bunched his shirt in his hands and tried to match her tone. "It's not the same if you wipe it off with a towel."

Evidently he wasn't as successful as she at hiding his feelings. She looked more closely at him.

"We shouldn't play these games with each other."

"I'm not playing. I don't think you are, either." Jack took a step, but slipped through the icing on the floor. He caught his balance at her side, grinning as she exploded in nervous laughter. He cupped her chin.

"Not so close." She held him off with stiff fingers on his chest, mesmerizing him with a smile that made him feel proprietary all over again.

"I want to touch you even when I know you won't let me have you." He traced the line of her upper lip. "You feel the same, India. Surely yesterday and today have proved to you that what's between us is supposed to be. Could we feel so right together if we were wrong? Why are you afraid?"

She tried to lower her head. "Trust me to know what's best."

He took a deep breath and a big chance. He jumped to a new conclusion that made sense to him. "You don't have to leave town because you think I'll get you pregnant, then abandon you."

India stared straight into his eyes, holding him off. "You think you know everything, Jack Stephens." She curved her mouth in a plea for understanding. Her smile quivered with echoes of the love they'd nearly made. She caught his hands, smoothing her thumbs against his palms. "You do know quite a bit. You know things I haven't even dreamed of till I met you, but you also don't know anything."

She lowered her voice, and her still-tender gaze grew serious. "I gave up a child. My choice hurt my family in ways that can never end. I won't hurt Colleen, too. I couldn't bear to hurt Colleen."

Jack shook his head at her, bewildered. "Give me a chance to understand what's wrong."

"What's wrong is that you make me lose control." She was lying, but Jack realized he'd already lost whatever edge her need gave him. She wiped the frosting off him. "I've given up control before," she continued in a reflective tone, "and the end result was too harsh. For everyone."

Jack studied the pulse beating in the hollow of her throat. She'd spoken matter-of-factly, not as if she were crying over the past. She'd made one mistake she refused to discuss, and she wouldn't let herself make another. He admired her quiet courage, though it stood between them.

He tightened his jaw. She wouldn't even welcome his praise. She'd tell him he had no right.

He put his hand behind her head and pulled her against him. Although his body still howled to make love to her, he offered her comfort, patting her back as he had Colleen's when she'd wakened from childhood nightmares. He held her until she relaxed against him. "You'll have to trust someone someday," he said. "Might as well be me."

"With that red frosting in your hair and on your sweatshirt, I'm not sure you inspire trust. Now the brown we used for the mast, that's a more sober color—but red—I don't know."

"I'm serious."

"I know, but Colleen is upstairs, and we won't solve anything tonight, and your friends—"

"What friends?"

"Colleen said you were having a party."

"You're full of surprises tonight. Are you sure?"

She nodded. Somehow, her faintly tilted nose looked as if it would like to be kissed. He closed his eyes.

Remember: Comfort. Reassurance. Don't frighten her any further away.

"I'm sure she said it was a party." India reached for the towel again and lifted her gaze to the ceiling. "Let's clean up before she comes down."

Jack unrolled a stretch of paper towel and soaked it beneath the faucet. He bent to swab up the frosting they'd all slalomed through. An uncomfortable idea straightened him. "What if you're the party?"

She stopped her arm in mid-circle. "Excuse me?"

"What if you're the only person Colleen invited?" Jack rubbed at the floor. "That calculating look she threw at us before she went upstairs. I don't trust her."

India stared from him to the trawler cake. She pushed the towel to the back of the counter and leaned against it. "How much can you eat?"

Jack laughed.

"None of this is funny. Why can't you see how dangerous getting her hopes up could be?" She grabbed the towel and went at the counter again, twisting her lean hips as she wiped.

Jack eased out a breath. "You've got a little frosting on the waistband of your jeans. Can I get it off for you?"

She dropped the towel and turned, frustration plain in her blue eyes. "Your voice kills me. Every thought in your head pours through it."

He shrugged. "If only you shared my unwavering devotion to honesty." Her flinch increased his confusion.

"I have to go home and change." She tossed the towel at his chest. "I swear to you—and in this I'm being completely honest—if Hayden and Nettie come back alone, if Colleen hasn't invited anyone else—" She sputtered, as though she couldn't come up with a threat to meet the occasion. "I will walk out of this house, birthday or not. That girl of yours is too devious."

Jack laughed out loud, taking inordinate joy in her loss of the control she valued so highly. "Like you're one to throw stones."

INDIA SHOWERED and put on a white turtleneck and a long forest-green corduroy jumper. As she brushed her hair, she stared at her face in the bathroom mirror. Her eyes glowed blue fire. Inner heat flushed her cheeks.

An image of how she and Jack must have looked, struggling together on his kitchen counter flashed through her mind. She was in big trouble.

She was falling in love. Maybe she'd loved Jack the first moment she'd seen him, ready to pound a boy who'd threatened his daughter. Maybe she'd loved him the first time he'd stared with hurt and longing at the child he'd never know they shared, the young woman she'd come to love as a person, not as a memory who'd branded her heart fifteen years ago.

India faced herself. "I came here to make sure she was safe so I could go on with my own life. Now I want to make a life with them."

The eyes that stared back at her were wounded. Worst of all, Colleen seemed to want the same family. She had to prepare Colleen for the fact she'd be gone soon. Not tonight. She wouldn't ruin Jack's party, but from tomorrow until she left, she had to make sure Colleen understood she wouldn't be back, that Jack and she would never be parents together.

India set her brush on the counter and clasped her hands tightly. Surely Colleen had invited other friends.

She quickly twisted her hair into a knot and prayed Nettie and Hayden and a crowd of birthday partyers would be rioting at Jack and Colleen's house by the time she returned. She felt like a coward as she forced herself down her steep stairs into the cold night. The trip to Jack's house took no time. He answered his door on her first knock.

His gaze swept her and he grinned. "You're a quick-change artist to go with your other many talents."

"I'm back too soon?"

He took her coat and leaned down for a swift, firm kiss that left India's lips tingling and her perspective in ruins. In his arms, she forgot all the reasons he'd have to throw her out if he knew the truth about her. He pressed his lips into her hair, drowning her in his strength. Frightened at years of forever without him, she couldn't pull away.

"You need warming up," he said, his mouth hot against her forehead.

"Where is Colleen?"

"Wrapping something."

"No one else has arrived yet?"

He turned her toward the living room, the hand on her back both comforting and erotic. The comfort frightened her, because it suggested a bond that added to their physical attraction. "I wouldn't count on anyone else coming. She hasn't said anything."

"Would she if they were a surprise?"

"I asked her point-blank, and she said she hadn't planned a surprise."

"Not for you, anyway." India shook her head. "She shouldn't have tricked me."

His smile annoyed her. "I believe you've hit the nail on the head. She must realize you don't want to be here."

India lifted her head. "You know I do, but I'll only hurt

all of us if I stay much longer. I'm tired of hurting the people I lo—I care for."

He grinned. "I'm glad."

India shook her head in despair. "Every time I look at you I feel guilty."

"You haven't done anything yet to feel guilty about. Let me at least enjoy the sin before you start paying for it." His shirt brushed her arm. He curved his hand around her throat and tipped up her chin with his thumb. "Face it. No one is on your side around here."

Pushing his palm away from her, she sidled out of his reach. "Back off," she said. "I suspect with you a wall is as good as a kitchen counter."

She turned at the living room door and looked back at him. She longed to be in his arms again, safe, where she could persuade herself he might trust her enough to believe her if she told the truth.

"What, India? Why are you looking at me like that?"

She shook her head. "I wish we could always be the way we were this afternoon."

His eyes darkened in the dim light as he came to her. "I wish we could be alone." He pressed his mouth to her forehead and then tilted her head to cover her mouth with his.

Passion spiked between them as though it had never waned since this afternoon. India pushed her fingers through his hair, pulling him closer, pressing her face to his.

With a tortured groan, he stepped away. "You'd better go on in there. Colleen will come down any second. I'll be along when I can." He smiled. "One look at what you do to me, and the so-called party becomes a scandal."

Before India could answer, the doorbell rang. Jack laughed at her and untucked his henley as he went back to answer it. She paced to the fire and put her hands out to the flames. She couldn't let this go on. She loved Jack. She couldn't hurt him.

"Nettie, Hayden." His voice rumbled from the hall. How she dreaded not hearing his scraped-over-gravel voice again. "Come on in," he said. "Did you forget your keys?"

"Hayden left them at a restaurant in the city," Nettie said. "Hayden, go get our things out of the car. I told you Jack and Colleen must be here, and I'm perfectly capable of entering an empty house by myself anyway. The man thinks I'm doddering, Jack."

"Nonsense. Can I help, Hayden?"

"No, thank you. She's enjoying herself too much. All the way back, she kept reminding me that she might get herself into little snafus occasionally, but she's never left your house keys in a public restaurant."

"I also thought to call the restaurant, and they've saved them for us, so we can go back and get them. Tomorrow. Not tonight when we would have missed your birthday if we'd turned back."

India chuckled. From Nettie's tone, they'd also discussed those logistics in the car.

The front door closed. Nettie and Jack came into the living room, Jack peeling Nettie's coat off her shoulders. "Let me take this. Do you know if Colleen invited anyone else?"

"She said just India." Nettie saw her. "Oh, you're here already. Hi." She glanced back at Jack. "She suggested we keep it to family tonight."

"Good." Jack donned a flawlessly unconcerned expression. "I'm about to order pizza, and I wanted to make sure we had enough. Go warm yourself by the fire, Nettie. I'll see if Hayden needs help after all."

The older woman joined India. "Where's that granddaughter of mine?"

"Upstairs, wrapping Jack's cap, I guess."

"You've seen it then? He'll love it even if he looks horrid in it." Nettie patted India's shoulder. "What's wrong, dear? You look tense."

Trying to cover, India lifted her elbow to brace herself carelessly against the mantel. She missed and almost tumbled into the fire. Nettie grabbed her arm, looking as if she suspected some sort of meeting with the cooking sherry. While Nettie stared at her, the front door opened again, and Jack and Hayden stomped inside.

"What's wrong, India?"

Nettie's question echoed in the quiet room. India looked guiltily at Jack, who offered no assistance at all.

"Grandpa! Grandma, when did you get back?" Colleen shouted from the stairs. Tumbling into the room, she threw herself at her grandparents with all the exuberance she normally disdained. "Come see the cake."

They exited the room, a twisting, happy mass of human hugs India regarded with envy. Jack didn't allow her to envy them long.

"Are you all right?"

"Even Nettie's starting to notice," she whispered.

He took her hand. "You're supposed to be here. Don't worry."

"I'm *supposed* to be anywhere else on the face of the earth."

"You look as if you're dancing on hot coals. Relax."

India flashed a glare at him. "Colleen sees us as some sort of family."

"She's excited. She's always like this at parties. That's how she ended up with spiked punch." Jack leaned closer and brushed India's mouth with his. "I'll have to congratulate her on her guest list. She plans a mean party." He moved away then, his mouth curving with hedonistic promise. "I'll go make some coffee. Nettie drinks it night and day, with every meal."

Gazing, lovesick, at his back, she shivered and touched her lips, still warm from the whisper of his. Before India was ready to face her, Colleen came back alone. "The cake looks great. Even better, now that I'm not peering through a face full of frosting. Thanks, India."

"I had fun. Thanks for letting me help." She hesitated but plunged on. "You know you made me think you'd invited your father's other friends to celebrate his birthday, too."

Colleen lowered her gaze. She reminded India of Rachel again, trying to come up with a good excuse for the docent incident.

"I know," she said, "but we only needed you."

CHAPTER FOURTEEN

INDIA LEFT THE SO-CALLED PARTY as soon as she decently could. The next morning, she started painting Leon Shipp's house by herself. For two days, she worked, realizing she hadn't inherited her father's painting skills after all. He must have worked around her since they'd come.

She valued the gift of his time so much she couldn't call and ask him to leave her mother early. Unfortunately, painting at such a pace gave her plenty of time to think. She dreaded leaving, but she had to go. Soon. For Colleen's sake and for Jack's. Maybe for her own. Much more of this island and these people she'd grown to love so dearly, and she'd latch on to any flimsy excuse to stay.

She avoided the library, or any place where she risked running into Jack or Colleen. At the end of the second day, Jack showed up while she was packing the van in twilight. He rose almost out of the growing darkness, but he didn't surprise her.

"Evening," he said.

She sniffed the salty air he brought with him. Even fish and the bay smelled good on him. "You've been busy."

He took the paint can she held. "Not as busy as you. Why are you avoiding us?"

"Avoiding you?" Trying not to snatch the can out of his hand, she took it back. "Why would I? You think highly of yourself, Mr. Stephens."

"Don't try to joke me out of this conversation, because

you can't make me walk away. Colleen said you didn't show up at the library last night.''

She'd known Colleen was due to volunteer after school. ''I called Mrs. Fisher to let her know.''

''You gave her some story about a cold—which I see was a lie.''

''Maybe you should ask Mrs. Fisher to tell Colleen she doesn't need her at the library until I leave.''

''Why?''

''Why pretend you don't understand?'' India shoved the paint can inside her father's van and slammed the double doors shut.

''How soon are you leaving? And why can't we arrange to see each other after you leave?''

''You've got to be kidding.''

''Stop saying no without giving me a reason. I care for you.''

India sagged against the truck. ''This is a dead issue. You can't care for me. I'm breaking my heart over you and Colleen. We live different lives. I don't want to be here, and you can't fish for a living in Charlottesville.''

''You could stay. What's wrong with our library? Do you care more about where you work than who you're with?''

''Mrs. Fisher runs your library, and I have to help my father with his business. And you don't know me, Jack.''

''I haven't proposed marriage. I'm asking you to stay so we can see what's between us.''

''Nothing between us is real, and Colleen wants us to be together. We don't have time to get to know each other. I have to paint this house and get out of town.''

''See me when you can. We'll do this your way. I don't want to hurt Colleen any more than you do.''

''I don't want to see you. Why won't you hear me?''

"Because you put me off, or you lie." Jack stepped in front of her, but she danced around him.

"Marcy could be dangling out of her bedroom with her ear to the ground." India shook her head. She wasn't making sense. "Have you felt like this about any woman since Mary died?"

He lifted his chin. His gaze remained steady. "No," he said.

"You've been alone for three years. You're cutting your emotional teeth on me, but you'll find someone more suitable."

"I want you. I'm not a lovesick boy, and I'm over my grief. I know my own mind."

"Believe me, Jack, I will hurt you more than Mary could, because I'll leave you and I won't tell you why. She tried to make your marriage work. She was honest with you. I won't be, so you have to leave now, and stay away."

She saw when he began to believe. Believing put confusion in his eyes. "Aren't you being a little melodramatic?"

"Listen to your instincts, Jack. They want you to pay attention. Even if you think I'm a kook, let me go."

"What do I tell Colleen?"

"I'll come to say goodbye, casually, like we all knew this was coming. I'll tell her the truth. My sabbatical's up, and I have to decide whether to go back to my old job or look for a new one. I'm more sorry than I can tell you for the misunderstanding I've caused, but I'm doing the right thing now. For all of us."

Jack backed away, his hands open. "You won't give us a chance?"

"I can't." For the first time in fifteen years, India made no attempt to disguise what she felt. All the love, the excruciating pain and the longing she suspected she'd only just begun to understand. She looked Jack straight in the eye, bare naked in her emotions.

His breath caught in an audible gasp. He opened his mouth, but he couldn't seem to produce sound. Finally she'd convinced him words couldn't matter. She hated her own success.

He turned and walked away. She sagged against the cold doors and pushed her hands over her face, into her hair. Tears came silently to her eyes. She'd kept back no strength to fight them, but she couldn't give in. Marcy might be watching, and Marcy would tell Colleen everything she saw or suspected.

India slogged around the side of the truck and dragged herself into the driver's seat. She started the engine. Jack was still climbing the driveway. She drove past him without looking his way.

WHEN COLLEEN LEFT SCHOOL that afternoon, she found her grandmother waiting. She thought first of her father. "Is something wrong with Dad?"

"No, he's fine." Nettie took her arm. "What do you say we have a burger at the drugstore?"

Maybe her dad was okay, but someone must be in trouble. "And a milk shake from the fountain?"

Grandma nodded "A double."

"Deal."

The news must be terrible. She didn't speak as her grandma drove, preferring to take comfort before the bomb dropped. They sat at the polished marble counter and ordered cheeseburgers, fries and milk shakes. Chocolate for Colleen. Vanilla for Nettie. Jean, who was married to Al, the pharmacist, worked the fountain.

"When are you coming to work for me, Colleen?"

"Are you serious?" She licked her lips with an eye on

the chrome spigots from which all good things flowed. "I'd love to work here."

"I figure we'd save if we paid you in kind." Jean poured the chocolate shake into a tall glass and set it on the counter. She placed the rest of the shake in its silver cup beside the glass and began the process from scratch to make the vanilla shake. "When will she be old enough, Nettie?"

"Next year. I'm just not sure you could afford her if you let her take her pay in the food and drink."

"Oh, we'd make her earn her keep. Let me finish this and start those burgers for you."

Colleen stared down the long counter at the mirror that reflected her and her grandmother and the old-fashioned fixtures. Her father had sat here before her, and her mom used to bring her here when something bad happened, like shots at the doctor's, or a low grade on a test after she'd studied hard. People knew her here. People looked after her. For the first time, she understood the sense of community her father preached. This was home.

"What do you need to tell me, Grandma? Might as well get it over with."

Nettie nodded. "Not too subtle? I don't think you'll want to hear any more than I want to tell you, but India Stuart is leaving."

"What do you mean she's leaving?" Colleen's hand trembled on her glass. She'd begun to include India in her life. India made it better and bigger in a way that made her feel more safe.

"Her father came back yesterday afternoon. As soon as they finish Leon Shipp's house, they're going home. He has enough work in Charlottesville, and India's returning to her job."

"Did India tell you? I didn't know you talked about personal stuff."

"Your father told me. He wanted to tell you, too, but he had to help Tim with an emergency on his boat, and we were afraid you'd hear through the grapevine."

"What did you all think? I'd fall apart like a baby? Where's Grandpa?"

"We thought you might be upset." Nettie glanced toward the wide double doors. "And Grandpa's probably waiting in the street, to make sure I don't let you run away from home."

"Was he like that with my mom?"

"No." Nettie shook her head. "Well, maybe sometimes. He'd be too stern, and let up, only to feel he was being too easy. He tries to be perfect with you. We want your dad to feel safe when you're with us. He loves you, though—Grandpa."

"I know. I just wish he'd be like he is with Dad. They joke together like friends, but he's always got to crack the whip with me."

"You're young, but you have to understand adults the way we try to understand you. Maybe Grandpa worries something will happen to you—we never imagined we'd lose your mother in a car accident. He wants you to be careful when you choose to trust your safety to others. Just try to look in from the outside and understand what goes on under the surface."

Colleen thought. Her mother's death had changed their lives in too many ways. "Why are you and I the only ones who talk about Mom?"

"I think your dad tries not to hurt you by making you remember, but if you told him you want to talk, he'd try." Nettie sipped her own shake. "Now, what about India? Are you okay with her leaving?"

"I sort of thought she might like to stay here. I thought she and Dad were getting...close."

"I thought so, too, but we can't know what happened

between them. She's not from a small town. What would she do here?''

Be part of our family. ''You don't think Dad said something to make her go away?''

''No, but their relationship is their business.''

Colleen twisted her straw in the thick chocolate. ''I like the way I'm old enough to understand anything you all think I should, but I'm too young to do what I want. Adults use youth as an excuse to keep underage people in line.''

Nettie dug beyond her complaint to one of those moments of understanding. ''You care about India, and you don't want her to go. She's been a good friend to you.''

''I wish Dad would do something to keep her here. He could persuade her.''

Jean pushed through the doors from the kitchen, two cheeseburgers and two orders of fries on wide, thick white plates. ''Hope I'm not interrupting. You two look pretty serious.''

''You're just in time,'' Colleen said with half a smile at her grandma. Why did India have to go? She belonged here.

INDIA'S HEART POUNDED in the back of her throat as she marched up Jack's sidewalk. Night was falling fast. She swiped her bangs off her forehead. The weather had warmed dramatically, as if the snowstorm had offered winter's last punch.

Mick had said goodbye to Colleen earlier, at Leon Shipp's house after India had already gone back to the hotel to pack. She'd called Nettie and arranged to come by this evening.

Jamming one hand into her pocket to grip the opal pendant her mother had given her when she was thirteen, India rapped on the door with her other fist. Nettie opened it right away.

"I'm sorry you're leaving, India. You know we'll miss you around here."

She tried to smile. "Thank you. I'm so glad I've gotten to know you all." Hayden appeared in the hall behind his wife.

"You really have to go?" he said.

"I'm afraid so. I need to get back to my job, and my father's business has picked up."

"I'm glad things are looking better for him."

Warmth crept up her neck. Soon she'd be lying like her mom. "May I say goodbye to Colleen?"

"She's in the living room."

Jack stood with his daughter as India entered. Hayden and Nettie continued on to the kitchen. Jack lifted the television's remote control and turned off the evening news. His hair gleamed in damp curls. A small circle of razor burn reddened his throat beneath his jaw. He'd taken a shower recently. Against her will, India imagined water beating against the lean angles of his beautiful body.

She cleared her throat and looked to the girl at his side. Colleen lifted a hurt gaze.

"You're really going?" She seemed more child than young woman. "When?"

"In the morning. I wanted to say goodbye."

Colleen lifted her chin slightly in a brave nod that looked familiar. Probably Rachel again. "I'm glad you came," she said.

India's throat threatened to close altogether. *Let's just finish this.* She searched Colleen's face hungrily, trying to memorize every expression, every line and color she'd never see again. She fished the pendant from her pocket and dangled it by its chain.

"I brought something for you." Suddenly she realized she should have asked Jack first if he minded her giving Colleen a present. "Jack, is it okay?"

He nodded. His taut face hurt her as much as Colleen's open pain. India crossed the creaking wooden floor that already sounded too familiar to her.

"My mother gave me this for Christmas when I was thirteen. My grandmother gave it to her."

Colleen touched the back of her finger to the opal teardrop. "It's beautiful. It's too beautiful. I don't think I can accept this."

She looked to Jack for advice, but India forged ahead. Maybe she'd never give her daughter anything else, but this pendant connected the maternal generations of her family. She wanted Colleen to have it.

"Please." She looked to Jack, too. "I want to give it to her. I asked my mother if she'd mind, and we both want Colleen to keep it."

Jack hesitated, and India flattened Colleen's open palm and dropped the pendant, chain and all, onto her daughter's young hand.

"It's yours. I hope you'll think of me sometimes when you wear it, and remember what your friendship—your entire family's generosity has meant to my father and me while we've been here. This was a hard time for us, and you've all made us welcome."

"Thank you, India." Colleen closed her hand. "I'm sorry you're going. I'll miss you."

Swiftly she twined her arms around India's neck, but she ran away almost before India realized she'd hugged her. India wanted to cry at the loss of her daughter's arms. She turned away, but Jack wouldn't let her go, his hands at her waist comforting rather than demanding a response.

"You don't have to go," he whispered.

"I do. I'm going to miss you, too, Jack. I really am."

He turned her. His eyes swallowed her whole. She must have looked the same, staring at Colleen. Suddenly, Jack pulled her to his heart. Held tight against him, she opened to his hunger. She tasted her own salty sadness on his tongue. She couldn't seem to hold back tears anymore, and they fell into his mouth and hers.

Comfort and longing burned into desire. India arched her breasts against his hard chest, wanting him to love her and make her forget the reasons she had to leave, but sanity returned. She couldn't let him change her mind. She couldn't beg him to change her mind, though she would if he held her a second longer. She pushed away.

"Goodbye, Jack."

She turned and blindly reached his door. She yanked it behind herself, but it didn't shut as she fled across the small porch. She didn't look back.

TWO WEEKS AFTER India and Mick left, Jack helped Hayden pack the car and saw his daughter and in-laws on their way to Washington, D.C. Colleen had been ecstatic at the idea of a trip to visit Nettie's cousins.

After they'd gone, Jack showered and found the iron, so he could press a pair of khakis and a blue denim shirt. He packed clothes for the weekend in a duffel bag he was hoisting onto his shoulder as the front doorbell rang.

Oh no. Not some local disaster. Not today.

His caller turned out to be a florist's deliveryman who held out a bouquet of wildflowers, wrapped in dark green paper that crinkled as Jack took them.

"Flowers?" They didn't truly seem to suit him.

"Don't ask me, buddy. I just deliver 'em."

Jack ignored the man's ironic comment. Inside the house again, he took the florist's card from its envelope. It was covered, front and back, in a long note.

"In case you've forgotten how to impress a girl," it read. "Love, Colleen and Nettie. P.S. Get a new card and write a note from yourself. A *good* card, Dad!"

Jack shook his head, laughing softly. A little thing like

tact didn't hinder Nettie or Colleen. Still he tossed his duffel bag into the back of his truck, but made a nest of his jacket for the flowers and hoped they wouldn't dry out by the time he reached Charlottesville.

He'd thought he was being so clever, arranging this trip for Colleen with Nettie and Hayden. He'd suggested it innocently enough, not intending any of them to realize he was heading for Charlottesville the moment they pulled out of town.

Two weeks. They'd stretched between him and India like a desert of silence and loneliness. At least he hoped she was lonely for him, too. He'd thought—long and carefully about his situation with India and with Colleen. He'd recounted every conversation in his head again and again. He didn't know what to believe. He remembered India's wistful expression as they'd looked at Colleen's baby photos.

He couldn't forget her expression of horror when he'd reacted to the news that she'd given up a child of her own. She'd expected—maybe she'd hoped for some other response from him. Maybe he'd let her down.

Maybe she would have trusted him with her secrets if he'd taken a moment to think before he'd condemned her. Anyway, he had to go to Charlottesville. He had to find her and persuade her to give him a chance. To give them all a chance. Did she really believe these feelings came along twice in a lifetime? He could tell her they didn't.

He just hoped Colleen wouldn't be disappointed in the results of his fight. He couldn't persuade himself India would listen, and he was grateful Colleen hadn't told him she knew what he was up to before she'd left.

As always, traffic crawled around the D.C. Beltway. West of the city, Jack turned the truck toward Manassas. Noon rolled around as he entered the city of Charlottesville. He drove from phone booth to phone booth until he found one that still possessed a directory. Fortunately, Mick ran an ad in the Yellow Pages. Jack called the office and asked for directions without identifying himself.

He hung up the phone, scrunching the sheet of paper he'd written the woman's directions on. He'd half hoped India would answer her father's phone. Had the woman on the phone been Rachel?

The woman who looked up from the receptionist's desk was neither Rachel nor India. A hum of business activity rose from the room behind her small reception area. Mick's business couldn't have improved this quickly.

"Can I help you?" she asked.

"I hope so. I'm looking for India Stuart."

The woman assessed him, her blond hair perfect, her lipstick glossy, her eyes confident but mistrustful. She'd toss him if required. "India doesn't work here," she said.

"Can you give me her address?"

"If you have painting needs, I can find a salesman to speak to you." She sized him up. "Most of our clients are corporate, mind you."

Something was wrong. "I have a personal matter to discuss with India. How about just her address?"

"Sure. Can I offer you her tax return, too? Possibly her medical records? Do you know what year this is?"

Jack stared at her, taken aback. "Maybe I'm used to a smaller town."

"Maybe I could call her and ask her if she wants to speak to you? She can give you her address if she wants you to have it."

"No." She'd call India anyway and alert her. He turned away from the desk. He wanted to ask India about her father's prosperity before she had a chance to prepare an answer. "I'll stop by her parents' house."

"Mr. Stuart's in the back. I'd be happy to page him for you."

Not a chance. Mick had gone along with the business-in-trouble farce. Jack didn't need any more lies.

"Thanks, but I don't want to interrupt him. I'll just speak to Rachel."

If he hoped knowing Rachel's name would give the receptionist second thoughts, she disappointed him. She let him leave without another word, but he figured she dialed India's home number the moment the glass door swished shut at his back.

He reversed his truck out of the lot and drove toward the main street. At the last minute, out of sight of the receptionist's desk, he turned left, down an access road that ran alongside the building. In the back, he found four vans just like the one Mick had driven to Arran Island.

Men and women circled the vehicles, loading equipment and paint. They paid no attention to Jack as he parked. He looked from van to van, trying to determine which employee would be most likely to spill India's whereabouts.

He almost struck out. On his third try, he persuaded a kid who looked nearly as young as Colleen that he just wanted to return something India had left on the island.

It wasn't a lie, necessarily. As silly as it sounded out loud, she'd managed to walk away with his heart. Maybe he'd come to retrieve an extremely personal effect.

The kid gave him India's address, along with good directions. She lived in an apartment near the UVA campus. Once there, Jack parked his truck on the road below her tall brick building.

She wouldn't welcome him. She'd resent him for coming. Whatever she might say, he'd rather hear it from her than guess about it from the curb.

He took the flowers from where they lay on his jacket and opened the door. Sheepishly carrying the bouquet, he avoided an elderly man's arch smile in the elevator. Jack's face felt too strained to smile in return. By the time he reached India's door, unexpected nervousness made him forget the flowers.

He knocked before he could change his mind. India took so long to answer, he wondered if she'd seen him from her windows and decided not to be home to him. At last she came to the door—in the plaid skirt she'd worn the night of the festival and a purple sweater.

Her hair, freed from its usual ponytail, fell in a curtain of pale gold silk around her shoulders. Translucent black hose hugged her thighs, and a pair of black suede flats looked as soft as butter on her feet. She didn't look like the same woman he'd known on the island, and yet she made him feel as if he'd come home.

He stared at her face again, to find her eyes wide, searching his body, with the hunger he shared. Tenderness and crushing desire overwhelmed him at the same time.

"Jack," she whispered in a hungry tone that sliced through his heart.

He tugged at his shirt collar, seeing part of what she'd run from, the responsibility, the ties. A certain amount of danger accompanied them. Loving made a man vulnerable.

She gripped the doorframe hard enough to turn her knuckles white. Edging forward, she would have pushed him farther into the hall, if he'd allowed her. He didn't.

"Why did you come to Arran Island? Why did your father pretend his business was in trouble?"

Her pupils dilated. A pulse pounded crazily in the hollow of her throat. She was afraid. He saw her more clearly here on her home ground.

"Why have you come?" she demanded. "How could you come here?"

He wanted her honesty. He gave her his own. "I needed you."

CHAPTER FIFTEEN

FURIOUS PINK COLOR SHOT from her neckline all the way to the roots of her hair, but his confession only upset her. "You didn't think I'd be glad to see you?"

"I hoped you would." At that moment he remembered the flowers, but he felt like a five-year-old kid as he thrust them at her. "These are from Colleen," he said.

"Colleen?" She peered over his shoulder. "You didn't bring her?"

"No, she bought them for me to give you."

India hesitated again, but she took the flowers from his hand, careful not to touch his fingers. She turned away from him, and Jack followed her inside.

A huge expanse of glass covered one wall and most of the ceiling. Colleen would love this studio. India picked her way around a blanket spread in the middle of the floor, to the kitchen area. Distracted by the gentle sway of her bottom, the graceful dance of soft strands of hair over her shoulders, Jack remained still, an intruder just inside her apartment.

She only looked at him again once she'd put the room and the wide kitchen counter between them. "I don't suppose you'd turn around and go home where you belong?"

"No, I won't. I don't enjoy constant rejection, but I had to see you. Can we talk?"

India ran water into a vase. She looked at him carefully as she spread the bouquet on the counter. "About what?"

Her voice cracked like breaking glass. She'd volunteer nothing.

"What if you tell me exactly why you came to the island?"

"You know I had a reason to go?" His knowledge hardened her gaze. She took a different tack. "Colleen knows you're here?"

"I didn't tell her, but she's a smart girl. She guessed."

She placed the first flower in the vase, averting her eyes. "I don't know how many ways I can tell you I don't want to hurt her or you. I'm trying to protect you."

"I don't need protection. Let someone protect you for a change." Blind to consequences, he followed his instincts across the room, stopping only to drop his coat on a chair before he went around the counter.

India backed away from him, but he caught her shoulders. In a moment's clarity, he made a plan. Maybe he could teach her to trust him. "Give me today. Let me pretend you asked me to come for you, that you'll come home to the island." Mistake. Her eyes narrowed as he called the island her home. "Give me today, and I'll go home and never see you again if you tell me that's what you want."

"No. Pretending wouldn't be fair to either of us." India shook her hair over her shoulder, a feeble attempt to hide. "I have to survive this, too."

Had she ever leaned on another human being? "Trust me, India. I've promised I'll go. I'm just betting you won't be able to send me away." He hoped today would show him how to put the pieces of her puzzle together. Sliding his hands around her back, he leaned toward her and kissed the sweet perfume of her hair. "Let me stay. I accept the risk."

"Jack…"

He put her hands around his neck. In a second that took

eons, she hesitated. At last, with a sigh that came from deep inside, she pulled herself closer to him. His body hardened with desire. He recognized the curves she fit so perfectly against him.

"Let me start with that skirt. I'd like to take it off you with my teeth. Interested?"

She didn't move or answer. He wrapped his fingers in the soft weave of her sweater and stroked her back, impossibly aroused as the heat of her body seeped through the yarn to warm his palms.

India turned, gently pushing him away. "Undressing me with your teeth is a little too intimate."

"What do you want to do?" A step back, he pushed his hands into his pockets. "Are you hungry? Do you want to go for a walk? Can I borrow a cold shower?"

Her uncertain smile reached inside his heart. "I was about to have lunch, but maybe you'd like to see Charlottesville?"

Jack eyed her somberly. "I don't give a damn about Charlottesville."

She lowered her head, her sudden shyness testing and charming him at the same time. She went back to arranging her flowers. "I grilled chicken and made some potato salad. And I have strawberry shortcake for dessert."

"You cook when you're upset?"

"Trust you to be so sure I minded leaving you behind." She folded the green florist's paper into neat squares.

He frowned. "You fold your rubbish?"

"You said Colleen ordered the flowers." She tucked the paper into a drawer. "I'm keeping it."

How could her sentimental attachment to green paper make him want her more? He'd better use these hours wisely to find out.

"Colleen would love your apartment."

India glanced around the large room. "I've had my eye

on it awhile. I planned to stay with my parents when I came back, but a real estate friend told me this was available.'' She shrugged. "My phone's not even connected yet.''

So her father's receptionist hadn't called. Jack was glad. After seeing Mick's business, he knew they'd come to the island for a reason. Maybe normal talk instead of pressure would make India comfortable enough to tell him the things he needed to know. "Where did you live before?''

"After the accident, I stayed with Mom and Dad. I couldn't afford to keep my apartment while I wasn't working.'' She gestured toward the open floor beyond the counter. "I also couldn't afford to store all my furniture. My dining table had to go, because my parents didn't have room for it.''

Jack nodded at the one big soft chair and the antique dresser beside the door. She'd kept bits and pieces, obviously family things, obviously precious to her. "That's the part Colleen would like best. Your apartment is like camping out.''

She turned from the counter, her hands on her hips. Her gaze brushed him with her doubts. She didn't know if he was insulting or teasing her. She clearly didn't know what to do next. He might be getting somewhere.

"Trust me,'' he said again. Whatever she'd done, she didn't believe he could forgive her. His wayward thoughts tried to supply answers, but he'd learned from his mistakes with Mary. He refused to suspect the worst, that her reason for going to the island had something to do with his family.

India dropped her hands to her sides. "I know a tavern by Monticello where we could get lunch.''

"I only have one day. I don't want to share it with strangers. What about your chicken? Were you planning to use that blanket as a picnic table?''

She hesitated again. He waited for her. He wanted to

talk—or listen—not sightsee. Taking a deep breath that
lifted her slender shoulders, India picked up Colleen's
flowers in their vase and carried them past him to set them
on the pine planking. "Sit down," she said. "I'll bring
everything over. Do you mind your chicken cold?"

As she straightened, her sweater hugged her full breasts
like a loving embrace. Cold anything sounded like a good
idea. "Do you have wine?" he asked. He'd passed a market down her street.

"No." She opened her fridge door. "I can get some."

"I'll go."

INDIA REACHED INTO THE FRIDGE for the plate of chicken,
glad for a few moments out of Jack's all-knowing gaze.
Why was today different? Why was he different?

Why had he run out to the market? She closed her eyes.
"Please don't let him try to figure me out."

She took the food to the blanket in consecutive trips and
then laid out plates and silverware. A knock at her door
made her jump. She hurried to open it for Jack, but his
speculative glance worried her. She stood back for him.
"You were quick."

"We should talk."

"About?" He looked determined. She pretended not to
notice. Taking the wine, she went to the kitchen for a
corkscrew. "Do you want to talk about Charlottesville?
Your trip over here? Where is Colleen anyway?"

"Nettie and Hayden took her to visit family in D.C.
Why don't we talk about the things we need to say to each
other?"

She opened the wine and placed the cork on the counter.
"You mean the things you think I should say."

"I mean the truth." He sat cross-legged on the blanket.
She loved the graceful way he moved, the rhythm of his

long, lean legs. She ached for his arms around her, for the depth of the love she believed him capable of giving.

Nothing of all she treasured about him could belong to her.

Avoiding him in his less understanding mode, she took two glasses from a cupboard and came to the blanket. Whatever happened, she mustn't answer his questions. She mustn't persuade herself he could go on with his life as he had before if he knew the truth.

"What about the boy, India?" He stared at her. "Your baby's father?"

She tightened her grip on the wine bottle. "Where did that come from?"

"Whatever happened to him?"

She sat on the blanket, trying to look as if none of this mattered. Thankfully, Gabe was the only part of the past she'd been able to put behind her. "I don't know."

"You don't know? Didn't he matter to you?"

His determination unnerved her. "What happened to you at the market?"

"Did you leave him? That's what I asked myself on the way to the market. All of this must have something to do with the fact you gave up a child. So, where is her father? How does he affect your decisions now?"

She spooned out potato salad and placed a chicken breast on a plate and passed it across, deciding what she could say. "As a matter of fact, Gabe left me. When I told him about the baby." She lifted her chin, defying him to feel pity. "My father turned rustic. He grabbed Gabe back and tried to force us down to the Justice of the Peace. He was furious with me when I refused to get married, but Gabe was relieved. He sneaked out during the fireworks." She shrugged. "I haven't heard from him since."

Jack stared at her. "How old were you?"

What could she safely tell him to put him off and not give herself away? "I was a junior in high school."

A muscle ticked beside his mouth. When he spoke at last, his voice was low. "All those years, when I resented people who could have babies when Mary couldn't, I never thought of little girls whose fathers might be angry enough to force them into marriage."

She shook her head, relieved at the subtle change of subject. Jack's soft heart might save her yet. "Dad has a temper, but he cools down. His situation made him angrier. He and Mom couldn't afford to help me." Enough, enough! "Did Mary ever get over it?"

He blinked as if he'd lost the train of her thought. "Over not being able to conceive? I think so. Colleen took away most of her regrets."

"And you, Jack?"

"I gave her Colleen. It made her grateful."

India flinched at Jack's bitterness. The woman who'd worked to feed hungry people and couldn't resist a stray pet had lost her way with a man who was capable of loving with great faith.

"I meant did you have regrets?"

He spoke as if had to make each word just right. "I loved her, even after she told me about her affair. I still cared for her. I tried to keep our marriage alive, and I've done everything since to keep her memory alive for Colleen. I'm sorry I didn't love her the same way after she told me the truth."

India shivered. She couldn't compare the wrong he'd think she'd done with Mary's, but she believed her truth might hurt him more. Colleen had made him want to stay with Mary. He would have suspected India had done everything with an eye to taking Colleen away from him.

"You changed the subject." He rose on his knees and climbed over the dishes between them to sit by her side.

He didn't touch her, but the passion they both felt when they touched swirled between them. "Why are you so afraid when I get close to you?"

"Because I want you close."

India saw herself in Jack's eyes before he leaned toward her, tenderness softening his gaze. His mouth curved in a smile she knew he'd never give anyone else on earth.

He kissed the corner of her mouth and moved to brace one knee behind her back, wrapping her in himself. He slid his hand beneath her hair. "I don't want to imagine going home and not seeing you again."

Holding back from him grew ever more difficult. If she touched him, how would she send him away? The truth crept into her mind. She'd never hold Jack again, but she could take today, the free day he'd offered her.

She lifted her hands to his face. "This is goodbye." He smiled, and she didn't ask what he meant. In wonder, she stroked his rugged cheekbones, basked in the heat of his gaze. Lifting her mouth to his, she suckled his full lower lip, taking for the first time. When he deepened the kiss, she opened to him, following where he led in a dance of intimacy whose steps she'd have to forget after today.

Afraid, enthralled, wary even as he moved over her, she gave herself up to him. She loved him. With all her heart, with all her will, with all that she would ever be. Tucking herself into the strong curve of his body, she slid her hands around his neck. Eyes open, she met his kiss. With her mouth and her hands, she took as he gave, and she demanded he give more.

"India—" He broke off, his voice as tortured as his hands stroking restlessly over her waist, over her breasts as she swelled against his palms and his fingers. "Not here," he muttered. "Not on the floor with lunch all around us."

Unable to speak, she pulled his shirt from his waistband

to scrape her nails gently over his broad, protective back. He shivered in her arms.

"Up there, in the loft," she said, aware she shouldn't.

She pointed to the stairs, but Jack was already standing. He pulled her up with him. He reached for the hem of her sweater and tugged it over her head. His gaze burned through the dark purple lace of her bra. Shivers chased across her skin as if he'd already reached for her again. Taking his hand, she climbed the first several steps ahead of him. He held back, and she turned to see what was wrong.

But he stood below her, his eyes hot on her body. He met her gaze and then flattened his palms on her legs, stroking from her calves to her thighs, melting her muscles, lighting a liquid fire in her center. India would have fallen if he hadn't launched himself upward to catch her.

"I've dreamed of touching you." He held her so tightly she almost believed tomorrow wouldn't come.

His heat rose all around her. His denim shirt scratched at her skin, escalating her need. She put her hands between them to unfasten his buttons. Somehow they made it to the top of the stairs.

Taking the first steps of a new life she wouldn't be able to keep, she pulled his shirt free and pushed it off his shoulders. She turned her face to his musky scent. Jack cupped her head as she pressed her lips to his strobing pulse. As his name sang in her mind, she kissed a path to his nipple, washing his skin with the passion he drew from her.

Groaning, he tilted her face to claim her mouth. If this day was the only one they ever shared, this day would mark her as Jack's, and she meant to mark him as well.

She pulled at his belt and managed to unbuckle it, but Jack caught her hands. "You'll want to be careful," he said self-mockingly. "I've wanted you very much for a long time."

India felt powerfully feminine as she unzipped his khaki trousers. "We have some time." Twenty-four hours. He'd promised.

With a rumble deep in his throat, Jack caught her hands again and pulled them behind his back. He scooped her hair away from her throat and scraped her neck with his teeth, but then he traced the tracks of his teeth with his tongue, building fiery pleasure.

He ran his index fingers over the straps of her bra, and India leaned back to meet his steady gaze. He massaged her nipples with his thumbs and she whimpered at exquisite sensation that struck her body like lightning.

She couldn't look away, but she couldn't bear to let him see what he did to her, either. She lowered her head as he reached around her for the catch to her bra, and she watched his hands as he delicately pulled the lace away from her body.

He cupped her heavy, swollen flesh. Her breath caught as he leaned forward. He took one nipple into his mouth and loved it with his tongue.

India threw back her head, groaning at the relief and the torture of Jack's mouth on her. She plunged her fingers into his hair and held him to her breast, but he moved to her other nipple to bathe it in the same pleasure. Back and forth he turned his head, kissing, holding, teasing, worshiping.

Her knees shook beneath the strain of such unlooked-for bliss. He helped her to her bed beneath the skylight. Kneeling on the edge, she pushed his trousers away from his hips, seeking the taut muscles of his backside, the hard expanse of his thighs. Not letting her play, Jack bent her over his arm, trailing a line of kisses across her throat. He opened his mouth on her collarbones, breathing heat on her skin, as if he couldn't taste enough of her.

He lowered her gently onto the bed and knelt between her legs. Blinding her with a smile of pure yearning, he pushed his hands up her thighs and lifted her skirt. India raised her hips to meet him as he curved his palms over her.

He muttered her name. She answered with his in a fierce rush of breath. He made her feel whole. He made her wanton. She shuddered, inwardly admitting her intense love for this man.

He pushed his fingers into the waistband of her hose and peeled them downward, seemingly intent on the contrast of his tanned hands against her pale skin. India splayed her fingers across his shoulders, her arousal growing on the strength of his.

As he rolled her hose to her ankles, Jack blew softly against her belly. She moaned at the feathery brush of his mouth. He rose on his knees again to open the leather clasp at the waist of her skirt, and she lifted herself so he could take the skirt off. He pulled slowly, tormenting her with the slow slide of the cloth against her flesh.

"Please," she begged, unable to stop herself.

He kissed her swiftly, binding her to him, but then, he rolled away and stood to kick off his pants. India stared at his dark blue boxers. She twisted to her knees and lifted her arms to his shoulders. He stared at her, trying to read her expression, but she closed her eyes, fearful he'd see her love. Jack cupped her face and forced her to look at him again.

"You won't have regrets?"

She hardly recognized his hoarse voice. "Millions," she admitted, "but I want to be with you." She pushed her hands inside the waistband of his boxers, but Jack stopped her again.

"If you touch me, I will die," he said simply.

I love you. The words throbbed in her head, but she bit them back. She pressed her face to his stomach and whispered her love against his tensed, straining muscles, in silence, in need, in fierce, luminous happiness she had not expected.

"India," he said through gritted teeth.

When she tugged at his boxers again, he pulled her hands away and pushed her back onto the bed. He slid his hands between her legs and caressed her. India groaned, in relief, in desire. Jack tugged at her panties. They tore away.

"I'm sorry," he muttered against her mouth. "I'm sorry."

"I don't care."

She pushed his boxers down his legs, kicked them off the bed. He parted her thighs and pressed himself against her. India looked into his eyes, his dark, fathomless, amorous, loving eyes. Sweat began to bead on his forehead, and he pulled away again.

"Wait."

She groaned, but she watched him lift his trousers and search in the pockets. He opened a foil packet and covered his erection, and she groaned again, because she would have liked to do it for him. He turned his face to her, surprise mixed with humor in his gaze.

"Hurry," she prompted him.

He leaned over the bed, running his hands down the insides of her legs. He feathered his fingers against her center, pushed her to the border of a place she didn't want to go without him. She lifted her hips off the bed. And he was there. He entered her with a fierce, sweet delicacy that stretched her body and ached in her heart. She convulsed around him, gloried in the strong, hard force of him.

He lowered his face to her throat, holding still for a

pulsing, primitive moment. But the next second, he rose and moved inside her again. India cried out. He opened his eyes and caught her in a blaze of want, a blast of fire she would never escape. She caught his rhythm and followed him. When he tried to hold back, she reached for him. She didn't want to be alone anymore. She belonged with this man. She belonged to Jack.

I love you. She put the words in her eyes. She wrapped them in all the force of her will and sent them to him, but she didn't speak them. Not even when he lifted her hips and poured himself into her. Not even when her body clenched around him, with ecstasy, with triumph, and he shuddered in his own drenching release.

India kept her secret as she opened her mouth to Jack's fevered, frantic kisses. She sang the words in her head as he fell against her, unable to hold himself above her any longer. She chanted them as he rolled to her side and pulled her into the shelter of his long, large body.

"I love you, India."

She froze. Jack's heart pounded against her shoulder. Her own heartbeat thudded in her ears.

"I love you." His rich tone betrayed the relief of saying it out loud. India envied him. She clung to him because she knew she was going to hurt him. She had to hurt him, and she had to do it now, because the pain would be greater if she waited.

Gradually he quieted in her arms. He turned his head and his body froze against her. She felt the difference before she understood, and she pushed herself to her elbows. When he looked at her again his cold eyes stated his complete emotional retreat. India followed the line of his gaze as he turned again to the picture at her bedside.

She flinched. She'd never put that photo away, a picture of her parents, taken the summer she met Gabe, the last summer they'd been a real family. Her father had tossed the camera to her as he'd put one arm around her mother, who looked too much like Colleen to be anyone but her blood relation.

Jack nodded at the picture, and he looked heartbreakingly young and vulnerable. "Say you aren't Colleen's mother. Tell me you didn't come to the island to make us love you."

She stayed very still, fighting agony that racked her. "I didn't go to make you love me." If she didn't move, she'd be okay. If she fought, the pain would best her.

"India!"

She lifted her hand to his face, but he ducked away from her touch. If she could take it all back, everything, maybe even the bliss of knowing her daughter, she might, to keep from hurting Jack.

"I'm sorry."

"Sorry?" He sat up. "Sorry—what the hell does sorry mean?"

"I didn't do it to hurt you."

"Do what? Tell me, India. Tell me now, when you think you have me where you planned all along." She shook her head, but he held her chin. "Tell me. Say the words, and say them clearly. I don't intend to forget or forgive."

She twisted out of his hand. How many times had he asked her to trust him? "I'm Colleen's mother. I gave birth to her fifteen years ago. Colleen is the child I told you about. Colleen is the child I gave up for adoption."

CHAPTER SIXTEEN

HE CLOSED HIS EYES.

"Jack, please try to understand. I gave her up, but I didn't realize— No wait, I'm not saying I planned to take her back. I just had to make sure she was all right."

He'd known. In his heart he'd known, even as he'd tried not to put the pieces together. He'd hoped he was wrong. When India had talked about the baby's father, her sudden appearance in his and Colleen's lives began to make sense. She'd come to take his daughter away from him.

Her quick affection for Colleen, her reluctance to commit to any relationship with him. It all made too much sense. After fifteen years she was now sorry she'd made such an idiotic, heartwrenching mistake, and she wanted Colleen back. She'd used him, just as Mary had, to reach Colleen.

"I left. If I'd planned to try to take her from you, I would have stayed, wouldn't I?"

Rolling away from her, he snatched his pants from the floor and stumbled into them. What was her next step? A lawsuit? "You can't have her. I won't share her, and I won't give her up." He glared contemptuously at her. "Like you did."

She sank into the pillows. For a moment, her pain hurt him. For a moment.

"You think I deserve that." She grabbed a shirt, his shirt, and wrapped it around herself, as if she felt her nakedness. "Maybe I do, but please, let me explain."

"Explain what?" Jack zipped his trousers and pushed both hands through his hair. "Your idea of a custody agreement?"

"I only wanted to make sure she was safe." India grabbed his arm, but Jack twisted out of her reach. He didn't want her to touch him. She talked around the tears that pooled in her eyes. "I gave her to strangers when I was sixteen years old."

"After fifteen years," Jack said derisively, "your concern touches me." Fear drove him. He'd once believed he'd put his fear of this moment behind him. He'd learned to love his daughter as if no one except he and Mary ever had any right to her. "What's the point in talking now? You were right all along. You and I will never have anything to say to each other."

He took the loft stairs at a breakneck pace and seized his coat from the chair where he'd left it. His shirt, he left behind. He didn't need it. It had touched her skin, her lying, lovely skin. When he came to the door, he stopped. He had to know one thing.

He turned, putting his coat on over his bare back. India was all but doubled over the rail at the top of the stairs. His shirttails brushed her thighs. She clenched his collar in her hands, and heaven help him, he hardened for her again.

He raked at his hair, enraged she could still make him want her, irate he could still burn with this bleak passion. "Did you think I'd love you so much I'd give you my daughter?"

She shook her head, and her hair whispered across her throat. Ice-cold misery splintered in her eyes. "I love you and her so much I wanted to tell you the truth. I'm sorry you found out this way."

Jack found the doorknob at his back. He gripped the

cold metal tightly. Any tighter and he'd pull the door off its hinges.

"I don't believe you." He'd made love to a stranger, a stranger who'd crept into his life and into his heart on a magic carpet woven of lies, just so she could take his daughter away from him. "Maybe you were willing to give her up, but I'm not." He stopped, halfway over the threshold. "You won't have her or me again. You've lied to us both."

India nodded, experimentally, as if she feared her head might roll off her shoulders. Her eyes glowed, two dark bruises in her pale face. "I wanted to tell you on the island. I was falling in love with you, but I knew you'd think I'd betrayed you."

He curled his fingers around the doorknob and yanked the door open. "So, you were right." He had to get out of here. Without another look, he stalked out and slammed the door on her.

INDIA SANK TO THE TOP STEP. She pulled her shirt around her shoulders and discovered it was Jack's. She buried her chin in his collar. His scent rose from the cloth, from her skin. Too bittersweet to feel him so close and know she'd lost him.

Her body still vibrated with the aftertremors of their lovemaking. He filled her mind, her heart. He should be angry. She'd never been honest with him, but she needed him, still. Despite all the times she'd reminded herself she couldn't trust in the forgiveness he'd offered before he knew her secret, she'd hoped she was wrong.

Maybe if I'd told him before I had no choice.... No, she'd never find words to persuade Jack she hadn't used him. Maybe no one could love that much. She rubbed her fists against her burning eyes as she recalled his words. "I couldn't love someone who'd lied to me about Colleen."

She buried her face in her hands, but tears slid across her palms, and she snapped her head up. For fifteen years, she'd made herself numb. She'd refused to feel anything at all and called her emotional distance strength. What good had her false strength done anyone she loved?

She'd pushed her parents into helping her make sure about Colleen. She'd planned to mosey into her child's life and mosey back out again. How could she have been so blind? She'd refused to see the truth.

Deep inside, in places she never let herself look, she'd ached to love again. And Jack had found those places with unerring aim. He had opened her to life again, and taught her to love. He'd almost made her feel safe. How could she expect him to believe her when she'd lied to him from the start?

She'd left him no more choices than she'd given herself. Mary had asked him to work their marriage out so they could keep Colleen. He believed she'd made love with him for the same reason. She'd known all along he'd turn his back on her if she told him she was his daughter's mother.

HE LET HIMSELF INTO a dark house, most of his drive home a blur. Walking into the living room, he dropped his keys onto the coffee table and sprawled in the chair. His chair in his home, where he and his daughter lived.

He sank his head into his hands. Not again. Not another woman's lies. Silence pressed in on him, its weight brutal. He lifted his head and stared into the hallway. No one home. Colleen was still with Nettie and Hayden in D.C.

He needed to hear her voice. Know she still belonged to him. Her mother—her birth mother, who'd given her up, wouldn't know where to find her.

He did.

He dialed the number Nettie had left him and asked for Colleen when a woman's voice answered. Within seconds, his daughter spoke across the line. Her curious hello sounded impossibly young, terrifyingly vulnerable.

"Colleen?"

"Dad, did she like the flowers? What are you doing about dinner? Take her someplace special."

He closed his eyes. "We haven't decided about dinner yet." He didn't want to explain he hadn't stayed.

"Are you sick, or something? You sound funny."

"I'm fine. Are you having a good time?"

"Great. We went to the zoo to see the pandas. Tomorrow night, we're going to a concert on the mall. Grandpa's taking champagne, but he said I had to drink sparkling grape juice."

That sounded relaxed, for Hayden. "I guess I'd better go. I just wanted to hear your voice."

"Oh. That's weird. You sure you're okay?"

"Positive." But he wasn't covering his tracks well, and he couldn't demand she return to the certainty of the house she'd grown up in. "I'll see you Sunday."

"Okay, love you, Dad. Bye."

"Bye." Her end of the telephone line clicked before he finished the word. He collapsed back into his chair. At least he wouldn't have to be on guard for her reaction this time. She didn't have to know.

Did she?

INDIA OPENED BURNING EYES to an orange glow that stole across the skylight, painting her walls in its fierce color. The sun, finally coming up after an endless night.

She rolled to her side, her muscles screaming with pain. She ached with Jack's leaving. Where had he gone last night? Home, to hold on to Colleen?

No, he wouldn't want her to ask questions. The sea would call him. He'd park in the spot all the other fishermen acknowledged as his. He'd talk to any one of those brawny men who all stood together and find the comfort only longtime friends knew how to offer. But he wouldn't be able to tell them the truth.

With a shuddering sigh, India curled around her pillow. She could stay here, alone and guilty, knowing she'd left no one for Jack to talk to, because she'd given him a terrible secret to keep.

Or, this time, she could fight. She could prove to Jack she hadn't gone to Arran Island with a plan to hurt him or his child. She'd ask for one gift. She'd never asked anything for herself, but she hadn't hurt him on purpose, and she'd risk whatever he demanded for the hope of a second chance with him.

With him. She loved him quite apart from her love for Colleen. Would he ever find it in his heart to trust her again?

The night of the costume party, Jack's utter faith in Colleen about the punch had taught India a lesson. Sometimes, you had to love and hope for the best. Sometimes you had to believe when believing felt reckless.

Jack had loved her when she'd lied to keep from hurting him and Colleen. If his love had been true, maybe he could forgive her when she was honest. She had to find out.

HE SLUNG HIS JACKET into the back of his truck. Spring had finally settled to stay over Maryland. With the passing of each of the nine days since he'd walked out on India, the sun beat down hotter.

He opened the driver's door and climbed inside. He was tired, bone weary, but his fatigue had more to do with sleepless nights than hard work he welcomed. Sleepless nights full of dreams of a deceitful woman who still had her small fists wrapped around his heart.

Every time he answered his door he expected to see India, demands for his daughter clutched tightly in the hand he'd loved and lost. She wanted Colleen. She didn't like to need anyone else, but what wouldn't he have done to see Colleen in her place?

He shook his head. He refused to become an adoptive parent who lost the child he'd raised. He slammed his fist on the steering wheel. Adoptive, hell! He was Colleen's father, always had been, always would be, and India had better learn to live with it.

He pulled into the street and headed for the high school. She'd stayed late to rehearse for her part in the end of the year play. He rubbed his chin and grimaced as stubble crackled. He needed to shave.

He needed a lot of things he'd taken for granted before India came to town. Security. Faith in the future. Trust.

No. Be honest with yourself. You learned not to trust long before India showed up. She only managed to reinforce the lesson.

Still, he'd better clean up his act. He couldn't let Colleen know he was mooning over a woman who'd lied her way into town. Of course, Colleen didn't know the truth about her supposed friend—about her mother.

Her mother. The title India didn't deserve landed a blow to his chest as strong and heavy as a balled fist.

He swung into the school parking lot, and Colleen broke off from a group of girls clustered around the door. She dashed across the pavement, anxious to keep her friends from getting a good look at him. Jack tested his stubble again. Definitely time for a shave before his child declared to the world she'd risen from the proverbial cabbage patch.

Unfortunately, she hadn't. Jack stared soberly at her as she crossed in front of the truck. Each day she lost a little more of her gawky adolescence. Each day she looked a bit more like—like India. Graceful, sure, self-sufficient. To a fault.

She opened the door and got in. He wanted to slam on

the gas and run for parts unknown, where no one could come for her. What would she think if she knew the truth about India?

"How was practice?" He forced his voice into a normal range as Colleen put on her seat belt, and he drove away.

"Fine." Her expression sharpened. She had something on her mind. "I have some homework to do. I may need to go by the library tomorrow."

Jack swallowed the cold taste of panic. The library. India. She must haunt the place for Colleen as she did for him. He'd steered Colleen away from any mention of her. Now he let silence play out between them.

He didn't have to tell her the truth. She'd forget soon enough, if India stayed put.

But he glanced his daughter's way as he turned down their street, and he saw all she'd lost at too young an age. He could add love to her life with a few words. The same few words that might send her away from him. He didn't want to talk about India, and yet, he mentioned her first. Unbelievably, he felt guilt at keeping her and Colleen apart.

"You miss her, don't you?" he asked. Idiotic question. Even he felt empty without her here.

"When will you tell me what happened?"

Colleen was too smart. She'd catch on soon.

"What do you mean?" he asked. Stall for time. Stall.

"With India. What happened between you two while I was in Washington?"

He nosed the truck toward the curb outside their house. "Nothing happened." He took the unapproachable adult routine. "If anything had, I'm not altogether sure it would concern you."

"I'm not a baby, Dad. When will you figure that out?"

"India is still none of your business."

Colleen opened her door, grabbed her book bag and her

jacket, and stormed up the walk to their door. Jack followed more slowly. Maybe now was too soon to deal with India.

By the time he reached the doorway behind her, Colleen went on as if she hadn't departed from their conversation in a huff. "Even Grandma noticed something going on between you two. That's why she helped me with the flowers." Just inside the door, she dropped her things on the hall floor. "What did you do, Dad?"

What had *he* done? Colleen already took her side. "Pick up your belongings, Colleen, and put them away."

She frowned as if she were the adult, and he made absolutely no sense. Staring at her quizzical expression, he bit back anger. He'd bet anything Rachel Stuart had looked exactly like Colleen at her age. Their resemblance was too strong to miss.

Unless you were blind.

"You won't even discuss her?" Colleen persisted.

Shaking inside, he took a deep breath. "You're my daughter, not my keeper. I'm an adult. India's an adult, but you are a child."

"And if you upset her and made her think we don't want her around anymore, I'll never see her again." Snatching up her things, she fled toward the stairs. "What's worse, you love her. I know you do, and you can give her up. If you're mature I want no part of it." She hurled herself out of his sight.

Guilty relief washed over him. Deep in the ritual of a good sulk, she'd have to let up on the interrogation.

He didn't know what to do about India. Mary had lived a lie with him, but India had topped her. He didn't care for women's lies.

But he couldn't deny loneliness that made no sense. Desire that pounded him to an emotional pulp. Loss that possibly eclipsed Colleen's.

Groaning, he rubbed his chest. His heart pounded like a steam engine. He still loved India. He still thought of her, wondered where she was, what she was doing, why she had really come to Arran Island. He wanted to know how on earth she could possibly have decided to give Colleen, his Colleen, to people she didn't know.

Craziest of all his self-discoveries, he found that loving India, he didn't have to trust her. He just didn't want to settle this time for love without trust.

But Colleen—now she felt differently. Something had happened between her and India that day they worked on the costume. They had established a bond, and the blizzard, and the frosting fight, and Colleen's flowers had only intensified their connection.

Colleen's mother had come for her. In a way he couldn't begin to understand or accept, Colleen had seemed to recognize her. She'd opened herself to India as she had to no one else since Mary's death.

True, India no longer retained any right to Colleen, but what were Colleen's rights? What would she want if he gave her enough information to make a decision?

How would he face his daughter if one day she came to him and asked him why he'd pushed her mother out of their lives? But how could he tell her the truth and risk losing her?

Jack turned into the kitchen. He pressed his fist to the doorjamb. He wasn't a violent man, but just now he'd like to hit something. Hard.

AS INDIA CLIMBED OUT of her car, her father rose from the lower step outside her building's door. She took a deep breath. Was she ready for this confrontation?

"Hello," Mick said.

"Dad."

"Where have you been? Why haven't you called? My

receptionist told me today, some guy came looking for you weekend before last.''

''Jack. He guessed the truth.''

Mick stood too still, but she'd learned one thing in Maryland—her mother and father would love her no matter what. He didn't ask for details.

''I take it he didn't welcome the news?''

''He took it the way I deserved. I went to Arran Island with a bag full of lies, all made up just for him.''

''You've always been too hard on yourself.''

She shook her head. ''No, Dad, I've always hidden from the hard things. I thought I was being brave and strong, but I just tried to put what I'd done behind me instead of learning to live with it. I can't any hide anymore.'' She sagged against the stair rail. ''Maybe if I'd faced my mistakes back then. Maybe if I'd tried to make a home for Colleen—''

''Forget all those maybes, India. They're poison. You did right for you and for Colleen. How were you supposed to make a home for her? Would you have finished high school? Would you have gone to college?

''You know your mother and I would have done anything to help—I'll be honest with you. We never argued about what happened—about your being pregnant—but we had a tooth-and-nails doozy about how we were going to pay for child care once the baby came.'' Mick paused for breath. ''That's why we've felt guilty. We let you convince us you couldn't take care of a baby, because you were trying to save our feelings, and then we let you drift to the edges of our lives because we couldn't face you.''

''Let's not waste any more time on guilt. Let's just forgive each other and move forward.''

''Can you?''

She shivered. ''In a way, I wish we'd never gone to Arran Island. You were right when you said leaving wouldn't be easy. You were one hundred percent right. Colleen isn't a baby anymore, and she did learn to care for me. And I love her."

Empathy roughened Mick's voice. "Have you thought of telling her? Does Jack plan to?"

"I don't know what Jack plans. He thinks I want to take Colleen away from him."

"Give him some time to cool off. If you stay here, he'll have to see you never meant to take Colleen from him."

"He'll think I'm biding my time. That's what I would think. I want to explain, but I don't know how to persuade him to listen."

Mick patted her hand. "Do you think he'll want to talk to you?"

"No, but I've held back too many times. I wouldn't even hold Colleen when she was born. I didn't give her a name."

"If you had, could you have given her up?"

"Maybe that's the point. Every day since she went to Jack and Mary, I've regretted giving her up. I know they were good for her. I know they were her parents, and wonderful parents. But I couldn't go on with my life. I went through the motions, but I've been dead inside since I let her go. I haven't let myself care for anyone, because I didn't allow myself to love her."

"If you hadn't loved her, would you have gone to Maryland? If you hadn't loved her, would you have risked all this?"

"I didn't allow myself to be her mother. I truly believed what I did was right, and I still think it probably was when I contemplate the life she would have had with me, but emotionally, it was all wrong. Emotionally, I've been lost without my daughter."

"So talk to Jack, but just don't expect him to understand."

India shook her head, restless and frustrated and wary of doing the wrong thing again. "I can't help believing in possibilities. Look where you and Mom and I were a few months ago."

"What if *they* don't want you?"

"You know, don't you?" She closed her eyes. Her father always knew.

"Of course, I know you're in love with Jack." He paused a moment. "Are you prepared if he tells you to leave?"

"I'll face what I have to. If Jack sends me away and decides not to tell Colleen, I'll learn to accept it." India stared at the row of houses across the street, all much like hers, filled with men and women and children, people who fought life's struggles every day, people who didn't turn their backs on the fight. "I have to face the end, Dad."

"When are you going back?"

"Soon. I figured Jack might need a break from my face."

"INDIA?"

Colleen. India's gasp must have carried through the receiver. She was willing to fight for Jack, but he had to decide what happened next between her and Colleen. She doubted he'd sanctioned this call.

"You are angry with us." Colleen's adolescent awkwardness tore at India's heart. "I knew you must be upset. Dad said you were too busy to call, but I knew it had to be more than that. I talked Mrs. Fisher into giving me your number."

India bit her lip. Now that Jack knew the truth, Colleen seemed more her daughter than ever. But Jack had said she was busy. At least, after causing him so much trouble, she could back him up.

"You know how school is at the end of the year. I've

gone back to work, and my father's business has picked up again,'' she added with sudden inspiration. ''How are Nettie and Hayden?''

''They're okay. They've gone home, but they come back when Dad panics and wants someone to look after me. You're sure he didn't say something to keep you away?''

''What do you mean?'' Lying on the fly didn't come easy despite her recent acting job.

''You haven't avoided calling us because you and Dad argued?''

Her heart went out to Jack, unknowingly accused. ''He didn't say anything—or do anything. Really, I've just been busy.''

''Maybe you should come back here. Mrs. Fisher is getting older. She could use the help, and the island is too big for one librarian.''

At Colleen's hopeful tone, a wave of frustration rolled over India. How could she have fallen in love with her daughter's father? How could she have run so roughshod over Jack's and Colleen's lives?

This had to stop.

She tried to firm up her voice to show Colleen nothing like that would happen. ''I enjoyed helping Mrs. Fisher, but I have work here that my colleagues kept for me. How are you doing in school?'' She steered the conversation onto safer ground, looking for a break where she could point out the call was long-distance. Soon she did. ''But I'm so glad you called, Colleen. Take good care of yourself.''

''I will. You, too, India.''

''Thanks again.''

She hung up. She was still lying, but she owed Jack her silence. Colleen would tell him they'd spoken. India braced herself. Barely twenty-four hours after Mick had asked when she was going to see Jack, Colleen had forced both their hands.

Each day for nearly two weeks, she'd asked herself if she was waiting for Jack or afraid. She'd tried to give him time and distance to figure out what he wanted. Colleen was a connection they couldn't break, but she wasn't the connection India wanted to bind her to Jack.

She wanted his love, true and faithful as the love she'd return for as long as he wanted her. If he could ever want her again. Tonight she'd call. They had to talk. He might refuse her, but that was his mistake to make.

JACK, WHO HARDLY EVER BOTHERED to fold his laundry, found himself ironing a pair of jeans to make himself presentable for India Stuart again. Colleen had come home with some wild idea that he should have a word with the city council about Mrs. Fisher needing help in the library.

Hearing her out, he'd realized his time was up. Colleen couldn't just let India fade into history, and she refused to let him. Maybe she had a right to know the truth. He'd never lied to her before, and he didn't know how to start now. Keeping this secret was like nursing a ticking time bomb.

India had filled the empty place Mary's loss had left in Colleen's life. He wouldn't have chosen this path, but now that he knew who her natural mother was, he couldn't persuade himself Colleen didn't have a need to know India.

What sort of relationship would his child want with her mother once she knew the truth? What sort of relationship had India forced on him? She'd turned his life upside down. He'd fallen in love with a stranger, only to trip over her feet of clay.

Jack put on his jeans and a green plaid flannel shirt. Nettie and Hayden had come back to be with Colleen in case he got home late. He hadn't told them the truth about India, but they weren't surprised when he'd told them he wanted to drive back to Charlottesville.

He had plenty more time to think on the way, but he tried everything to shut off his thoughts. He blasted the radio. He shouted the words to the songs. Finally he recounted coastal landmarks from Maryland to Maine.

His heart began to pound long before he parked in front of India's building. Anyone would feel nervous at seeing his child's mother. He wasn't about to blurt out how much he'd missed her.

Jack got out of the truck and put one foot in front of the other until he came to the elevator in her lobby. All the way to her door, he came up with reasons he should go home without talking to her, but he jabbed the doorbell. Almost at once, he heard footsteps, light elegant footsteps.

She opened the door and backed away from him, shock widening her eyes. He took her run for cover as an invitation. He followed her inside and shut the door behind himself.

"I tried to call you," she said, her voice a little tight as she lifted her hand to her throat.

"When?" Hardly hearing her, Jack stared in undeniable hunger. Her jeans hugged the legs whose long length he knew intimately.

"About an hour ago. Colleen answered so I hung up."

Across the front of her sweatshirt, the letters *UVA* curved over her breasts. This woman had wrung the truth inside out, and still he wanted her. "We need to talk," he said in a low tone.

She nodded slowly, a sleepwalker. "I can't believe you're… Is Colleen all right? Did she tell you she called me?"

He shrugged out of his jacket. The studio felt like an

oven. "She said she tried to persuade you to move back to the island."

She blushed, a pale pink stain that painted her cheekbones and sharpened his longing. "I tried to tell her it was impossible without hurting her feelings. I didn't know what to say."

"She said you'd backed up my story about being too busy to stay in touch with her."

India looked at him sharply. "She put it that way?"

"She's positive I did something to make you leave." Even to himself, he sounded defensive.

She pointed to the sofa and perched at one end. Settling slowly, she looked sore from the inside out. He joined her, though he put the length of the couch between them. Might as well get this over with.

"I still don't trust you. That I want to, after all you've done, makes me angry."

Hope sprang to life in her eyes. No—she could forget that. She had to, because he couldn't trust her.

"I need your help with Colleen."

She leaned toward him. "I won't let her think you're at fault."

"I don't need you to protect me." He didn't want to owe her.

"You can't let Colleen blame you, either. I've seen you together. You're her father. She loves you, and she'll come around. She just got too attached to me, and she thinks you've picked some kind of fight with me."

"You've seen us together," he repeated. Did she think he couldn't guess what she'd looked for? "You mean you had to make sure I was a good parent. I don't need your approval."

She had the nerve to look hurt, which annoyed the hell out of him.

"In a way, I did come to see if you were a good parent," she admitted. "I needed to know I actually gave my child the better life everyone promised." She threaded her fingers together, tension etched in every clenched-tight line of her. "I tried not to love her. I tried to forget her. I tried as hard as I could to believe she was better off wherever she was all those years, but for nine months I was allowed to love her. I nurtured her and kept her safe in my body. I couldn't turn off the feelings I already had for her."

She compounded his fear with every syllable. "You can't forget." He filled in the blanks. "You can't stop loving Colleen. You wonder if a judge could withhold custody from a woman who so obviously made a mistake?"

"I never meant to tell you who I was. I thought I'd find out about her life and leave when I knew you and Mary had made her a good home."

"What happened?"

She bit her lip, that same old gesture that made his hand automatically reach to soothe her. "Chris," she said simply. "And then you and Colleen. That first night I wondered why you let her date a boy like Chris. And then, every time I saw you together, you were at odds. I didn't expect to see her. I thought I'd hear gossip if anything was wrong, and I did."

He tried to ignore her broken tone. "How much truth did you expect to find in small-town gossip? Where did you get the arrogance to come to my home and judge us?"

"Concern isn't arrogance. I abandoned my child, Jack. I did it legally, but in my heart I've always believed I abandoned her. I convinced myself that keeping busy, going to school, working hard, was dealing with what I had done. Everything I did, I did to make her proud. I was just some egg donor. She had a real mother. I just wasn't sure her real mother could love her as much as I wanted to."

Mary. She might not have loved him enough. "Oh, she

loved Colleen all right. It must have been hard for you to hear about her.''

"About Mary?'' India's eyes darkened—amazingly in grief. Impossible, if she was the woman he now believed her to be. ''I was glad for Colleen. She had the mother I couldn't have been, the mother I would have wanted to be. I'm not just saying that, Jack. I wish I could tell Mary. I wish I could thank her for all she's done for Colleen.''

"You expect me to believe you?''

''I've told you the truth. I went to Arran Island to make sure Colleen was safe and to find a way to go on with my life without her.''

''Don't tell me any more.''

''But I want to tell you—''

''Nothing.'' He cut her off.

''I do love you. I'm sorry I hurt you. I never would have set out to cause you pain. If you believe I love Colleen, how can you think I'd hurt the father she adores?''

Though he closed himself off from her declaration of love, her real pain twined around him, goading him to comfort her, to let her persuade him. Jack shook his head again. Images of India hurting made him uncertain.

He saw her and Colleen, showing off the costume they'd made, proud of their work, joined in the job they'd done. An image of the two of them swan-diving through his birthday cake frosting brought an unwilling smile to his mouth.

He remembered the way India made love. Like she meant it.

''I've decided to tell her the truth.'' His voice scratched his throat. He'd said it quickly, before he could change his mind, before she could go on.

Then he looked straight into India's eyes and dared her to gloat.

CHAPTER SEVENTEEN

HE'D NEVER BEEN ABLE to predict India's responses. In one swift movement, she rose and came to sit beside him. Concern blanched her lovely face. "I've left you no choice," she said.

He hesitated. They'd get nowhere if he continued to accuse her and she kept on denying her guilt. "I can't keep you a secret. Now that I know, I have to tell Colleen." He allowed her to see how much her betrayal hurt, if she cared to look for it. "Why didn't you tell me when you first arrived?"

"Would you have believed me then, any more than you do now? What if I'd asked for a relationship with her?"

"I don't know. When Colleen came to Mary and me, I had to make myself believe you wouldn't come back for her."

"I never learned how to give her up and yet not love her," she said.

Astonished at his own weakness where India was concerned, Jack wanted to soothe the trembling from her vulnerable mouth. He cared too much for her. After Mary had told him about her affair, he'd had to dig for empathy. Even though India's lies had hurt him at least equally, he kept stumbling over compassion for her.

He tried to distance himself. "I'd like you to come back to the island when I tell Colleen who you are. She'll want to know why you gave her up, and I can only stand to have this discussion once."

She nodded, but the wary tilt of her head told him she wasn't sure how Colleen would take the news. "When do you want me?"

She amazed him. He'd forced himself to sound like a businessman setting up a meeting, and she was brave enough to concede to his demands. Nothing felt natural between them.

"Tomorrow. She won't have school until Monday, so she'll have a couple of days to absorb whatever you have to say."

Jack stood. She'd agreed. Colleen had become their only connection.

India rose as well. "I'll start as soon as I pack, and I'll take a room at Viveca's."

"I'll talk to Colleen in the morning, and then I'll call you if she wants to see you."

"And if she doesn't?" Her voice broke.

Jack refused to comfort her. "I'll let you know, whatever she says."

Staring at India's tousled hair and tired eyes, he realized how hard these past few weeks had been.

Could she have planned everything?

"If Colleen knows the truth, that you're her mother, and I—if I fall in love with the real you, you've caught us."

She shook her head. "I don't want to 'catch' you. I want to be part of your life—and Colleen's. But, you, Jack, you're the man I love. I made a horrible mistake that hurt you, and I don't know how to make up for it."

"Not by using me to keep a child. I've already lived that life."

"I'm not Mary. I'm not as good as she was, nor as bad. I'm just the woman who gave birth to your child and who loves you desperately."

"I have to go," he muttered.

She stepped back. Her silence scraped at him, as harsh

as her tortured gaze. Searching her face, he pushed his fingers into his pockets.

"How am I supposed to believe in you? You gave up my daughter, but now you want her back. You wouldn't have come to the island if you didn't want Colleen. I don't believe in that much altruism."

"But I absolutely believed I could see her happy and healthy and know I'd done the right thing for her. I thought I could back out of her life once and for all."

"I'd do anything to keep Colleen with me. How can I believe you feel any differently?"

Her eyes went blank. "You can't unless you decide to. I know what I've done, but I never planned it. I didn't, Jack." She narrowed her gaze, and her determined blankness fled before anguish that made him ache to hold her. "Why don't you know me well enough to know I couldn't plan to take her? Even if you don't believe I care for you, why would I hurt Colleen?"

Jack suddenly remembered the moment he'd leaped off Bill Pearson's boat onto the safety of the dock. She'd held him as if letting him go would be impossible, and he'd thought it would be, too.

"I'd doubt you every time I held you. And when I touched you, I'd wonder if I was the price you're willing to pay for a life with Colleen. You'd know, just like Mary knew. I won't settle again."

Jack didn't wait for her to answer. What good were more empty words? He turned and left her. He still had to figure out how to tell Colleen.

TURNING INTO ARRAN ISLAND'S short main street was like coming home. She let down her window to taste the sea salt that weighted the humid air. A slow smile started from her insides out as she passed Al's drugstore, a Victorian monarch, all bustles and bows, spilling a small crowd of people through chrome and glass doors.

Jack would know all those people. They'd know him. They'd rally to his side now, when he needed them most.

Light rain began to fall, and India lowered her window farther, welcoming the sting of raindrops on her cheek. She passed the town square where men and women were pulling down the stalls they'd sold from all day. She began to hum as she passed the library, stationed like a sentry in modern brick, with tiny windows like half-shut eyes.

Trying to find out about her daughter, she'd opened herself to this place. The day they'd rescued Mr. Pearson, she'd been a citizen of this town, though now the other citizens wouldn't welcome her unless Jack did. Maybe this place seemed like home because she'd learned to love him here. She'd been a mother to Colleen for a few, spare seconds. Her heart lived here, with them.

India checked into the Seasider Inn again, thankful Viveca was out and her young assistant was a stranger. She ended up in the room her father had occupied. She didn't unpack. She had to anticipate Jack not asking her to stay. She set her purse and bag on the bed and walked to the window. Almost time for school to be over.

Before long, children came down the sidewalk, turning into their homes. She recognized Colleen by her walk, Rachel's loose-limbed, graceful walk. Colleen made her slow way toward her own street, stopping to pet a cat, pausing again to talk to a little girl who swung on a gate with her face to the misty rain.

Looking at Colleen, India became afraid. She backed away from the window, stopping when a chair bumped the back of her thighs. Easy to be brave and swear she'd fight from the safety of her anonymous life in Charlottesville. Jack hadn't believed her. Why should Colleen?

She folded her hands to keep her fingers from trembling.

All the way from Charlottesville she'd tried to think of what she would say to her daughter. Words wouldn't form in her mind. The clock ticked off seconds, a minute, an hour. She swigged water from a sports bottle. It tasted like acid.

A sudden knock at the door made her jump.

Jack had said he would call, but maybe he hadn't the heart to tell her on the phone that Colleen didn't want to see her. She hurried to the door. He'd been kind to come and tell her in person.

But Jack wasn't waiting on her doorstep. India opened the door and found Colleen, looking a bit taller somehow and not a little stunned. Even the frustrated, disjointed explanations India had tried and discarded disappeared from her mind.

"I look like your mother, don't I?" Colleen asked.

"That's the last question I expected."

Colleen laughed shortly. "It was the first thing I thought."

"Would you like to come in?"

"No." She might have been rooted to the ground. "Dad said he promised to tell you what I wanted to do, but I can speak for myself."

India nodded. Colleen's adult voice chilled her. These were consequences. Killing consequences.

Colleen held up her hand. "I have to tell you the person I thought you were would never turn me out. No matter what, she would have fought for me."

India swallowed. "I wish I had."

"I love my Mom. Mary Stephens. She was my real mom."

"Yes."

"I'm mad at you. You should have told us."

"I would have if I'd known how I would hurt you and

your father anyway. I only wanted to make sure you were all right. I never meant to get involved with your life.''

''That's what Grandma says. She says that's why you always acted as if you didn't want to come in. All I know is my dad looks like he did when Mom died, and I feel a little that way, myself, so I don't want to talk to you, and I don't want you around my dad.''

India took a shuddery breath, her heart shattering. How could she argue? She'd done the one thing she'd sworn not to do in coming here. ''Okay,'' she choked out.

Colleen turned away. She stopped at the top of the stairs, but she didn't look back. ''I don't mean we won't ever want to talk to you, but right now, I need my dad.''

And not you lay plainly between the lines. India gripped the doorknob until she could let go without falling. Then she went to the phone and dialed Jack's number.

He answered quickly, but India cut him off.

''She doesn't want to talk. Should I go back home?''

''You want my permission?''

''I want your advice. You know her best. If I stay, will I hurt her more?''

''Damn you, India, how can you ask me?''

''I'm sorry, but she's more important than you and I are. You think so, too.''

He didn't answer at first. His breath whispered through the phone, in and out, in and out. Finally he cleared his throat. ''Stay.''

She waited for him to hang up, anticipating a click in her ear.

''Okay?'' he asked. ''India?''

''I'll stay. I'm sorry, Jack.''

''I have to go. She'll be home soon.''

He did put the receiver down this time. India followed suit, feeling numb. As much as she treasured each moment she'd spent with Colleen, she wanted to believe she would have given them up to keep from hurting her in the end.

"INDIA'S YOUR WHAT?" Marcy raised her eyebrow so far her little gold hoop all but disappeared under her hair.

Colleen watched, fascinated, even as she wished Marcy'd keep her voice down.

"I knew she didn't come to paint houses." Leah redid her ponytail for the third time since they'd left the school parking lot. "You don't paint houses *and* work in a library. Who'd do that?"

"Someone who was desperate," Marcy suggested.

Colleen eyed her friend in surprise. "To see me, you mean?"

"Well, yeah. Would you wear one of those paint things around if you didn't have to?" Marcy stopped as Colleen turned down the street that led to the library. "Where are you going?"

"Mrs. Fisher said I could pick up my picture from the exhibition today. I want to take it home." Colleen didn't care if Marcy and Leah thought she wanted her mommy. She did. Why did India have to confuse everything?

"Colleen?" Marcy said.

"Yeah?"

"Are you all right?"

Her concern startled Colleen. Mostly, Marcy talked about boys and tattoos. She hardly ever talked about her own parents. Colleen wouldn't have thought she'd care about anyone else's.

"You know how my mom and dad fight a lot?" Marcy said.

Colleen shared a look with Leah. They'd discussed their concern over their friend's home life before.

Marcy looked impatient. "Sometimes I wonder what it'll be like when they get divorced, because it's just a matter of time. Will I like my dad's new girlfriend? Will my mom's boyfriend's treat us okay? Will both of them be so happy to find someone else they'll forget about me completely?''

Cold whistled down Colleen's spine. ''What are you saying?''

''Is that why you're so mad at India? Do you think she's going to change your life into that?''

''I liked her, but she lied to me. She can't take me from my father. I'll be seventeen next summer. No one is going to put me anywhere without my say-so. I wouldn't let them.''

''She told you she was sorry. What do you want her to do?''

''I don't know. Is saying she's sorry enough?''

''Would it be different if she'd told you the truth from the beginning?'' Leah asked.

Colleen considered. ''I guess it might have been worse. I'd have been afraid she was going to try to take me from Dad, no matter what she said.''

''Do you miss her now?''

Colleen began to grow uncomfortable with their inquisition. ''Well, yeah, kind of. I thought she was my friend. She kind of made up for—''

''For your mom being gone?'' Leah finished.

''Yeah, but I feel guilty thinking that.''

''My mother thinks wearing my clothes makes her my friend,'' Marcy said.

Colleen bit her lip. Compared to Marcy's parents, India was an Andy Griffith episode, but she shouldn't have lied.

''Maybe you're mad because of your mom,'' Leah said. ''Maybe you should think about how long you want to stay mad.''

''I thought you'd be on my side.''

''I am, but you're my friend, and you're in trouble. I

don't want you to make things worse because you're hold
ing a grudge. What good does that do you? What doe
your dad say?"

"Not much. I think he loves her. I think he must hav
asked her to marry him or something, so she finally tol
him the truth." She scooped her hair away from her face
"He tries to talk to me, but I don't want to. He an
Grandma and Grandpa watch me all the time. They tol
him about that seventeen-year-old thing. They were in th
kitchen, and they thought I couldn't hear. I'm sorry he'
worried, but this is *my* problem. I told him he'll always b
my father, and Mom was my only mother, but I did lik
India. I thought she and Dad would end up together." Sh
covered her mouth with her fingertips as they reached th
library. "Shut up, now. I don't want anyone else t
know."

Marcy and Leah looked up at the library door. Lea
caught Marcy's arm. "We'll wait for you out here," Lea
said. "Mrs. Fisher's too used to having help now, and wh
knows what those little kids are doing today?"

Colleen grinned. "I wonder if the job you want coul
be genetic."

"Who knows?" Marcy lounged against the low wal
"Don't make us wait out here too long."

Mrs. Fisher gave her the picture of her mother and f;
ther. Colleen peeled the paper wrapping back to make sur
it was the right photo. She was still staring at her mother'
face when she rejoined her friends outside.

Marcy peered over her shoulder. "What would *she* thin
about this whole India thing?"

"She used to look at Dad just like in the picture." Wit
all the love Colleen secretly hoped to feel for her ow
husband some day. "She was never afraid of how thing
looked. She would have said what I feel is more impo
tant."

"What do you feel? It's not like India stormed into town, claiming you as her long-lost baby girl."

Colleen bridled. "Mom wasn't a saint. She wouldn't tell me to start planning for next Mother's Day or something." Leah and Marcy gaped at her, like two fish. "All right," Colleen muttered. "Maybe she'd tell me not to be mean to India."

"Maybe she'd point out you were already trying to get India and your dad together," Leah said in a perfectly serious tone.

Marcy exploded in a derisive snort. "Yeah, right!"

Colleen laughed with Marcy, but she stopped laughing first, and she thought about what she'd planned for India and her father. Exactly why had India come to Arran Island, if not for her?

INDIA'S HEART STOPPED when she opened the door to Colleen again. A few days without contact had strained her hope to breaking point.

Colleen jutted her chin with familiar belligerence. "Are you still willing to talk?"

India tried not to leap at the chance. More than anything, she longed to explain herself to Colleen. Truthfully, she hoped Colleen would hear her out and decide not to send her away. Her heart pounded so fast, she could hardly find her voice.

"I'll tell you whatever I can," she said.

"I want my dad with us when we talk. I think he needs to hear your explanation as much as I do, but I asked him if I could come up and get you, because I wanted a few minutes alone."

Picking up her room key, India nodded. Colleen barely stopped for breath.

"See, I already picked you out as my mother. I already thought of you as my mom. Not like my real mom," she hastened to add, "because you can't take her place. She took care of me when I was a lot of trouble. She fed me and diapered me, and she gave me everything. She's always going to be my real mother, but I might have room for you."

Startling even her, hot tears burned India's eyes. Colleen saw them.

"Oh, I'm still mad. Don't think I'm not. Like Dad, I don't appreciate the lies. And, India, Dad and I are family. It doesn't take blood, you know."

Without answering, India quietly followed Colleen out of the room and closed her door. Everything Colleen said made sense. She had made the mistakes here, not Jack or their child. She just hoped she'd have the chance to make it up to them, to fight for them, and maybe to stay.

"Do you understand what I'm trying to tell you?" Colleen asked.

"You don't want a relationship if your father wants me gone."

"For now, anyway, because *he's* my family. I won't hurt him."

"I understand."

"Good." She took a deep breath, as if she'd gotten a weight off her chest. "It's easier for me. Whatever your reasons, you came here for me. I know you wanted me."

"I do love you, Colleen. I love both of you."

"I know."

India sneaked a peek at Colleen's averted face. Her calm self-assurance came straight from Mary and Jack, but had the quiet acceptance come from India? If so, India didn't trust it, because it had never been real with her. The other shoe always dropped, even if it took fifteen years.

Colleen walked slightly ahead of her, making conversation impossible. They found Jack waiting in his living room. He stood, searching both their faces. He lingered on India with distrust and then turned to Colleen.

"Are you all right?"

She nodded.

India stared at them, the rangy, long-limbed man and the coltish, more-mature-than-she'd-realized girl, all of the love she'd ever dreamed of. She prayed for the right words, that she wouldn't squander this one last chance. For the first time, she might have the right to love her daughter. And her daughter's father.

CHAPTER EIGHTEEN

JACK BRACED HIMSELF. The silence grew and thickened. Not even Colleen was willing to help India. But he didn't want Colleen's loyalty to him to hold her back. No matter how threatened he felt as her father, he didn't want to come between India and Colleen, if Colleen decided she wanted a relationship with her birth mother.

"I was fifteen when I became pregnant," India finally began. "I was a junior in high school." She raised a level gaze to Colleen. "I was one of the smart girls. Until I met Gabe. He was eighteen, but my parents thought he was younger.

"My father's business was in big trouble. I didn't even understand how deep the trouble was, until we lost our house. They tried to cover up, to protect me, but their protection backfired. I thought they treated me like an infant who wouldn't understand, but Gabe treated me like a woman.

"I wasn't allowed to car date, but Mom and Dad let me go out with my friends and meet Gabe. They thought he lived with his parents, and I didn't tell them any differently. You see, they thought I couldn't handle a guy who had his own apartment, but I knew better. Before long, I'd meet Gabe with my friends, and he and I would go back to his place. The more my parents tried to protect me by not telling me the truth, the more I identified with the life I led as Gabe's girlfriend. They didn't need me. He most definitely did. Until I got pregnant.

"My mother guessed on my sixteenth birthday. I'd worn baggy clothing, but I couldn't seem to shake off the morning sickness, and I never should have eaten that slice of birthday cake."

"Was she angry?" Colleen broke in. "Rachel didn't seem like the type to blame you."

"She did at first," India said quickly, nervously. "What else could she do? I mean, it happened back then, maybe even as often as it does now, and it wasn't as much of a stigma as it might have been a couple of decades before, but my parents always thought they were open and liberal. They couldn't manage liberal or open this time." India took a deep breath and went on. "Mom and Dad promised to help if I decided to keep you, but we all knew they didn't have the money to support another child, and a desperate promise wouldn't feed or clothe you." She straightened. "I gave you up so you could have a family and a life I couldn't give you, myself."

Jack lifted his hand to Colleen, who caught it in both of hers. This was his daughter, the child he'd loved all her life. He'd do anything to help her avoid hearing this. He hoped she'd see how much India must have loved her to do what she'd done. She'd never rejected Colleen.

The realization drew his gaze to India, whose sorrow was plain, written all over her body, as she held herself tight as a bowstring.

"My parents took me to Mother Angelica, and she arranged for me to stay at the home until you were born. She arranged for your adoption." India forged ahead with a ragged breath. "It wasn't what I wanted. It was never what I wanted. I loved you. I wish I could make you believe how much I loved you. All I had was love, but you needed diapers, and baby food, a place to sleep, a future. Love didn't seem as good for you as a mother and father who could give you everything. I believed I would have been more cruel to have kept you with me.''

"What about this Gabe?'' Colleen demanded.

India's gaze shifted to Jack, swept him with open flames of longing and regret. Clearly she didn't want him to think of anyone else as Colleen's father. He didn't. He'd always be Colleen's father. She looked back to Colleen.

"He took off. My dad brought Gabe back to town, but I refused to marry him.'' Though her story obviously embarrassed and hurt her, she didn't flinch. Colleen was more important. "My marrying Gabe would not have given you what you needed. His specialty was football, not life.''

"Where is he now?'' Colleen asked.

India blushed, a reminder of the sixteen-year-old girl she'd been. "If you want to talk to him, I'll help you find him, but I don't know where he is.''

"Why did he run away when you told him about me?''

Hearing his daughter's sadness, Jack walked around the sofa to put his arms around her. For once, she didn't fight a public display. She needed him, as he needed her.

"He didn't know you, Colleen.'' Jack pushed her hair behind her ears. "He couldn't reject the best chance he ever had if he didn't wait around to see what a lovely girl his chance was. Don't let his poor choice change you.''

He glanced at India, whose gaze softened on them, as if she liked seeing them together. Jack smiled back before he realized he'd let down his guard.

"He was scared,'' India said. "He didn't know what to do.''

"Didn't know how to be responsible you mean?'' Colleen retorted. "He was eighteen.''

India grimaced. "I don't know how well I learned responsibility, until I came here. I ran from what I'd done, too. I just ran within an acceptable system. A little while back, I was in a plane crash. I spent some time in a fire and then on my back with a broken leg. Plenty of time to look at my life, the people I'd given up, the fear I'd never faced. I came to find you because I couldn't forget you. I couldn't go on without knowing what had happened to you, but it wasn't until I came here that I began to face my responsibility for all the mistakes I made.''

"Didn't you miss me? Didn't you ever want to know about me before?"

Jack tightened his arms around his daughter. She couldn't look at India and not see how urgently she'd needed to know about Colleen.

"I had no rights. I told myself I was building a life you'd be proud of, if you ever came to look for me. But nothing I did ever made me feel completely whole. After I crawled out of that airplane wreckage, I realized the something missing was missing in me. I could laugh. I wouldn't let myself cry. I worked as hard as I could, but I never let myself slow down long enough to truly *feel*. I'd think, 'This sun is setting over my daughter's head. This day is ending where she lives. Someone is tucking her into bed. Someone is loving her.' On your birthdays, I tried to picture what you were doing, what you looked like." India stopped with an uncomfortable smile. Jack's heart skipped a troublesome beat in response to the fragile curve of her mouth. "Somehow," she continued, "I pictured you looking like me and Dad. I never guessed you'd be Mom's mirror image."

"Why didn't you tell me who you were?"

India hesitated. To think of an answer that would win Colleen over? But she tilted her chin as if to take a blow. "I promised myself I wouldn't interfere with your life. I'm an outsider with no rights to you, and I thought if you found out who I was, you could be so upset it might change everything for you with your parents. I had already made one life-altering decision for you—I couldn't make another.''

''But you told my dad.''

India's blush deepened. Jack remembered the moments before she'd told him with too much clarity. He moved away from Colleen, needing distance.

''He figured it out,'' India said. ''But I'm in love with your father.'' She looked at him. ''I wish I could show you both I never meant to hurt you.''

Wasn't that love in her eyes? Didn't they glow with love for him? Jack wanted to trust her, to believe. He wanted to forgive and find the life he'd glimpsed with her.

Enough! He couldn't stand much more. He believed India had loved Colleen even as she'd carried her. The same fears she'd described had driven him half-crazy after he grounded the boat. At sixteen, how had she found the courage to let her child be adopted?

''Colleen, do you have any more questions for India?''

She turned slowly, her gaze curious, as if something in his voice surprised her. ''Do you, Dad?''

''Colleen.'' He made himself stern. Because right now, she mattered most, and she needed time to take in the changes India brought to her life. He knew his child. She hadn't fully formed her response yet.

He didn't trust her quiet mood, her calm acceptance. Maybe she had more in common with India than all of them realized. As had happened when they'd lost Mary, she was already trying to act as if she'd moved on. If she didn't find a way to examine her feelings and accept them this time, he'd find a way to help her. He hoped the dam would burst a little sooner this time.

''I'm all right.'' Colleen hugged him. ''I wished India could be a mother type to me. I just didn't know how real she was going to be.''

As he took in her brittle voice, Jack glanced India's way.

She also looked concerned. He patted Colleen's shoulder. "Do you want to talk?"

"Actually, I'd like some time to myself." Colleen twisted out of his arms. She stopped in front of India. "I'm glad we finally know the truth."

India bit her lip, struggling for an answer. "Your father and mother were the parents I would have chosen for you if I could have," she said finally. "You're a beautiful young woman, inside and out, and I'm proud to have gotten to know you."

"This isn't goodbye." Colleen turned slowly toward the hall. She stopped at the doorway. "This is 'let me get used to the idea.' Like Dad, I already loved you." Her voice wavered. Jack moved swiftly to her side, and Colleen reached for him. "We can't say goodbye. We know who you really are." She buried her face in Jack's shirt. Her shoulders began to shake as the dam crashed wide-open.

Jack sighed in her hair, relief washing over him while India stared in horror.

"She'll be all right," he said, surprised to find himself reassuring her. "I hated to let her go up to bring you down by herself, because she reacts this way. She's quiet until everything hits her."

"I'm like that, too." India inched forward, as if her feet pulled the rest of her body along. She eased her hand against Colleen's hair but Colleen wasn't ready for a physical connection. She moved, dragging Jack with her. He curved himself protectively around his daughter.

"I believe you, India," Colleen uttered brokenly into Jack's shirt, "and I wouldn't change my parents, but I still wonder why you didn't find a way, why you gave me up."

India hesitated. "I thought I was giving you everything a child should have. I didn't see any other way."

"How am I supposed to know you don't just care for

me because you love Dad? How is Dad supposed to know you love him when you came here for me?"

India shook her head tiredly. Her suffering was as real as Colleen's. He knew it as surely as he knew his own name, but he couldn't reach out to her. Like Colleen, he wasn't ready.

"I'm not the woman I was when I let you go. I never let myself truly care for anyone after. It hurt too much, and I was too afraid."

Colleen turned in Jack's arms. "And now?"

"And now, if you want me—" Breaking off, India looked to him.

And he pitched into an ocean storm. Now or never. He had to decide. He had to know in this moment if he had room in his life for India. The thought of living his life without her trapped his breath in his chest.

Eventually he and she would have to figure out where she fit. His daughter's life could never be whole again without her. But neither would his. He would not feel whole again if India left. So sharply he wasn't sure she'd see, he nodded. He couldn't form *I love you. I want you to stay.*

He improvised. "I don't want you to go."

INDIA SAGGED WITH RELIEF. At least he'd agreed to let her say she would stay as long as Colleen needed her.

"If you want me, Colleen, I'll be here."

Colleen seemed to find that answer satisfactory. She swiped at her eyes with the backs of her hands. "I hate it when I cry. Maybe you're right about not using mascara, Dad." Pushing away from him, she glanced nervously at India. "I'm okay, really. You two don't have to study me as if I'm on the verge of a breakdown. In fact, I may be the least of your problems. I'll be fine, but what about you?"

She swept from the room with fine dramatic flair and took the stairs double time. Within seconds, a door slammed above. India turned to Jack.

"Should you go to her?"

"I will," he said. "She's mature enough to know when she needs time alone."

"Thank you for letting me talk to her, and for letting me tell her I'd stay."

Jack pushed his hands into his pockets in a gesture India recognized. He looked so lean and out of sorts when he did it, he made her want to soothe him, with her hands, with her lips. She fought for a little control over her own haywire emotions.

"Will you stay?" he asked.

What did he mean? Could he forgive her? "Do you want me to stay?" She didn't let him answer. This was not the time to make sure she was safe before she admitted she wanted to be with him and Colleen. "No, don't. Of course I'll stay."

He lifted his dark gaze to her. "For Colleen?"

Through dry lips, she admitted her true feelings. "I'm afraid to tell you the truth, because I don't know what you're thinking, but I'll stay because I want to be with you."

"Even if I can't find a way to trust you?"

Her heart banged around in her chest so hard she would have sworn he could hear. "I'm not a martyr. I'm not asking for penance, but I did wrong, and I understand your mistrust. I'm willing to fight for us if you aren't. At the moment, I believe we can have a life together, but you don't. Someday, you'll have to fight, and I'll lean on you."

She hoped her leap of faith didn't put him off. She was so new at loving him. Revealing this much trust nearly drained her of all her trust resources. His unsmiling silence hardly lessened her uncertainty.

Finally he cleared his throat and turned toward the door in an unmistakable gesture. He wanted her to go. "Just stay on the island," he said in a thick voice.

AS SOON AS THE DOOR CLOSED on India, he wanted to call her back. They should talk this out together. The day Mary had told him the truth, they'd begun lives that kept them separate from each other in intimate ways neither ever acknowledged. He would never be able to say for sure she'd known their marriage had changed. Part of his grief at losing her had stemmed from never being able to love her the same way. But this—this was as different as night and day, as different as loving India.

She'd wakened him, brought him back to emotional life, with her hunger to live, her determination, her joy in simple things like an afternoon at the sewing machine with Colleen. India loved his daughter. He'd already begun to think of them as a family before he'd found out the truth.

Which version of the woman he loved was real? He'd lost his ability to trust before he'd known her. For a long time, he'd been a means to an end. A man wanted to be more.

What had she said? Someday he'd have to fight? She'd met his demands. She'd stayed with no promise of tomorrow, and he believed she'd continue to stay. Maybe today was a good day for a clean start, and maybe she was a woman worth fighting for. Worth fighting with, for a love that made them both equal and whole.

SHE'D MEANT TO GO BACK to her hotel room, but she turned toward the bay. Jack's bay. Maybe the people of the Chesapeake thought it belonged to all of them, but this patch of it, embraced in the somewhat narrow arms of Arran Island's harbor, dark green, heavy with mist and salt, belonged to Jack Stephens. Being near it meant being near him.

India had already started down the steep stairs to the dock when she heard him call her name. She must be imagining his voice. As she turned, her hair whipped across her face, almost veiling his long, lean body from her. She hooked her index finger through the strands and pulled them away as he descended the stairs on surer feet than hers.

"I need to ask you again." He stopped, just a fraction of an inch too close to her for comfort. "Will you stay? Will you stay for me?"

Such an easy answer, if only he could find a way to believe her. "I would have left if you or Colleen had asked me to, but I don't want to be anywhere else. I wish I had told you who I was before, but I was in so deep, I couldn't see a way out. I didn't want to hurt you, and I couldn't hurt Colleen. I made a terrible mess of everything, but I love you. I always will. I am constant, and I will abide."

The deep rise and fall of his chest told her more than his stern expression. At last, he pulled her left hand into both of his. He stroked her fingers, sensuously, seductively, deliberately.

"No more lies? None from me, and none from you?"

"Not even to save your smallest feelings," she promised fervently.

He smiled, and tiredness fell away from the lines beside his eyes. "You'll have to move in with us," he said in the rumbly tone she loved so well, the one that ravaged her senses and reduced her to aching desire. "I can't fish in Charlottesville, and how would Colleen survive without Marcy and Leah?"

India bit back a cry of pure delight. Was he serious? Had he forgiven her? "Do you mean what I think?"

"I'm asking you to share my drafty house and a mortgage on the boat and school lunches and tantrums about makeup and hair coloring, and love that will never end and never fade away. Oh, and grandparents, too.''

She hesitated. What if his change of heart was a dream? ''I like Nettie and Hayden, and I love that never-fade-away part, but do you believe me?''

''I saw how careful you were to tell Colleen the truth, and to spare her feelings where you could. Maybe I should have waited for your explanation that day in your apartment. I can't know what I would have done in your shoes, but I know you love my daughter, and I believe you love me.'' His love blazed at her, warmed her, protected her. ''Your lies protected us. You didn't protect yourself. Maybe it's time you did. Maybe it's time for you to take what you want.''

She sank against him, reveling in the knowledge he wouldn't pull away. ''I want you, Jack. I've fallen in love with you.''

He tightened his arms, his possessiveness a forgivable sin. Grasping a handful of her hair, he gently tilted her head. ''I want you to be my wife and my lover. I want you to be my daughter's mother.'' He kissed her temple. ''I want us all to be together, without any secrets between us.''

''I'm cured of keeping secrets.'' India laughed softly, giddy in her relief, in happiness she almost couldn't take in. ''I'm not so sure about my mother, though.''

Jack brushed the line of her brow with his disturbing mouth. ''Your mother?''

Languorous and hungry in his arms, she began to lose her focus. ''All that stuff about being a docent.''

His laugh rolled through her body, leaving her indecently weak. He pressed his lips to hers. ''You don't think she'll be a bad influence on her granddaughter?''

India laughed against his throat. "She felt so bad about lying she's signed up for docent school at Monticello."

"You're all so quirky, you Stuart women."

India lifted her face for his kiss, impatient for his love. "You like quirky?"

"I love quirky." Covering her mouth with his, he ended the conversation. Mutual need heated the gentle seduction of his kiss. India gave as good as she got, meeting him, breath for breath, sigh for luxuriant sigh. When he lifted his head, she whimpered in unashamed frustration, but he gathered her so close she felt a part of him. "I love you, India Stuart."

This time she knew how to answer. This time, she got it right. "I can't wait to start a lifetime of loving you, Jack Stephens."

EPILOGUE

JUNE SUNSHINE STREAMED THROUGH the window as India fumbled with the last button on her going-away suit. She was too happy. Her happiness hurt deliciously.

"India, are you sure you have everything? Grandma said to make sure you packed plenty of hankies, because brides tend to cry for no good reason."

India drank in Colleen, who glowed with heartwrenching beauty in her ivory bridesmaid's dress. "Hankies? Are you kidding me? She meant tablecloths."

Colleen laughed with her, sharing the joke. Rachel had cried a lot lately herself. India still couldn't get used to the freedom of sharing her life with her daughter, but Colleen had no time for sentimentality.

"You'd better hurry. I'll die of humiliation if Dad breaks down the door with everyone outside, and I wouldn't put it past him."

India closed the latches on her suitcase. "You don't mind our going away?"

"I'll be fine with Grandma and Grandpa. We're going to visit that cousin of Grandma's again near D.C., and then we head to Mick and Rachel's, before we go back to Baltimore."

Jack kept telling India Mick and Rachel would soon become Grandpa and Grandma Stuart, and she hoped he was right. And she was grateful to Hayden and Nettie for making room for her parents during their week with Colleen.

Heading for the door, she paused, her suitcase thumping between her and Colleen. "I'll miss you."

With a big grin, Colleen reached over the suitcase to envelop her in a huge hug. "I'll miss you and Dad, too, but married people shouldn't start out with a nearly grown daughter."

"India, Colleen—psst!"

The pitch of Rachel's whisper all but shattered the windows in the room, and India burst into laughter. Colleen opened the door for Rachel, and all three Stuart women laughed together, just because they could. Jack and India had kept putting off their wedding, thinking Colleen wasn't ready, until one day, she'd asked when they planned to make each other legal. Today, they'd tied that knot, with overwhelming happiness, surrounded by a family that was gradually forming itself around them.

"Jack sent me up," Rachel said. She eyed India with an accusation. "He asked me a lot of pointed questions about Thomas Jefferson. You may tell him for me, your little Monticello joke will soon lose its humor." She ignored India and Colleen's renewed burst of laughter. "He *says* to hurry up. Mick has introduced Colleen's other grandfather to the wonders of his family's moonshine recipe, and then someone brought up lock picking. Mick mentioned you might be able to teach a class."

"Let's get down there." Hoisting her suitcase, India fled down the hall, but Rachel and Colleen only giggled conspiratorially behind her.

"We're the only ones who know about the lock, and Mick would never bring out the moonshine," Rachel whispered to Colleen loudly enough for all of Maryland to hear, "but Jack thought it might speed her up a bit."

India turned back with longing and love. She couldn't resist Stuart women any more than Jack could. "It would

serve him right if I showed up in a cat burglar's mask. Got
a pair of stockings, Mom?''

"I dare you," Rachel said.

India stared at her in smiling horror. "You are a bad
influence. Colleen, when you come back here, consult with
Dad before you agree to any scheme of Mom's."

Colleen only giggled harder as Jack topped the stairs.

"Are you nearly ready?" His mock tired, male voice
walked down India's spine like fingertips.

She went to him. "As soon as I talk to Dad about blab-
bing my trade secrets."

Jack looped his arms around her waist. His gaze locked
on hers so tightly India couldn't catch her breath. "Rachel," he said, "remind me you cannot keep a secret."

"I'll do that," she promised with all seriousness.

India looked askance at her husband. "Mom already
admitted you put her up to it."

His smile was lethal, but he turned off the voltage to
lift one beckoning arm to Colleen. "Come say goodbye,
and promise you won't run away and join the circus while
we're gone."

"What*ever*, Dad." Though exasperated, she hugged
them both.

India's eyes welled with happy tears. "Don't move,"
she said, holding Jack and Colleen tight. "I want to remember this moment all my life." She kissed her husband's solid cheek and then Colleen's softer skin.

Colleen tightened her arm briefly before she backed
away. Her cool friends might bounce up the stairs at any
second. "You two have a great time. Don't forget to call
me."

Jack ruffled her hair. "India made a list of phone num-
bers, including your grandmother's cousin's." He turned
to India, who was loath to leave her daughter, even for so
happy an occasion as a honeymoon.

"It's time," he said gently, understanding.

He was good at that. Jack made her trust in forever. Forever with him and Colleen.

"I'm ready." She squeezed her daughter's shoulder one last time.

Fed up with mushy stuff, Colleen gave them both a gentle push. "I'll be fine. I won't even pierce my nose. I think I could talk Rachel into letting me, but Grandma still remembers the makeover."

Jack shared a long-suffering smile with India as he linked their fingers. "Let's go then."

They raced down the stairs and clambered into his truck through a hailstorm of birdseed and good wishes. Tucked against his shoulder, India looked back at their family stacked on the steps of his house. Colleen stood, happily cocooned between Mick and Hayden and Nettie and Rachel.

"Close your eyes," Jack said.

"Now? But I want to see them as long as I can. They're our family, Jack, yours and mine."

"Now is good."

She closed her eyes, because she'd declined to include "obey" in the vows, and she figured she owed him a little something in return. He started the engine and the truck pulled forward.

"I wish you'd tell me where we're going, and why I have to close my eyes."

"Because it won't take long, and this is your surprise."

Sure enough, within a few minutes, Jack turned the truck sharply and they rocked over some lumpy surface before they jolted to a halt.

India opened her eyes to musty dimness. "Where are we?"

"In the shed behind Mrs. Henderson's new, fully renovated honeymoon cottage. When I put in a skylight for her, it reminded me of your apartment, so I asked if we could be her first guests. I thought you and Colleen might like to plan a family vacation for all of us during her last two weeks of summer.''

Delighted, India clutched him in a bear hug. ''It's the perfect wedding present.''

Looking pleased with himself, he opened the door and pulled her out behind him. They edged through the yard and sneaked to the door.

''Why are we hiding?'' she asked.

''I don't want anyone else to know we're still here.'' He turned serious for a moment. ''I told Mick and Hayden, of course.''

''Setting aside the chauvinism of telling only the men, you've given me the sweetest gift.''

''I asked Mick to lay in a large supply of frosting.''

India laughed, but he yanked her through the door. She didn't see icing, but someone had positioned a beautiful antique sleigh bed directly beneath the new skylight. Beside it sat a bottle of champagne on ice and a flowing bouquet of the same wildflowers she'd carried down the aisle.

''Mmm, lovely, Jack.''

''We couldn't find a picnic blanket. Mick looked at me funny when I told him I had to.''

''You amuse me, but I only fall for practical jokes once a day.'' India strolled lazily to the bed. ''Are you tired?''

''No, I'm wildly in love. I am a good and circumspect father, but I'm ready to be a husband, too.''

Turning on her toes, India fluttered her fingers his way. ''I am a wife at your command.''

An irresistible, stalking cat, Jack edged her against the bed and reached for her buttons. ''As I recall, you left that part out.''

"Are you in a hurry, Jack? You're going to break them."

"I'm in a hurry. This marriage thing has piqued my interest for days, in case you hadn't noticed. Who'd have guessed it would be even more provocative to make love to my wife than my lover?"

India tapped his nose. "Especially when she's the same woman."

"And both of them all mine."

He caught her mouth with his as he reached the buttons at her waist, and India found he was right about that marriage thing. She arched against his scandalously stroking hands as he pushed her jacket off her shoulders.

"I knew you weren't wearing anything under this," he muttered.

"Just the skirt," India returned as she reached for his shirt. But his buttons wouldn't give. She tugged harder, and they suddenly flew into the air and bounced onto the floor. India laughed into Jack's heavy-lidded eyes. "More confetti."

"I love you."

"Jack," she sighed on a long breath that required more kissing, more stroking, even less control.

Somehow, they managed to divest themselves of all their inconvenient clothing. She knew she had come home at last as Jack covered her with his body.

"Slowly?" he whispered in her ear as he stroked her.

She lifted her hips. "Plenty of time for that later."

He laughed, a wicked, affection-filled laugh that melted the last of her restraint, but this time as he pushed deep inside her, as he claimed her—this time she spoke the words out loud. The litany she'd locked inside her head. This time she shared the truth, her only truth with the man she loved, the man who was more than her daughter's father, the man who was her husband, lover, friend.

"I love you, Jack." She twisted her head to meet his virile mouth, swollen from their life-giving kisses. "I love you."

HARLEQUIN®
SUPERROMANCE®

**They look alike. They sound alike.
They act alike—at least some of the time.**

Two Sisters by **Kay David**
(Superromance #888)
A sister looks frantically for her missing twin.
And only a stranger can help her.
Available January 2000

The Wrong Brother by **Bonnie K. Winn**
(Superromance #898)
A man poses as his twin to fool the woman he thinks
is a murderer—a woman who also happens to be
his brother's wife.
Available February 2000

Baby, Baby by **Roz Denny Fox**
(Superromance #902)
Two men fight for the custody of twin babies.
And their guardian must choose who will be their father.
Available March 2000

Available wherever Harlequin books are sold.

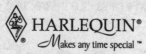

HARLEQUIN®
Makes any time special ™

Looking For More Romance?

Visit Romance.net

Look us up on-line at: http://www.romance.net

Check in daily for these and other exciting features:

Hot off the press

View all current titles, and purchase them on-line.

What do the stars have in store for you?

Horoscope

Hot deals

Exclusive offers available only at Romance.net

Plus, don't miss our interactive quizzes, contests and bonus gifts.

PWEB

Come escape with Harlequin's new

Series Sampler

Four great full-length Harlequin novels bound together in one fabulous volume and at an unbelievable price.

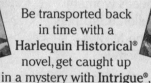

Be transported back in time with a Harlequin Historical® novel, get caught up in a mystery with **Intrigue**®, be tempted by a hot, sizzling romance with **Harlequin Temptation**®, or just enjoy a down-home all-American read with **American Romance**®.

You won't be able to put this collection down!

On sale February 2000 at your favorite retail outlet.

♦ **HARLEQUIN**®
Makes any time special ™

Visit us at www.romance.net

PHESC

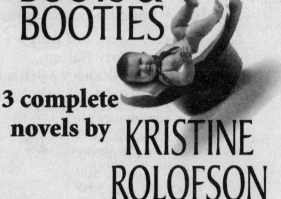

Return to the charm of the Regency era with

GEORGETTE HEYER,

creator of the modern Regency genre.

Enjoy six romantic collector's editions with forewords
by some of today's bestselling romance authors,

**Nora Roberts, Mary Jo Putney,
Jo Beverley, Mary Balogh,
Theresa Medeiros and Kasey Michaels.**

Frederica
On sale February 2000

The Nonesuch
On sale March 2000

The Convenient Marriage
On sale April 2000

Cousin Kate
On sale May 2000

The Talisman Ring
On sale June 2000

The Corinthian
On sale July 2000

Available at your favorite retail outlet.

HARLEQUIN®
Makes any time special ™

Visit us at www.romance.net

PHGHGEN

**A cowboy town in cowboy country.
This is a place a woman could love.
These are *men* a woman could love!**

Priscilla Prescott is new to the town of Glory, where
she opens a much-needed nursery school. Rancher
Jeremiah Blake immediately decides she's the
woman for him—although Cilla just as quickly
decides this cowboy's not for her.

Jeremiah knows there has to be a way to change her
mind.... And he's right!

Read and enjoy **The Rancher Takes a Wife**
by Judith Bowen (Superromance #900),
on sale in March 2000.
It's the newest installment in this popular series!

Available at your favorite retail outlet.